DELIVERANCE

OTHER BOOKS AND AUDIO BOOKS BY H.B. MOORE

Out of Jerusalem: Of Goodly Parents
Out of Jerusalem: A Light in the Wilderness
Out of Jerusalem: Towards the Promised Land
Out of Jerusalem: Land of Inheritance
Abinadi
Alma
Alma the Younger
Ammon
Daughters of Jared
Esther the Queen
The Moses Chronicles: Bondage

OTHER BOOKS BY HEATHER B. MOORE

Women of the Book of Mormon: Insights & Inspirations
Christ's Gifts to Women
Divinity of Women: Inspiration and Insights from Women of the Scriptures
Athena
Ruby's Secret
Tying the Knot

THE MOSES CHRONICLES
VOLUME 2
DELIVERANCE

A NOVEL BY **H.B. MOORE**

Covenant Communications, Inc.

Cover image *Moses and the Burning Bush* © Friberg Fine Art, www.fribergfineart.com.

Cover design copyright © 2016 by Covenant Communications, Inc.

Published by Covenant Communications, Inc.
American Fork, Utah

Copyright © 2016 by H.B. Moore
All rights reserved. No part of this book may be reproduced in any format or in any medium without the written permission of the publisher, Covenant Communications, Inc., P.O. Box 416, American Fork, UT 84003. The views expressed within this work are the sole responsibility of the author and do not necessarily reflect the position of Covenant Communications, Inc., or any other entity.

This is a work of fiction. The characters, names, incidents, places, and dialogue are either products of the author's imagination, and are not to be construed as real, or are used fictitiously.

Printed in the United States of America
First Printing: March 2016

22 21 20 19 18 17 16   10 9 8 7 6 5 4 3 2 1

ISBN: 978-1-68047-935-5

In loving memory of my cousin
Lee Oblad-Fritsch Morikawa
1974–2015

PRAISE FOR *THE MOSES CHRONICLES: BONDAGE* BOOK 1

"An engaging and interesting story that feels authentic to the time period and cultures, which Moore seamlessly uses in the story to her advantage." —Christine Rappleye, *Deseret News*

"Strong characters, a compelling plot, realistic background, an educated vocabulary, prose that flows beautifully, along with a spiritual element that feels right and natural make *Bondage* a pleasure to read and an impressive start to a new series. This book is easily my favorite H.B. Moore book." —Jennie Hansen, *Meridian Magazine*

"This book was so rich and full of life. I could easily imagine the scenes and the people as I went through this book. I loved the alternating points of view of Miriam and Moses. It really helped me create a firm personal connection to them both." —Aimee Brown, blogger

"I highly recommend this book because it is an engaging story with suspense, romance, and truth from its biblical roots conveyed in a way that made me feel a connection to a story that is thousands of years old." —Rachelle J. Christensen, author

And God heard their groaning, and God remembered his covenant with Abraham, with Isaac, and with Jacob.

(Exodus 2:24)

CHARACTER NAMES

*Denotes Historical Figures

*Moses
*Zipporah, daughter of Jethro
*Jethro, also called Reuel in Exodus 2:18
Qurayya, wife of Jethro
*Hobab, son
Tema, daughter
Madiama, daughter
Cozbi, daughter
Jael, daughter
Tayma, daughter
Abigail, daughter
Oreb, son of Cozbi
Sihon, husband of Cozbi
Peor, brother of Sihon
*Gershom, oldest son of Moses and Zipporah
*Eliezer, youngest son of Moses and Zipporah
*Seti, Pharaoh of Egypt
*Ramses, crown prince of Egypt and son of Pharaoh Seti
*Bithiah, Moses's adoptive mother and daughter of Pharaoh Seti
Asif, Hur tribe
Zur, Badrayan
Evi, chief of the Badrayans

CHAPTER ONE
MOSES

1280 BC

Moses's bruises had long since faded from deep purple to mottled blue, and finally to a pale yellow like the sand that stretched beneath his feet. Yet the scars still remained, running along his forearms and chest, red against the ever-deepening color of his skin.

But Moses didn't need scars or bruises to remind him of his final days in the land of Egypt. They were etched deeply into his heart. Scars of killing the Egyptian taskmaster. Scars of sneaking back into the palace that had been his home for as long as he could remember. Scars of listening to the woman he'd called "Mother" his entire life tell him he wasn't her child.

Scars of learning that he'd been born a Hebrew slave, then wrapped and hidden away in a woven basket, and pushed into the River Nile . . . to meet his fate.

His life had been left in the river god's hands, or was it the god Amun? Or perhaps the Hebrew god had orchestrated Moses's life so that he did not meet the fate of all other male infants born in the Hebrew settlements and ordered dead by Pharaoh.

Moses exhaled and pushed forward across the desolate terrain. Nearly a moon had passed since he'd crossed into the wilderness, leaving behind everything he knew, and leaving behind questions that he could never answer. He kept his focus on the rocky outcrop of the hill ahead of him as the merciless sun baked his skin. Hoping to find shade beneath an overhang, or better yet, a cool, dry cave, Moses ignored the fierce thirst battling in his throat and the labored breaths expelling from his chest.

His scalp itched and burned from the fierce sun and the new growth of hair. His head had been shaved his entire life, so he wasn't used to hair on his head. He tried to sleep through the days and travel only at night, but he'd soon changed that tactic. Too many snakes and scorpions were out in the dark, and the moon wasn't always a reliable guide.

When Moses reached the rocky outcrop, he nearly collapsed underneath a ledge that jutted out from above. The shade wasn't much cooler than the hot sand surrounding him, but at least the deadly rays of the sun were blocked.

He opened his goatskin satchel and pulled out the few remaining dates. He chewed slowly, letting the sweet, grainy taste fill his senses, not knowing when he might find another date grove in this desolation. Or another well holding water, for that matter.

Closing his eyes, Moses leaned his head against the rough stone and inhaled. Hot, dusty air surrounded him, and he thought of the fertile land surrounding the River Nile, where he'd spent his entire life. A life of privilege, of wealth, of esteem. A life that was now gone.

Moses hadn't realized he'd dozed until a rock skittered next to his feet. His eyes flew open and he looked up, afraid that the ledge above him was crumbling. Instead, a pair of bare feet, calloused and hardened with years of desert walking, dangled over the rock. Moses pulled his legs up and scooted back, not wanting to be seen; then the feet lowered, and suddenly a man with a coarsely woven tunic dropped to the ground. His hair was a long mass of matted curls, and his eyes were like piercing black daggers.

"Who are you?" the man demanded in a language that resembled Egyptian but was more guttural. The man's hand gripped a staff, his knuckles white with tension.

Moses raised his hands to show that he didn't hold a dagger or any other weapon. "I am just a stranger passing through. I'm here in peace." He spoke slowly, keeping his hands raised.

The man's eyes narrowed, and Moses could practically feel him taking in the whole of Moses's appearance. He'd been in the desert for three weeks, yet his dirty kilt was still finer than this nomad's. And there was no comparing the fine leather of his sandals with the nomad's bare feet.

The man's eyes were on Moses's satchel, and Moses's breath stalled as he realized what the man was about to do. Although the small gold statues his mother had sent with him were at the bottom of the satchel with his elegant robe on top to hide them, that wouldn't be nearly enough protection to deter a determined nomad.

"Stand up," the man commanded in his harsh language.

Notwithstanding their language differences, the nomad's instructions were clear, and Moses rose to his feet. His height and stature must have surprised the nomad because he took a couple of steps back. But Moses was too weak to feel he posed much of a threat. Even if his life depended on besting this man, the energy it would take to fight him would finish Moses off.

The nomad's eyes took in the measure of Moses's height, although it was plain to anyone that Moses was in no condition to fight.

The nomad whistled, and the piercing sound shot straight through Moses's head, causing him to wince. Moments later, two more men appeared. Three against Moses. The first nomad held out his hand, and Moses handed over his satchel.

The nomad grinned, his teeth nearly brown as if he'd never cleaned them in his life. "We will return your things after you pay for crossing into our land. We have owned this land for generations."

The other two men stared at Moses. The taller one, who was close to Moses's size yet looked as if he'd never spent a day inside a hut or cave, grabbed Moses's arm and tugged him forward. "Come with us," he said in a thick voice. "Our leader will decide your payment."

Out in the sun again, Moses couldn't think straight. He'd eaten those few dates, but it wasn't enough to clear his head or give him sufficient strength to defy three hardy nomads. They led him along the rocky ridge and down into a sand-filled valley. A sparse grove of pomegranate trees grew against the edge of the valley, and Moses's mouth watered as he thought of how the fruit might taste.

He stumbled, and the man who gripped his arm scoffed.

By the time they reached the collection of black tents with rolled-up sides, the occupants had come out to watch the new arrival. A dozen children and a handful of women, all wearing black, with thick scarves around their heads, crowded together, their eyes wide and appraising. Three men came from inside one of the tents, and a short man with a broad chest and belly looked to be the leader. He was older than the rest, his face wrinkled with age and the ravages of living in the sand and sun.

"Where do you come from?" the old man asked.

It took a moment for Moses to comprehend what the man had asked him. Moses had been educated in many languages, and if he concentrated, he could follow what these tribesmen were saying. Moses licked his dry lips. Standing here with the nomad still gripping his arm while the sun baked his shoulders, he felt as if he were standing before a great fire.

"I am from . . . across the border," Moses managed.

"You are a warrior?" the leader said. "Defected from your army?"

"I have fought in battles."

The broad-bellied man chuckled. "Ah, you have fought. You were strong in body, but not so much in mind. Now you are weak in body."

The first nomad who had taken Moses's satchel stepped forward and handed it over to the leader. "He was carrying this."

Right there, in front of the whole tribe, the leader opened Moses's satchel and pulled out his robe. The interwoven deep red and indigo and yellow threads combined to cast a purple sheen. It was made of the finest and softest wool, lighter than the crisp spring air. The old man held it up and smiled. "Beautiful! Like the sunset." Then, bringing it closer to his face, he squinted at the weave and stitching. "Very fine. A woman made this for you? Perhaps your mother?"

At the mention of his mother, Moses felt his knees give. He gritted his teeth together, trying to stay upright.

"Oh, and you have gold," the leader said, pulling out the gold statues from the bottom of the satchel. He turned one over in his fingers, then bit down on one of the edges. "You have come from another land. Have you heard of us—the Hur Tribe?"

Moses hadn't.

The man continued without waiting for a reply. "The Hur Tribe is known for harvesting frankincense, which some believe is more precious than gold. But if any of the surrounding tribes knew we had gold, our women and children would wake up with slit throats."

Moses exhaled, his head spinning as he tried to comprehend what the leader was implying.

The man put the gold back into the satchel and stuffed the robe into it as well. Then he looked up at Moses. "We will put you to work, and if you succeed, you will get your useless gold back." He nodded to the nomad gripping Moses's arm. "Give him water and food and let him rest. Then guard him until he wakes up."

CHAPTER TWO
ZIPPORAH

Holding the goat steady, Zipporah finished milking the fat animal. If there was one thing she could take credit for in her settlement of Midian, it was raising goats that produced the creamiest milk and the most delectable cheese.

She patted the goat, and it trotted away, joining the small herd Zipporah kept corralled by the mountain's edge. The Sarawat Mountains rose steadily and proudly above her, a dependable and familiar landmark Zipporah had known her entire life. Her settlement spread out below the mount, a massive collection of haphazard tents. To a nomad, Midian might look unorganized, but to Zipporah, it was comfort and security. Everywhere she walked and turned, she ran into a family member or friend.

As the third daughter of seven, Zipporah was just another disappointment. Her parents had one son and seven daughters, but that single son was showered with the most esteem and privilege. Zipporah let out a sigh, knowing that wasn't exactly true. Her father adored his daughters. Truthfully, he spoiled them, purchasing goods from passing caravans, then presenting them to each daughter with delight. Olives from Jerusalem, silk scarves from India, frankincense from Punt, colored stone carvings from Damascus. In fact, the daughters of Jethro were envied throughout Midian. Her mother, Qurayya, made no such motions for coddling, leaving it up to her husband. Zipporah's mother was set on one thing. Grandchildren.

And in that, Zipporah had failed miserably. Her older brother, Hobab; two older sisters; and one younger sister had all married and produced babies. Zipporah had failed to capture the attention of any desirable man, and that included the butcher. Last year when the butcher, Sihon, had made an offer for her hand, Zipporah had spent the next few days lying on her mat, overcome with nausea. There was nothing inherently wrong with Sihon. He was cheerful, energetic, and always had a laugh about to surface. But marriage to him? She couldn't keep anything down, and each time she thought of marrying Sihon, she stumbled to the clay pot and retched.

Her parents kept her plight hidden for days, but when Sihon learned the truth from Zipporah's never-quiet younger sister Cozbi, he'd taken back his offer. Oh, the shame. Her mother had ranted for hours, and Zipporah could only huddle on her mat, feeling sick all over again.

When Cozbi joined in the ranting, Zipporah had finally had enough and shouted, "You marry him, then! See if that doesn't wrench your very heart out as it has mine."

Cozbi had shut up then, but her expression turned contemplative. A month later, Cozbi and Sihon were happily married. And now Cozbi had just given birth to their first child—a healthy son, of course.

It wasn't that Zipporah didn't want to marry, although her mother had a hard time believing that. "Why don't you speak to the men? You are too quiet," Qurayya declared. "You are too serious. Laugh and smile a little, and the men will come around. One will surely ask for your hand in marriage."

Zipporah tried to imagine herself acting carefree and sweet toward the available men in Midian; however, whenever she was around one of them, it was as if her tongue was weighed down by stones.

"There you are." Her mother's voice was extra shrill today. It had been a hot few days, the sun merciless in its heat. "It's time to take supper to Cozbi—and be quick about it. A new mother has a large appetite."

Zipporah rose from the ground and brushed off the bits of sand and pebbles from her tunic.

"You need to stay out of the dirt, Zipporah," her mother said, placing her hands on her wide hips. If anything could be said about the Jethro women, it was that they had ample curves—a sign of their family's wealth and pride. Well-rounded women equaled wealth and position. "Sihon's family will be around as well, and you might consider looking your best for Sihon's brother."

Zipporah caught herself before she scrunched her nose in distaste or let out a rude noise. Peor had not quite grown into his coordination; he was more a boy than a man. He was two years younger than Zipporah, and she knew that even she, despite her panicked reaction to marrying Sihon, preferred a man over a boy.

Zipporah was in her nineteenth year, after all, and beyond her first childbearing years. According to her mother, a voice that was never quite silent in her head, Zipporah should have two or three children by now.

She picked up the clay jug of fresh goat's milk and walked past her mother, saying nothing, which just exasperated her mother even more.

"That scowl on your face will be permanent if you're not careful," her mother called after her. "When your father and I are gone, what will happen to you then? Who will take care of you?"

Zipporah's emotions tumbled against each other. She was tempted to laugh while at the same time her eyes stung with new tears. If something happened to *her*, who would take care of her parents? Her brother, Hobab, perhaps, or one of her sisters and their families. Maybe her mother had a good point.

She reached the large multisectioned tent and entered the cooking room. Inside, the heat of the day dissolved like a moving shadow, and Zipporah relished the brief respite. No one was inside the cooking area, so for just a few moments she had the place to herself.

One thing Zipporah had in common with her mother was the gift of cooking. She'd mixed spices and created mouthwatering garnishes that had impressed many of their guests, from the traveling nomad who stopped for a night of rest, to the settlement priests with whom her father spent a lot of time.

She moved over to the stone enclosure that contained a few embers. Next to it, her father had lifted a tent panel so that the smoke would rise straight into the sky. With a thick cloth, she pulled back the top stones and examined the sheep's meat cooking beneath. It could be said that goats and sheep were literally the life bread of Midian.

The savory smells rose, and Zipporah smiled in satisfaction. With two thick sticks she picked up the meat and set it into a heavy clay pot. This she set onto the heated stones, keeping it close to the embers, and then she poured a combination of spices over the meat. It would take only minutes to soak in, and the meat would be even more flavorful and tender.

While the meat simmered in the spice mixture, she pulled out the small dagger she kept belted around her waist, then speared the meat over and over, separating it into bits until it made a nice, thick stew. Zipporah knew that this particular meal was a favorite of Cozbi's. She was certain that Sihon would appreciate it as well. And it would be yet another offering she could make to him and his family to make amends for her ill treatment of him the year before.

"It smells divine in here," a voice boomed behind her. Zipporah turned to see her father. He was tall and lean, with a narrow, scarred face and crooked nose. One didn't become an important man with many herds without having to fight a battle or two. She smiled as he walked toward her, bent down, and kissed her cheek.

"How's my favorite daughter?"

The smile broadened. He called every daughter of his a *favorite*. Zipporah could just hear her mother now reproving her father about how he was spoiling their daughters so much so that they'd expect their own husbands to dote on them as well.

But it made Zipporah smile to hear her father's lavish praises about her cooking. And although he ate plenty of it, he never seemed to run too fat like the other older men in Midian.

"Are you taking this to Cozbi?" her father asked.

"I am, and it's almost ready." She stabbed at the meat and was satisfied that the stew was perfect. She picked up a thick piece of wool to keep her hands from burning while she carried the jar, then turned to her father. "Don't tell me you're here to give me advice about Peor?"

Her father's brows lifted in surprise, but his eyes gleamed.

"You were. Well, I'll tell you I'm not marrying an infant."

"Ah, Zipporah," her father said, placing a hand on her shoulder. "I ask myself a hundred times a day how my most beautiful daughter can be my most stubborn."

She felt her face start to heat, but she told herself he said that to all her sisters. Maybe not in that exact way, but Zipporah didn't want to think of herself as beautiful. Because that very fact would mean that one day, a man, not a boy like Peor, would possibly be interested in her.

"Father," she said, "I need to get this to Cozbi. Let me pass."

He chuckled and lifted his hand, stepping aside.

Zipporah moved past him and stepped out of the tent, walking back into the heat of the sun. But not before seeing the look of tenderness on her father's face. It made her feel terrible that she was letting her father and her mother down. But mostly her father.

How many times had he told her he was praying for her to find just the right man, that the right man would come along and Zipporah wouldn't be able to turn down his proposal? She couldn't think of a single man in Midian with whom she'd have any problem turning down a marriage proposal. And it wasn't as if a man was going to walk straight out of the desert and marry her.

Zipporah wove her way around their collection of tents and passed a couple of the younger camels that were still with their nursing mothers. Their main herd was kept in a corral closer to the center of the settlement where young boys were paid to guard them at night.

"Zipporah!" Abigail shouted at her, pumping her little legs as she ran toward her.

Abigail was Zipporah's youngest sister, and even at the age of ten, it was plain she'd grow into a beauty. Her dark eyes were huge, framed by thick lashes and golden skin.

Zipporah slowed and waited for Abigail to catch up.

"I love him!" Abigail said as she came to a stop.

"Whom do you love?" She looked down at her younger sister, wishing she could be so carefree and full of energy—but she realized this had never had been the case, not even when she was a child.

"Oreb," Abigail said, clapping her hands together. "He smiled at me."

Oreb was Cozbi's new baby. "Oh, I'm sure he did. Except new babies don't smile." She laughed at Abigail's enthusiasm. "I'm taking dinner to Cozbi now. Do you think she'll like sheep stew?"

Abigail shrugged her small shoulders. "I don't know. I'm going to tell Father that Oreb smiled at me."

Before Zipporah could say anything else, Abigail was gone, running toward their family tent.

For a moment, Zipporah forgot her errand and watched her sister hurry away, her excitement nearly palpable. A twinge of wistfulness passed through Zipporah as she wondered what her life might have been like if she had a different personality. Perhaps she'd be married with a child of her own and not walking alone to visit her sister, who was surrounded by family and friends celebrating the full circle of life.

CHAPTER THREE
MOSES

Moses crouched next to the nomads of the Hur tribe and reached for his share of flat barley bread and bitter goat cheese. These nomads were shepherds and spent their days feeding their flocks. The other nomads had all eaten their fill—as much as a desert dweller could be filled—and only then had they allowed Moses to eat what was left, which barely amounted to scraps. He'd been their virtual slave for three weeks now. A prince turned slave to a nomad tribe. It was difficult for even Moses to believe that he was currently cleaning the scraps of bones left over from their meat-filled meals. And that he kept guard all night long over their camel herd in company with other tribesmen and was now helping them collect several sheep that had somehow escaped to the top ridge and needed to be guided back down.

It hadn't taken Moses long to appreciate the desert food—when one had an empty stomach, one was not selective. And it was better than a steady diet of dates.

"Are those your tribesmen?" Moses asked, inclining his head toward two men below the ridge, keeping to the shade as they walked. Over the past weeks, he'd learned enough of their language to communicate reasonably well.

The nomads snapped their heads around to look, and then Asif, the first nomad who had found Moses, said, "Don't move. They haven't seen us yet. Let's see what they're doing."

"Who are they?" Moses asked in a low voice.

"Baal tribe," Asif said. "They are on our north side, but I haven't seen them come this far into our territory for years."

"You aren't friendly?"

Asif smiled, but it wasn't a kind one. "They stole my sister three years ago."

The Baal tribe was an enemy indeed.

The nomad next to Asif added, "So we stole two of *their* women."

"Did you get your sister back?" Moses asked, eyeing Asif and feeling an affinity he hadn't thought possible.

"We couldn't bring her back. She had been spoiled by a man of another tribe. She belonged to them now, but we took our revenge." Asif lifted a shoulder, his eyes tracking the men below the ridge the entire time he whispered. "My sister would have rather killed herself than face her tribe in shame."

Moses didn't know what to say. He was almost afraid to ask about the women they'd stolen from the Baal tribe.

Asif answered without him having to ask. "My wife is from their tribe—stolen, but we are married now, and it's as if she's always belonged to me."

Moses swallowed the bit of bread in his mouth, his throat suddenly dry. He stared at the tribesmen below and thought about the stolen women on both sides. Whatever these men's reasons were for trespassing on Hur territory, Moses knew that any interchange would not be friendly.

"Why are they here now?" he asked in a low voice.

Asif shook his head slowly. "We had some sheep go missing, and now I know who took them. They are trying to intimidate us. Disrupt the peace that's existed for a few years at least."

And then it happened. One of the tribesmen looked up. The nomads next to Moses were immediately on their feet, Moses right next to them.

The two tribesmen disappeared beneath the rocky overhang, and the nomads backed away from the ridge and started whispering among themselves, trying to decide what to do.

Moses stayed where he was, watching the spot where the men had disappeared. He knew they hadn't moved far or else they'd have to come out from under the overhang. He glanced back at the nomads, who were trying to decide whether they should try to make it back down the ridge and head for the settlement to get more help or simply try to fight them off with their staffs.

Then Moses saw it. A shifting shadow. The men were right below them. A stone's throw away, which gave him another idea.

"Give me a dagger," Moses whispered to the pair of nomads. They turned to stare at him, and Moses continued. "I have a plan. Give me your dagger, and I'll get their attention. They'll see me and be confused because they won't know me or why I'm yelling at them. Once they are focused on me, then you start pushing rocks off the ledge. That should convince them to leave."

Asif handed him a dagger but then said, "I don't want them to run and get more men. I want to finish this here and now."

Moses looked from one nomad to the next. "Then do you want the dagger back?"

"I have another one," Asif said, bending and pulling a knife from his food pack. He eyed Moses after he straightened. "Are you with us?"

"I am."

"Then follow our lead."

Moses followed the nomads down the snakelike trail that led them off the ridge and toward the large overhanging rock where the two tribesmen hid. Their steps sent rocks skittering along the ground, and one of the tribesmen poked his head out from their shelter.

When he saw them coming down the ridge, he called to his companion, and soon both men were standing out in the open, their bodies alert as they gripped their staffs in one hand and short daggers in the other.

Moses descended the ridge, hurrying to keep up with the more dextrous nomads. Although he'd been traversing rocky territory for weeks now, he couldn't quite match the agility that came from years of traversing the wilderness. And now Moses would be fighting a different battle for a different people. Fighting the Libyans with the Egyptian army was one thing, but out here in the wilds of the desert, there wasn't any protocol. He didn't have armor, spears or swords, or a horse-drawn chariot to give him an advantage.

It would just be him against the next man. At least they outnumbered the tribesmen. As they reached the bottom of the ridge and made the final turn to face the intruders, Moses finally got a good look at their opponents. The two men were shorter than Moses had at first thought, but their arms and legs were muscled well enough, telling Moses these men were not weak in body.

The black eyes beneath their heavy dark brows were alert and calculating. They had no problem holding their daggers aloft and standing their ground.

"Why have you crossed into our territory?" Asif demanded before he and the other nomads came to a stop.

The tribesman with the indigo scarf about his head spit on the ground. "This is our territory now." The man's dialect was similar to Asif's, although it had more inflections.

Asif chuckled, scraping his foot along the ground, pawing it like a beast about ready to charge its prey. "You have no rights here. We made this clear a generation ago. You can't change tradition."

"We have just as much right as you to this grazing land," the tribesman with the ruddy face cut in. "Tradition died with Serena."

Moses couldn't see Asif's face, but the man staggered back. "She's dead?"

The tribesmen kept their gaze steady and hard. "She is," one said.

Asif rubbed his face with his hand. "What happened to . . . my sister?"

"She died giving birth to a son." The man with the indigo scarf narrowed his eyes. "The child also died, so we were not compensated for her loss in any way. We are here to get our payment." He swept his hand, indicating the surrounding land. "We'll take this portion."

Asif was quiet for a moment, and Moses's heart twisted at the thought of the terrible news and what it must mean to Asif. He looked at the sky as if he could find the answer to his questions there, and Moses had to look away from the pain on the man's face.

Moments passed, and the tribesmen shifted their stance yet kept their daggers raised.

Finally Asif turned and looked straight at the man with the ruddy face. "You and me. We fight here. Now. Whoever lives will possess this land." He looked at the other nomads, then at Moses. "Each of you is a witness to this pact."

"Agreed," the ruddy-faced man said, stepping forward. He bent his knees as Asif approached, going into a half crouch.

Heat pounded through Moses's veins as he watched Asif make the first lunge and the fight began. Moses and the other nomads took a few steps back as Asif and the tribesman circled each other, periodically lunging and taking swipes. Asif drew first blood, and the tribesman cried out.

His face turned even redder, and he closed the circling distance, practically throwing himself at Asif. The two men tumbled to the ground, and Moses couldn't tell which arm or leg belonged to whom. The nomads were shouting, encouraging the fighters, and Moses found himself joining in.

And then, almost as suddenly as the fight had begun, there was silence. A pulsating silence of heat and sand and wind. Asif struggled to wriggle out from beneath the tribesman's unmoving body. Blood ran down Asif's face, and Moses didn't know if it was from a cut or a broken nose. Asif finally extracted himself with a groan, then rose to his hands and knees, taking deep breaths.

The fallen tribesman wasn't moving, wasn't breathing. He was lying on his stomach, his face half hidden by the sand. Was he dead? Memories of the day he killed the Egyptian taskmaster flashed into Moses's mind. The blood, the smell of death, the absolute and final silence of a man's soul.

The other tribesman rushed to his companion's side, sinking to his knees in the sand. He grabbed the man's shoulders and shook him. "You killed him!" he shouted, looking up at Asif. The man's mouth worked in silent anger, then he scrambled to his feet and charged toward Asif.

Asif barely had time to stand and catch his balance before the tribesman pummeled into him, knocking him over. Asif was completely taken off guard; his knees gave out as his body crumpled to the ground.

Moses's instincts kicked in, and before he could second-guess himself, he was on top of the tribesman, pulling him off of Asif. The tribesman shrieked with rage and turned on Moses, brandishing his dagger.

Moses barely managed to block the plunge of the man's dagger toward his chest, and the dagger pierced his forearm instead. Pain burst through Moses, but he twisted away and dove for the man's lower legs. The man dropped his dagger as he tried to brace himself during the fall. Moses gained the advantage and pinned the man to the ground. Holding one hand on the tribesman's neck while his other hand kept a dagger touching the man's jawline, Moses stared into the unblinking eyes.

"Jehovah save me," the man cried out, his voice thick and garbled. "Spare my life and I'll be your servant."

Moses kept his grip firm and the dagger steady, unmoving, waiting for the nomads to decide what they wanted to do with the tribesman.

"Let him go," Asif said in a rough voice.

Moses snapped his gaze to Asif, stunned at his command. "He tried to kill you. Don't you want to take him as prisoner?"

"I don't want this man as a slave, and I don't want him on our land," Asif continued, standing next to Moses and looking down at the tribesman. "He'll go back to his tribe with a tale of how we were merciful, even when he didn't deserve it."

Moses hesitated, staring into the tribesman's fearful eyes. Then he slowly released his pressure and stood up. The tribesman let out a choked cry, either of fear or relief; Moses didn't know which. While Moses and the nomads watched, the tribesman scrambled to his feet and crossed to his fallen companion. With a grunt, he picked up the man and started carrying him slowly in the direction of the dried lakebed that formed the border.

Moses stood with the nomads, watching the men go. Nothing good had happened today. First the intrusion by Asif's enemy, then the news of Asif's sister's death, and now the death of an enemy. Moses's pulse made a slow throb in his neck, and he let out a long breath. The sounds of the desert returned—the buzzing of the flies, the stirring of the wind, the scraping of the sand beneath his feet.

At this moment, he felt farther from his former life than ever. He'd almost killed a tribesman. Another death on his soul. Moses knew he was far from the person he thought he'd become. And it frightened him.

CHAPTER FOUR
ZIPPORAH

Zipporah cradled Cozbi's new baby in her arms. Marveling at the exquisite perfection of the small infant, Zipporah felt a stirring deep within. This baby was at the beginning of his life, with his whole future ahead of him. Gazing at his closed eyelids and the soft black lashes against his rounded cheeks, Zipporah felt a protective swell begin in her breast, mingled with a sense of pure love.

Oreb was adorable. Zipporah wanted to forget all of her chores and duties and sit and hold the child forever. She bent over him and kissed his soft cheek. The babe's eyes fluttered open and a tiny sigh escaped. Zipporah wanted to laugh and squeeze him to her chest. Instead, she just gazed at him, completely enraptured.

"Zipporah?" Cozbi's voice cut through Zipporah's infatuation. "Don't you have to get home? You've been here for hours, and it's almost dark."

She looked up, feeling surprised that so much time had passed. The sheep stew she'd brought over had long since been eaten by Cozbi and Sihon. All of Sihon's family had left, save for his mother, who now dozed on a mat in the corner of the tent. She'd been taking turns at night caring for the new baby.

"I can stay longer if you need me, at least until your mother-in-law awakes," Zipporah said.

Cozbi tilted her head. "You are funny, sister. I've never seen you like this. What's happened to you?"

Zipporah felt her cheeks heat up. She wasn't used to having her emotions on display, visible for everyone to see and analyze. But tears threatened. And she didn't even know why. "Nothing's happened," she said, barely managing to keep her unsteady voice in check. She handed the baby over to Cozbi, then slipped out of the tent, taking the empty clay jar with her.

The sun had settled against the horizon, its rays turning from gold to orange. The sky above was like a vast violet pool of shimmering water dotted with pricks of light. Zipporah's steps were slow as she walked back toward her family's tent. Strangely enough, her arms felt empty and her soul barren. While holding that baby, something sweet had swelled inside of her, filling her with a longing she'd never before experienced with her other nieces and nephews—a longing for her own child, a longing for her own loving marriage and a tent she could call her home, a longing for others to surround her and exclaim over the perfect being she'd helped create and bring into the world.

But Zipporah had none of that. She was alone, and unless she settled for a man like Sihon's younger brother, would she ever have the feeling of peace and contentment Cozbi seemed to have?

When she entered the cooking area of her family's tent, everything had already been cleaned and organized, which meant her mother had done Zipporah's work. She was sure to hear about that tomorrow, if not tonight. She knew her mother and other sisters had gone to her oldest sister, Tema's, tent in order to start planning the celebratory meal that would take place in a few days honoring the arrival of Cozbi's baby.

So for a while, Zipporah was alone with her thoughts. She scrubbed the clay pot with sand, then rinsed it with well water. She set the cooking jars in order, then walked out into the cooling night. Small fires burned in front of many tents as families prepared their evening meals, and the smell of cooking permeated the air. The sun had disappeared completely below the horizon, and the sky was a deep blue now.

Zipporah crossed to a boulder and perched herself on top of it, pulling her knees to her chest for balance. She turned her face toward the last remaining threads of light and rested her head on the tops of her knees.

As the warm breeze stirred around her, Zipporah thought about the intense feelings she'd had holding Cozbi's baby. The fierceness of the emotion had surprised her. She felt she'd caught a tiny glimpse of what it felt like to be a mother, and it had overwhelmed her.

"Zipporah," a male voice spoke from behind, startling her.

She turned to see Peor approaching. Why was he seeking her out?

"Your f-father said I'd find you h-here," he said.

The poor man was stuttering. What was her father up to? And what was Peor up to? "Is everything all right?" she asked, sliding off the boulder and standing to face him.

"Uh, yes," Peor said, now close enough that Zipporah could see his reddened face in the rising moonlight. "Your father thought we should . . . talk . . . get to know each other."

Zipporah raised a brow and stared at Peor. Was this his idea or her father's? The last thing she wanted was her father pushing someone like Peor in her direction. She didn't realize she hadn't said anything until he stuttered out, "But I-I didn't want to make you sick or anything. He said you are very shy and quiet."

Her mouth fell open, but then she thought better of giving a sharp retort. "Cozbi and Sihon are very happy," she said in a faint voice. "We should be happy for them and forget that he asked me to marry him before he asked Cozbi."

"O-oh, I am happy for them," Peor said. He took a step back and looked down at his feet.

Zipporah exhaled and decided that being direct was the best way to deal with this. "I'm sure my father meant well in his request that you come and speak to me. But I know we have a large age difference."

Peor looked up at her, a questioning look on his face.

"I don't think we need to let our parents force us together," she said. "I'm older than you and will someday find a husband, just as you'll someday find a wife. But it won't be each other."

It almost made Zipporah sad to see the look of gratitude on Peor's face. She knew her parents would be upset—more than upset—but she didn't want her future husband to quake at the knees and stutter every time they were speaking to each other.

He gave a brief nod, then turned away. She saw the relief in the set of his shoulders as he hurried away into the darkness. Zipporah told herself that it hadn't been a cruel thing she'd done, but quite the opposite, providing instead another possibility for both herself and Peor. Just as marrying Sihon had also been a possibility, but now he was happy and loved by Cozbi.

Zipporah climbed up on the boulder again and drew her knees in, wrapping her arms about her legs. The night sky had deepened to black now, and the stars were out in full force, vast across the sky, seemingly neverending. It was on nights like this that Zipporah felt there were more possibilities in her life, that the universe was so much larger than Midian, that living her entire life here seemed a minute chance. That perhaps something else was in store for her.

She'd known she wouldn't have to wait long before her mother and father discovered what she'd said to Peor. Sure enough, before the cooking fires had a chance to die out as the families of Midian settled in for the night, Zipporah heard her mother calling her name.

She stayed on the boulder as her mother's calling grew closer. "Over here, Mother." She cringed as she heard the rustle of her mother's robes as she approached.

Then, beneath the light of the low moon, her mother crossed to her and looked into her eyes.

"Cozbi told me about what happened when you were holding her baby."

This Zipporah didn't expect. A tongue-lashing about Peor, yes, but not this. She should have realized Cozbi wouldn't waste a moment in telling their mother.

"I thought you were at Tema's tent," she responded.

"I was for a short time, but your sisters have it under control," her mother said. "I made a final stop at Cozbi's to make sure they had all they needed. It bothers me that Sihon's mother won't leave—won't allow me to spend a few nights as well. But I suppose the baby doesn't need two grandmothers hovering."

Zipporah smiled at that. But she'd smiled too soon.

"What were you thinking, talking to Peor like that?" her mother continued. "You are ready to marry. You have been ready for too long, and it's time you cast aside your daydreams."

Zipporah opened her mouth to reply, but her mother rushed on. "Look around you," she said in a lowered voice. "Men die in battle with the other tribes, they are bitten by snakes and die, they fall off of ridges and break something, they drink poisoned water, they are robbed, and—"

"Mother, I understand."

Her mother moved closer, practically hissing now. "You *don't* understand. Life is valuable in the desert. Every life is precious. We don't have a wealth of choices in who we marry, but we marry because we must. And then we have children, and those children grow up to have more children. We work together, male and female, hand in hand, to create a strong settlement that will benefit and protect us all. And in order to do that, we must bear children."

Zipporah could no longer look at her mother, and she wished she didn't have to hear her chastisements.

"You need to understand, my daughter, that refusing to marry someone can severely affect your entire family's future," her mother said.

Her mother was right, although it was painful to be lectured. "I will marry," Zipporah said. "Just not Peor."

"Then who?" Her mother huffed out a breath. "And when?"

"I don't know." Whom *would* she marry? The question bothered her as much as it plagued her mother. Perhaps she would have to marry Peor. But would it be fair to either of them? She thought of the other men in the community and realized that she might never have hope for a marriage of love. Hers would be a marriage of duty.

"Well, I do," her mother said with finality. "You have *one month* to choose someone. And your father will agree with me. Or we will encourage Peor to propose to you, and you will accept his proposal."

One month. Or she would be betrothed to Peor. *One month.*

Zipporah exhaled and nodded. Her mother strode away without another word, apparently mollified for now. But Zipporah knew that her mother was far from finished lecturing her. Tomorrow it would be more of the same, and she'd also have her father's disappointed expression to contend with. Not to mention her other sisters—who would surely be informed at the earliest moment of Zipporah's conversation with Peor.

She stayed on the boulder, gazing at the stars and listening to the sounds of a settlement settling in for the night. When she was sure that everyone in her family had gone to bed, she crept back toward the tent and found her sectioned-off portion where she kept her mat and clothing. She fell asleep thinking of her mother's mandate and remembering the emptiness of her arms when she'd handed Cozbi's new baby back to her.

CHAPTER FIVE
MOSES

Moses studied the rocky terrain interspersed with patches of wild grasses where the sheep grazed. Today was his final day with this tribe. They'd promised him the night before that he could go free on the morrow. Ever since he helped defend Asif and the other nomads against the Baal tribe, he'd risen to a new level of respect.

But it had wrenched his heart when they'd arrived back at the camp with the news that Asif's sister had died. Moses had never heard such woeful wailing and keening as had come from those women who mourned their relative. It had resonated in his ears long after they'd fallen silent for the night.

There were moments when Moses thought perhaps he would stay with this tribe, live off the land like they did, herd sheep, trade with nomads. But he wanted to keep moving, put more distance between himself and his birth land.

He felt stronger in body now, and he'd grown accustomed to the barley stew with bits of meat and honey cakes prepared by the women and cooked over the fire. In fact, he craved it, especially during the long hours of shepherding in which he had only a few morsels of crusted flat bread and soft goat cheese with him.

Moses saw movement out of the corner of his eye and turned to see Asif approaching. "We'll return now to the settlement," the nomad said.

Moses drew his brows together. The sun hadn't even touched the evening horizon yet. "It's early."

Asif's mouth crooked into a smile. "The women have prepared a banquet to send you off to your new life."

Surprised, Moses suddenly felt overwhelmed. "I do not expect a banquet."

Asif clapped him on the shoulder. "We will not let you leave without enjoying our best desert hospitality."

And so it was. Moses and Asif, along with the other nomads, moved the herds back to the settlement before the sun set. The spicy smells of roasting meat reached them from across the small valley. Moses's stomach rumbled, and it was apparently loud enough for Asif to hear, since he laughed long and hard.

"You will miss our meals, I am sure," Asif said. "Out there," he waved his hand, "you will learn to love locust and rodent meat."

Moses knew this was true. His body had adjusted to the desert life, and he'd never felt more fit or energetic or more in tune with the earth and nature. They strode back into the settlement. Rugs had been spread out around the cooking fires, and Moses was to be the guest of honor.

He was ushered by two of the women to a large cushion that sat atop a rug, and the first dish of pomegranate mixed with a green plant was brought to him. Perhaps because Moses was facing the unknown in the morning, the food tasted especially savory and rich. Course after course came, including barley stew with thick chunks of meat, and cakes drizzled with syrup made from dates. Moses ate until he was quite full—a luxury he hadn't known for some time.

As the night advanced, the women herded their children into the tents, and the men remained, telling stories. Asif shared the history between the two neighboring tribes, and Moses learned that it had been tense for generations. And even though they had better relations with other tribes, those weren't necessarily stable either.

"You are best to stay away from this area where the Badrayan tribe lives," Asif said, drawing a crude map in the sand past the edge of the rug. He pointed out other areas and explained the intricate relationships of each group of people. "Midian is one of the larger settlements, and they are a decent people. They are strong in number, and most tribes are smart enough to leave them alone."

The other men in their gathering nodded. "The main thing to remember is that everyone has a point of desperation, especially in the dry season," Asif continued. "Tribal laws and truces have little meaning when a nomad thinks another has driven off his herd, or there is not enough water for everyone to coexist."

"Sometimes camels wander off, but sometimes they are stolen too," one of the men added. "Wrong assumptions are easily made, but there's not much civility in the desert. A wrong look or an aggressive move can lead to immediate death." The tribal leader picked up a bundle wrapped in a piece of cloth next to him. "We want to present you with this in appreciation for helping Asif and our nomads." He handed the bundle to Moses.

Moses unwrapped it to find a crudely carved bow, along with several arrows that were surprisingly straight.

"You will have to kill your own food now," Asif said, and the others chuckled.

Moses felt grateful yet nervous at the same time. "Thank you for this," he said with a broad smile. "I will never forget your tribe's generosity. Even though we got off to a rough start."

The men laughed, and Asif clapped Moses on the back. "You will get your satchel back too in the morning."

Moses's world had become small and focused on the essentials of living and surviving. His old life seemed more than a lifetime away and almost impossible to imagine now.

But the following morning, just as the dawn lightened the sky, the tribal leader presented Moses with his satchel, complete with his exquisite royal robe and both gold statues. And the memories came flooding back.

"We have no use for gold," the tribal leader said when he saw the surprise on Moses's face. "If we so much as attempt a trade with one of these, all of the surrounding tribes would band together and attack us just for the gold."

Moses had pulled out everything from the satchel before setting off. He held up the robe; its softness felt foreign in his fingers. The lustrous weave caught the early rays of sun that now spilled over the far hills. He didn't know if he'd ever wear the robe again, but it was from his mother, and he'd keep it even if it was impractical in the wilderness.

After a lot of pats on the back and several farewells, Moses set off on his own, carrying his satchel, a goatskin of water, a pack of food prepared by the women, and the bow and arrows. He knew he'd miss his association with the nomads, but he needed to figure out who he was now and create a new identity.

The wind blew hot for so early in the morning, yet Moses pressed forward, leaning into it and bringing the scarf the nomads had given him up around his nose until it covered everything but his eyes. He thought of the terrible sandstorms he'd experienced in Egypt and was sure they would be equally terrible here.

He avoided the areas Asif had warned him about and followed the route of the most public wells. He knew that shepherds had certain times of the day they'd go to the well. It was dangerous to be there when it was another tribe's turn. Battles had broken out and men had been killed over whose turn it was to water their flocks.

Moses kept his eyes sharp, looking for animal droppings or other signs of a recent herd passing through the lands he was walking on. As a lone man, he didn't expect to see fortune twice. Asif's tribe had been plenty fierce, but once they started to trust him, they'd become like brothers.

Although he'd never had a true brother, Moses had been close friends with his cousins Ramses and Pentu. Of course, now he knew they weren't his cousins at all. He had been educated side by side with these two boys he'd grown up with, had shared military strategy lessons, and had even fought alongside them in battle against the Libyans. And they had always believed Moses was one of them.

Surely by now they had given up on finding him. He wondered what Ramses, who was the crown prince of Egypt, thought of him. Had he learned that Moses was of Hebrew blood? Or would his mother, Bithiah, keep it a secret? There was no need now. Moses wouldn't be returning to Egypt. Even though only a handful of weeks had passed since he'd left his home, it felt longer. He'd already changed so much, and he knew he'd be hard to recognize.

There were no servants here to bathe or trim or shave him. His hair had grown for the first time in his memory, though it wasn't nearly as long and full as that of the nomads—not yet anyhow. Moses pushed on, taking the incline until he was walking on top of a ridge that overlooked the desert. There was barrenness as far as he could see, cut by the occasional groupings of trees in the bottom of a shallow wadi, a mostly dry riverbed.

In the far eastern distance, he could just make out a flock of sheep. The shepherds wouldn't be far behind, and Moses had no interest in encountering anyone today. Even though the sun was high now and making its usual scorching path across the sky, Moses kept moving. He turned away from the flock and looked for the landmarks Asif had told him about. Asif had said that when he saw shepherds congregating and the terrain sprouting more green, he should expect to see a well soon.

Moses watched as the shepherds in the distance led their flocks to a small grove. He assumed there must be a well there. He found an alcove among the rocks where he could rest and escape the fiercest part of the heat as he waited for the shepherds to leave.

He must have fallen asleep because he woke to a much dimmer sky, and when he stood and looked around, clouds had gathered and the sun was nearly to the western horizon. Evening had fallen, and the wind had picked up, the heat now dissipating somewhat.

Moses finished the last of the water in his goatskin and set off toward the grove of trees, hoping that his prediction was right and that he'd find a well there to refill his goatskin and refresh himself.

It wasn't until he reached the grove of trees that Moses realized how depleted his energy really was. The cool shade, mixed with the darkening sky, was like a balm to his skin. And the well situated in the middle of the grove must be what afterlife looked like for those who were preserved in death.

"Praise Amun," he said as he approached the well. He found a rope that had mercifully been left at the well and tied it onto his goatskin. Then he lowered the goatskin until it met resistance. After leaving it there for several moments, he finally raised it back up. It was significantly heavier, and Moses sighed with relief as he saw the water that had filled it.

He tipped the goatskin back and began to drink. After the first two swallows, he lowered the goatskin and spat the water out. It was bitter. Moses wiped the water from his mouth and stared at the well. The edges of the well weren't built up but were nearly level with the ground. Then Moses noticed something he hadn't before. There were animal droppings and urine stains around the well, and some leading down to the well. It was obvious that animals had been allowed to roam free, too free. Or wild animals had come to the well, sensing the water, and now it was bitter to the taste.

Moses looked around the small grove. Stone troughs sat several paces away—this was obviously a watering place for herds. He thought back to the traveling he'd done that day. He hadn't passed any bodies of water or any sort of stream or river. And Asif's explanations hadn't included what to do if the well water was too bitter with animal droppings to be palatable.

Moses's stomach felt sour, and he pulled off a hunk of the bread from his food pack. Chewing made him feel better, but what he really needed was water. With the desert sun finished for the day and the shadows turning to black, he knew he'd have to sleep through his thirstiness and hope for better fortune the next day.

He picked several dates from one of the palms, then settled beneath it for the night, hoping sleep would come quickly.

CHAPTER SIX
ZIPPORAH

"May I carry him?" Zipporah asked Cozbi as they walked alongside their other sisters. They were leading her father's flocks toward the well outside the settlement. It was reserved for the animals since the water tended to be bitter, especially during the hotter months. The men were busy this morning, caring for the camels of a caravan that had just arrived the night before.

Cozbi handed over Oreb, and Zipporah eagerly wrapped him in her arms. It was Cozbi's first trek farther than the settlement since the birth of her baby. Zipporah had hovered over the child every day, and today was no exception. She was glad Cozbi had agreed to go with them.

They moved as a large unit with their sisters and the sheep. The two oldest sisters, Tema and Madiama, had left their children with their grandmother, so it was a rare moment for the sisters to be alone together. And Zipporah was determined to enjoy the morning with them and not think about her mother's new mandate. Although she was sure to be asked about Peor at some point.

Oreb nestled close to Zipporah, his adorable little hand clutching her tunic, and her heart soared at the sweetness of it. She could almost agree with her mother that it was time to get married. She knew it deep down, but she had a hard time thinking of a man with whom she'd be willing to commit living the rest of her life.

Tema and Madiama lagged behind the group, talking rapidly, catching up on their mornings. Her three youngest sisters, Jael, Tayma, and Abigail, ran ahead as if they'd been confined to a tent for weeks, laughing when they made the sheep bleat. Zipporah stayed close to Cozbi in the middle of the group, enjoying the moderate coolness of the morning and the scent of the tiny desert flowers that had bloomed close to the approaching oasis.

When Oreb whimpered, both Zipporah and Cozbi fussed over him. He settled back down, and Zipporah gave a triumphant smile.

"I've never seen you like this," Cozbi said.

"Your son is a charmer," Zipporah replied, loving the softness of his skin against her neck.

"It's like *you* are besotted," Cozbi said. "You're a natural mother."

That caught Zipporah off guard. "I am besotted, but I don't know about being a natural mother."

Cozbi moved closer and lowered her voice. "I know what you said to Peor. He told me and Sihon. But he's a good young man, and you'll love being a mother with your own child."

"That's just it," Zipporah said. "In about ten years, Peor will realize what an old woman he married."

Cozbi was shaking her head. "You underestimate yourself, Zipporah. You're very pretty, you know. There's a reason that my own husband made an offer for you before me."

"He just asked me because I was the oldest unmarried daughter," Zipporah said.

"See. There you go again. Always putting yourself down." Her eyes narrowed. "You can't wait too much longer. Just think, if you marry in a few months, we can raise our children together."

"I can't imagine any child being sweeter than Oreb," Zipporah said. "I'll just plan on being the best aunt in Midian." Even as she spoke, she wondered if marrying someone like Peor or one of the other men she didn't particularly care for would be so horrible if she could spend her days caring for a baby as sweet as Oreb.

She released a silent sigh. If only she could already have the marriage part over and done with and a child or two to watch over.

"The frankincense caravan should be coming through soon," Cozbi said, nudging Zipporah. "You should go with the other young women to barter."

Zipporah laughed. "I did last season, and you know how that turned out. Besides, Father would never let me marry a foreigner."

"Perhaps there will be younger men this time," Cozbi said, amusement in her voice.

Zipporah could still picture one of the caravan riders in her mind. She'd gone to sell them fresh goat's milk and to browse through the wares they transported from exotic countries. Once in a while, a Midian woman would capture the eye of a traveling tradesman. But Zipporah couldn't imagine a life where her husband would be gone for entire seasons at a time.

Somehow Zipporah had attracted the intense interest of a man older than her father. He had only a few teeth, and his face had deep lines from the harsh desert sun and wind. Cozbi claimed that he wasn't as old as Zipporah thought he was, but even if the man had still had most of his teeth, she couldn't get past the fact that he'd told her he was in love with her minutes after meeting.

Zipporah and her sisters were close to the well now, and the sheep increased their pace. They knew they were getting watered, and they recognized the path. Zipporah noticed movement on the far ridge, and her breath caught when she saw several shepherds coming down the ridge, surrounded by their flocks, and heading straight for the well.

Without seeing them close up, Zipporah knew they were from the Badrayan tribe. They were supposed to water their flocks after the sun's zenith. Midianites watered in the morning, the Badrayans in the afternoon. It kept things simple, and now with only women in their group, Zipporah wasn't looking forward to any confrontation. The Midianites and Badrayans had a long history of conflict. When the rain was plentiful and the land rich, peace was more prevalent. But when harsh conditions forced men to scavenge the land, the Badrayans stopped at little to provide for their people.

Desert living could be difficult at times, so Zipporah couldn't completely blame them for their savagery. Yet everyone's lives were dependent on the same resources, which meant that following the unspoken desert rules was extremely important. It was because of this that unease pulsed through Zipporah at the sight of the shepherds coming toward the well at the wrong time of day.

"Do you see them?" she said to Cozbi.

Cozbi squinted toward the ridge. "What are they doing here so early?"

Zipporah looked back at her older sisters. They had increased their pace, having seen the approaching shepherds too. The women would reach the well before the other shepherds, and Zipporah hoped that the shepherds had come early just by chance.

"Perhaps they want to intermarry into our tribe," Cozbi said in a hushed tone, "and they are here to watch us."

Tribes never intermarried. Everyone was too fiercely protective of their own territory and didn't want it split or shared in any form. The only marriages that took place between tribes were those that were forced because of battle trophies.

The women traveled the last few paces to the well, and without even giving any instructions, they set to work drawing up the water and pouring it into the troughs for the sheep. They worked quickly and silently, and at one point Zipporah adjusted Oreb against her when he startled awake from her bending over so much.

"They're almost here," Cozbi hissed to Zipporah.

With dread pounding in her chest, Zipporah turned to look at the approaching shepherds. They weren't slowing down or holding off. Maybe they were here to talk. But what about? Zipporah and her sisters wouldn't be able to make any official decisions without their father or their brother anyway.

Zipporah tensed as the shepherds drew closer and closer, although she and her sisters pretended they weren't worried as they continued to transfer the water as the sheep crowded around. The sheep that had already been watered started wandering and nibbling at the desert grass.

The closer the shepherds came, the harder it was to ignore them. Finally, Zipporah set down the goatskin she was carrying, and holding Oreb against her, she watched the men. There was no greeting, no eye contact, and that alone sent a chill through Zipporah.

"Aiyah! Aiyah!" one of the shepherds called out, waving his staff at Zipporah's sheep.

She stared in astonishment as the other shepherds started to scatter the sheep as well. True to their nature, the sheep started to bleat and run off haphazardly; confused and not knowing where to go, they just followed each other.

Abigail and Jael chased after them, trying to get the sheep to turn around. But there were too many going in different directions, and the men were still shouting at the sheep and scaring them.

Zipporah's entire body heated with anger, and she started walking forward to yell at the shepherds, even though she knew it was foolish. What were she and her sisters against these five tribesmen and their apparent decision to bully Zipporah's sisters away from the well?

"Wait! Think about Oreb," Cozbi said, grabbing her arm.

Zipporah paused for a moment to collect her thoughts. Anger still burned through her, but if things turned dangerous, it wouldn't be good for her to be holding Oreb. She unwrapped the cloth that bound him to her body and was about to hand the child over to her sister when a new voice startled her.

She whipped around to see a man coming from the trees on the other side of the well. He was tall, his torso was bare, and he wore only a kilt. Zipporah's first impression was that he was one of those nomads who lived a savage life. Perhaps he was a Hippioprosōpoi tribesman. She'd heard tales of the cannibal tribesmen from the east, and they were said to have shorter hair and bare torsos.

The possibility shuddered through her, but she didn't have time to dwell on it as he lifted a bow and shot an arrow at one of the shepherds. It hit him in the fleshiest part of his shoulder, and the man screamed.

Zipporah stood in shock, her hands still gripping Oreb, as she watched the unexpected turn of events. The stranger ran toward the shepherds, yelling at them in some language Zipporah didn't understand, but it was clear that he was defending the women and attacking the men.

He nocked another arrow and sent it flying. It barely missed one of the shepherds. Now the stranger had everyone's attention. Cozbi snatched Oreb from Zipporah, and the women huddled together, adding their own screams to the commotion. Zipporah gripped one of her sister's hands as the shepherds charged the stranger, their staffs held high in their hands.

Four shepherds against one man. Zipporah's stomach felt as if it had turned inside out. Nothing about this battle could go the stranger's way. The man who was trying to defend her sisters would end up dead in the sand.

Zipporah fully expected the stranger to turn and run, to escape while he could. But the stranger simply nocked another arrow and shot again. The shepherds dodged it and continued to run straight toward the stranger. One of her sisters cried out, and it was only then that Zipporah realized Oreb was crying hysterically.

The stranger stood his ground, and just before he was trampled, he dropped his bow and pulled a dagger hidden in the waistband of his kilt. He lunged forward, knocking one of the shepherds to the ground. The other three immediately piled on top of him, and Zipporah wanted to run and help him. But knife blades, fists, and feet where flying so fast she couldn't tell who was who.

She was barely aware of the gasps of her sisters, the yelling of the men, or the crying of the baby. She could only stare in horror as men fought to kill each other like wild animals fighting over the last morsel of meat.

And then the stranger rose to his feet, blood staining his face and arms. He had been cut several times, but he was standing triumphant, looking down at the men who had outnumbered him.

One of the shepherds held up his hands, crying for mercy.

The stranger gave a nod and said something in his foreign language. The shepherd took it to mean that he was free to take his men and go.

Zipporah watched in amazement as the shepherds picked themselves up, blood on their clothing and arms, and started to walk away. Two were limping, and the other two crossed to the man who'd been shot by an arrow. They picked him up and started carrying him toward the ridge.

Zipporah had no idea if the man was alive or dead. The two shepherds with a limp didn't even have the strength to collect their flock. The sheep about the well were mixed in with the women's sheep, and it would have taken some time to divide the herds. With the water-filled troughs, it would be a while before even a master shepherd could redirect any part of the flock.

Next to her, a couple of Zipporah's sisters were crying quietly, but she had a new worry. The stranger who'd just saved their flocks, and possibly their lives, was bleeding heavily. He didn't seem to notice, though. He stood as still as a carved statue, watching the shepherds depart, as if he believed that by moving or attending to his wounds the shepherds would return.

Zipporah had never seen a man stand so still. But she couldn't endure the sight of the blood on his skin any longer, and she walked to his side. "You must sit down and let me check your wounds," she said in a soft voice, hoping not to startle him. She also hoped that he hadn't just chased off the shepherds so he could do fouler deeds to her sisters.

He blinked and turned his head toward her.

She kept her gaze steady and looked into his gold-brown eyes, a most unusual color, and she realized she was trembling. The past moments had been terrifying, and now her body was starting to comprehend what could have happened.

"You're injured," she said, pointing to his arm and the long, extremely painful-looking gash on it. "We need to bind your wounds." She didn't know what language he'd been speaking, but she hoped her gestures would make him understand.

He looked down at his bleeding arm.

"Come sit down," Zipporah said, motioning with her hand. He didn't move, so she reached out and touched his other arm.

Instantly, he took a step back.

Holding up her hands, she said, "I want to help you. You need to sit down so I can attend to your wounds." She pointed toward the stone troughs that were crowded with the sheep. "Come, and I'll wash the blood." She mimicked brushing at her arms.

Finally, he seemed to comprehend that she meant to help him. He followed her to one of the stone troughs. Zipporah shoved two sheep out of the way, then motioned for the man to put his hand into the water. When he did so, she gently splashed water on his arms, then removed the scarf from her head and soaked it in the water.

Her sisters had straightened from their huddling, and Cozbi was soothing Oreb. "Gather our flocks before it gets too hot," Zipporah commanded.

That seemed to pull Tema back to the present. She started sending the sisters in different directions, giving them orders. "And if a few of those tribesmen's sheep decide to follow, it will be their loss."

"Tema," Zipporah said in a sharp voice. "We don't want to start a tribal war."

Tema gave a bitter laugh. "I don't think they'll be coming back anytime soon." She looked at the stranger. "I'll gather some leaves for a poultice."

Zipporah turned her attention back to the stranger and began to wash the blood off his arms using her wet scarf. Over and over she soaked the scarf, and over and over she cleansed his wounds. He stayed utterly still and silent as she worked. He flinched a few times but didn't cry out. Being this close to a strange man and knowing he'd just saved her and her sisters did odd things to Zipporah's senses. She was alert to his every movement, his breathing, the blink of his eyes, and the way the desert wind stirred his short hair.

As she cleaned the blood from his chest and neck, she glanced at his face. His eyes were closed, as if he were enduring the pain as best he could. It gave Zipporah a few seconds to really look at him. His face didn't have the roughness of a desert man, and Zipporah knew that he wasn't a nomad—or at least hadn't been one for very long.

She'd never seen a man with such short hair. It was almost as if he'd kept it shaved like the Egyptians. She paused in her work. Was this man Egyptian? It would explain his language and his different ways of fighting. She realized the man's eyes had opened and he was looking down at her.

She turned back to the water trough quickly, her face heating up. She'd never been this close to a strange man before, never cleansed a man's body. His scent of sand and leaves and perspiration mixed into a spicy aroma. It took her a moment before she felt she could look back at him.

"Sit down, and I'll clean your face." She motioned for him to sit, and he perched on the edge of the trough. When he closed his eyes again she was relieved, and she continued to carefully wash the blood from his face.

CHAPTER SEVEN
MOSES

As the woman continued to clean his face, Moses tried to keep his body still. It was like trying to hold back a wild animal. He wanted to writhe in pain—it throbbed through every part of his body now. During the skirmish with the shepherds, he hadn't felt the pain. He hadn't felt anything, really, except for anger at the cruelty of the shepherds and the way they'd so shamelessly scattered the women's flocks and taken over the well as their own.

The woman who was administering to him spoke in soft tones, and her voice helped him relax. Then she stopped washing for a moment, and he opened his eyes. One of the other women had joined her, and they began to wrap strips of cloth about his arms. His skin burned fiercely, but he didn't move, allowing them to do their work.

He focused on the first woman's face, trying to distract himself from the pain while watching her expressions as she worked on him. Her eyes were deep brown, framed with heavy lashes, her skin darker than Egyptian or Hebrew. Since she'd removed her scarf to help him, her rich brown hair had tumbled from its captivity and spilled across her shoulders in abundance. She didn't have the refined beauty of the women he knew in the Egyptian royal court, yet her beauty was natural, almost wild, and Moses found that he could appreciate that very much.

The second woman spoke to the first woman, saying *Zipporah* more than once. That must be the first woman's name. Zipporah had been the one with the baby when he first saw them through the trees. He didn't understand what the women were saying, but he listened intently, trying to connect some of the words and sounds with his own knowledge of languages.

He hadn't been able to sleep during the deep of the previous night and had finally fallen asleep in the early hours before dawn. The air had already warmed with the morning sun by the time the sound of female voices talking and laughing had awakened him. For a moment, he thought he was back in Egypt, hearing women passing in the corridor outside his bedchamber. But the feel of the sand on his skin brought him to the present all too quickly.

By the time he'd stirred and sat up, the women's tones had changed. They sounded worried and fearful. He rose to his feet and walked through the stand of trees he'd slept under and saw seven women busily hauling water from the well and filling the stone troughs. Sheep crowded around them eagerly, bleating and pushing other sheep out of the way to get to the water.

Moses smiled at the animals, but then the smile dropped from his face as the women kept turning their attention away from the well and their flock. When Moses spotted the approaching shepherds and their flocks, he knew they weren't related to the women, nor were they a friendly tribe.

Scanning his surroundings, Moses confirmed that no men had accompanied these women and that they were quite vulnerable. None of them seemed to have weapons with them, and one even held a baby. It didn't take much to see that the shepherds had only mischief on their minds, and when they started scattering the women's sheep, Moses couldn't stay hidden one moment longer.

The shepherds had been strong and scrappy, but Moses had spent years training in battle, and he knew all of the weak spots on a man's body and could use that to his advantage. It helped that his first arrow had hit its mark, thus intimidating the other shepherds, letting them know that he was willing to risk his life and take theirs.

If there was a way to thank Asif and his tribe for the gift of the bow and arrows, Moses would find it.

Now the women had finished wrapping his arms, and the one named Zipporah was speaking again. To him? He opened his eyes and discovered that she was leaning close to his chest, as if examining the cut near his shoulder. The marauding shepherds had had staffs and a couple of them daggers. It had been a mean fight.

The woman raised her head and said something in a quiet voice.

"I don't understand you," he said, speaking to her for the first time.

She straightened, clearly not understanding him either. He wondered briefly how someone so slim could have such a new baby. The second woman put her hand on his good shoulder, and he was surprised at her firmness until Zipporah applied a poultice of some sort to the cut on his bad shoulder.

The stinging was immediate. He nearly jumped up and yelled, but the second woman continued to hold him in place while Zipporah applied the poultice. He could tell she was trying to cause him as little discomfort as possible. By the time she moved to the injuries on his face, the pain in his shoulder had numbed. Whatever they'd put on his shoulder was already helping.

As the pain receded, other physical ailments came to the forefront. Since drinking the bitter well water the night before, Moses hadn't had any water. He still had a bit of food in his pack, but he'd rationed it carefully since he didn't know when his next meal would come.

Now, sitting here in the cool shade after such a fierce fight, he was feeling weaker by the moment. His thoughts kept muddling together.

The woman was speaking to him again. He tried to concentrate on what she was trying to tell him. She was pointing at her chest and saying, "Zipporah." So it truly was her name. He repeated it aloud, the name sounding foreign on his tongue.

Zipporah smiled and then pointed to the woman next to her. "Cozbi."

He tried that name out too. Both women were smiling now. He tried to smile back, but he simply didn't have the strength. They both pointed to him, and he realized they wanted to know his name.

"Moses," he said, then everything around him darkened for a moment.

Someone grabbed his arm, and he opened his eyes again. He must have lost consciousness, and now three women surrounded him. Zipporah held a goatskin to his lips.

He didn't need any encouragement to be asked to drink. The water was cool and sweet. As he drank, he decided he'd never tasted anything more delicious in his life. The most exotic food at the grandest banquet in the Pharaoh's throne room didn't compare to sweet-tasting water in the harsh desert.

The water made him feel better, and next thing he knew, Cozbi was pressing a piece of flat bread into his palm. He took a bite, then another. He didn't care that the women were watching him eat and were probably surprised at how hungry he was. After he finished the first piece, he ate the next piece they offered. And then a third. Finally, he held up his hand.

Cozbi nodded with a smile, then took the baby from one of the other women. She held the child close, and Moses realized that the baby looked a lot like Cozbi. Perhaps that meant Zipporah wasn't the mother, and he wondered if she was yet married. He shook the thought immediately from his mind. He was just trying to survive, not fill his mind with thoughts of a woman.

His head felt clear now, and the pain of his wounds was only a dull throb. He was well aware of the approaching heat of the day and what it might mean for these women to be delayed in watering their flocks. Without a word, he rose to his feet and walked to where a couple of the women were working to fill goatskins from the well, then transporting the water to the stone troughs.

Moses grabbed a goatskin left by one of the girls who was rounding up the sheep and lowered it into the well by its rope. Zipporah hurried over and tried to tell him to rest, but he ignored her suggestion and worked to fill the stone troughs. The sheep crowded in as he worked, brushing against his legs, bleating in what he thought must be appreciation.

It didn't take long for the wandering sheep, as well as the sheep from the tribesmen's flock that had been abandoned, to return to the water. Nearly all of the sheep had drunk their fill when one of the younger girls crossed to him, and with her eyes wide, looked him over from head to toe.

Zipporah said something to her, but the young girl continued to stare. Then she grasped his hand and made a motion as if she wanted him to come with her. The other women gathered around while he stood holding a dripping goatskin, not understanding what they were talking about. They were all nodding and talking, then motioning for him to come with them. Where did they want him to go?

The young girl was hopping up and down with excitement. A couple of the other women tried to explain to him in their language. Moses decided they must want him to come back to their settlement. But he didn't know if he could again put himself into a situation where his belongings would be held as ransom while he worked his way into another tribe's favor before he could be set free.

He was just about to decline and wave away their offer when he caught Zipporah looking at him. She hadn't joined in the other women's coaxing, but with her dark eyes and slight smile, she was looking at him differently than the others were.

She was watching him quietly and wondering about him. He knew she could see his differences and may have already figured out that he was a runaway Egyptian. But he sensed she was curious, and for some reason he liked her being curious. He realized he was curious about her too. He liked her wanting to know more about him, where he was from, where he was going.

Moses dumped the water from the goatskin he held into the nearby trough, then he turned to the woman and said, "I will come with you." They seemed to understand he was agreeing, and one of the women handed him a staff. He realized it had been left behind by one of the shepherds. He waved it in the direction of where he'd slept, and said, "I have to get my things."

No one could have understood his exact words, but they seemed to understand they needed to wait for him. He walked to where he'd slept, favoring his right leg, which was the most bruised of the two. The only actual gashes he had were on his arms, chest, and face, but his legs and feet had been spared, so he shouldn't have any trouble walking to wherever these women lived. Although he hoped it wasn't too far. Zipporah and the young girl followed him, and when they saw that he meant to pick up his satchel and pack, the young girl reached for them.

It was only then that Moses realized that Zipporah was holding the bow and arrows and dagger he'd used in the fight. He took the dagger from her and replaced it in the waistband of his kilt. He motioned for Zipporah to carry the bow and arrows for him. He didn't know if he could sling anything over his back right now. She gave a small nod and kept the bow and arrows.

They walked to join the other women, and as they set off away from the well, back in the direction they must have come from, Moses thought about the evening in Egypt when his life had completely changed. It had started out with his fight with an Egyptian taskmaster and ended with the confession by his mother that she'd fetched him out of the River Nile.

How the events of that day had changed his life! Moses sensed that the events of this morning were about to change his life again.

CHAPTER EIGHT
ZIPPORAH

THE WALK BACK TO MIDIAN was slow, and Zipporah only walked as fast as the stranger did. Moses was his name. An unusual name, which further clarified that he wasn't a nomad who'd spent his life in the desert. She and her sisters had determined that he was Egyptian—it was the only thing that made sense. His clothing and short hair seemed to add up to that conclusion.

She stole frequent glances at him, appraising him and wondering about his life up until the moment he had chased away the shepherds from the well. She wondered why he was out here in the wilderness by himself. She knew the land of Egypt was populated with Hebrews who worked as slaves for the great Pharaoh Seti. Her father had told them plenty of stories he'd heard in his travels, and they'd heard more stories from passing nomads who stopped at Midian to trade.

She could tell by his irregular breathing and the way he favored one of his legs as he limped along that Moses was in pain. But his expression was determined, his gaze directed forward as if he were focusing on putting one foot in front of the other. As the sun climbed in the sky, the heat became almost unbearable, and Zipporah wondered if they should stop to let Moses rest.

She moved closer to his side, not wanting to startle him as she spoke. "Would you like to rest?" she asked, bringing her folded hands to her face and tilting her head. She pointed to the sun. "It's very hot, and"—she pointed to his bound arms—"you have many wounds."

Moses was watching her as she talked, and for some reason, her mouth felt dry. What was he hearing her say? Could he make out any words? If her own mouth was dry, he was probably even thirstier. She held up the goatskin she'd offered him before with the sweet water in it. Nothing close to what the well water would taste like during the dry season.

He slowed his walk and came to a stop. He took the goatskin from her fingers and drank a few swallows of water from it.

"Have some more water—as much as you need," Zipporah said, pushing it back toward him when he tried to hand it back.

He drew his brows together as he looked at her. She nodded encouragingly. "Please, drink more."

"Drink more," he said after her, imitating her language.

She smiled and said, "Yes, drink more."

He smiled back, then started drinking the water again, this time not just a few swallows, but most of what was left in the goatskin.

Zipporah just watched him and smiled, a sense of accomplishment and even pride coursing through her. They'd spoken the same language for a few words, and she'd convinced him to drink water. She was sure it would make him recover more quickly, and if she had a small hand in his recovery, she couldn't be more pleased.

If only her mother could see her now, standing beneath the hot sun with the desert wind blowing through her unbound hair as she smiled at a perfect stranger who wore only a kilt to cover his body. And with him smiling back at her. Zipporah's mother would certainly have an opinion about all of this.

Moses lowered the goatskin and handed it back to her.

"Thank you," she said in a quiet voice, suddenly feeling shy after all the smiling and explaining back and forth.

"Thank you," Moses said like a child imitating his mother's words.

The simplicity of it endeared this stranger to Zipporah. He was obviously skilled in battle, able to fight off five shepherds armed with staffs and daggers, adept at surviving in the desert on his own, yet *she* was teaching *him* something.

Zipporah was about to sling the much lighter goatskin of water over her back when Moses reached toward her and slid the bow and set of arrows she was carrying for him off her shoulder.

"I can carry it," she said, putting her hand on the bow as well.

He only smiled and pulled it away from her, then with a grimace that told her he was hiding most of his pain, he slung it over his good shoulder. When he held out his hand for the nearly empty goatskin, she shook her head. "No, I can carry this. You are the one who is injured."

His eyes studied her as she talked as if he were trying to separate and understand each word she spoke. "Injured?" He motioned toward his bandaged shoulder.

"Yes, you're injured," Zipporah said. She placed her hands on her hips. "You are hard to help, you know that? You should be resting in the shade somewhere while my sisters and I bring you tea and bread."

His eyebrows quirked, and he looked like he was about to smile again. She had spoken quite a lot, and she couldn't expect him to understand anything she'd just said.

"Sorry," she said. "Hopefully my father will be able to talk to you. He's traveled all over and speaks several languages." Again, there was no response from him. "All right, come on. We'll reach my family's tent soon enough." She started walking again, and he fell in step beside her.

They'd fallen quite a bit behind now. Zipporah's older sisters were following the rear of the herd as the younger sisters led the way. Her sisters were sending plenty of curious glances back at them, but Zipporah refused to let herself be bothered or embarrassed by their speculative expressions. She was simply helping the stranger who'd helped them.

Who knew where he was from or what his life had been like? Moses might even have a wife, or wives, and a brood of children somewhere. Perhaps he was traveling to meet them now. So many questions crowded Zipporah's mind that she didn't know what she wanted to know first, even if she could ask him. She hoped her father could speak with him, and then somehow she could find out more about him from her father without seeming too curious.

Zipporah's younger sister Jael waited for them to catch up. She was still carrying Moses's pack and satchel. He said something in that deep voice of his, and Jael merely stared at him. He gave her a gentle smile and took the satchel and pack from her. It seemed he was feeling stronger and wanted to carry his things now, but did that mean he wasn't coming with them to the settlement?

Zipporah's worry was for nothing. Moses continued on with them, and they walked in silence while Jael skipped ahead and caught up with Tayma. Zipporah found that she became more and more aware of everything about him. The way he walked, the way he held his head, and the way he kept his focus straight ahead without looking at her even once. He probably knew women who were sophisticated, who oiled their hair and bodies—not someone like her who must seem like a wild nomad to him. Hair undone, skin made even darker by the sun, and bits of sand clinging to her tunic.

Zipporah had never felt so relieved when the tents of Midian came into view. She directed the younger sisters to lead the sheep to their mostly parched field while her older sisters hurried ahead to be reunited with their young children. Cozbi went with them, looking forward to feeding her baby in the coolness of the family tent.

But Moses came to a sudden stop.

"What's happened?" Zipporah asked. "Are you all right?"

Moses scanned the settlement as if realizing how large it was. Or was it small to him? Zipporah wished more than ever she could communicate with this man. He grasped her wrist, the move startling Zipporah so much that she could only stare at him.

He gave her a sad smile and said something in his language that she didn't understand. Then he let go. "Thank you," he said clearly, in her own language.

At least she understood that much.

He gave her a nod, and before Zipporah could respond, he'd turned north and started walking away.

"Wait," she said. "Where are you going? You can stay with us until you recover from your injuries."

Moses continued to walk north.

She wanted nothing more than to run after him and stop him from leaving. It was the oddest feeling to watch a man she'd barely met and spoken to even less walk away from civilization into barren nothingness by himself. He had no water and, she suspected, little food, and he must still be in pain.

Anything could happen to him out there. The shepherds could track him down and take revenge. His injuries could fester and give him fevers. He could miss the next well and slowly die of thirst.

"Moses!" she called out, her pulse pounding in her throat. He was far enough away now that he might not have heard her. She couldn't run after him. But how would she convince him to come with her?

Perhaps she was overreacting. He was a stranger, after all. He'd helped them, gotten them safely back to Midian, and then left. Was that typical of men of his kind? Zipporah didn't know, but she did know she couldn't let him wander off by himself to meet a terrible fate.

She started running toward her family's tent. By the time she reached it, she was out of breath. Her mother and father and her sisters and their children had all gathered, waiting to meet the strange man.

Her father spoke first. "Your sisters tell me that an Egyptian delivered you from the Badrayans who threatened our flocks. Where is this man?"

"He is . . ." Zipporah started to say, trying to catch her breath. "He saw us to Midian but then headed north. He's injured, Father, and he doesn't have fresh water."

"Call him back," her father said. "We will feed him and watch over him as he heals."

"I tried," Zipporah said, her throat thick with emotion. "But he just continued walking."

Her father gave her a quick nod, then said, "Let's take the camels and fetch him. Perhaps if I speak with him he'll change his mind."

Zipporah hurried with her father to the camels tethered to the side of one of their smaller tents nearby. Within moments they were atop the camels, and Zipporah was leading her father to where she'd last seen Moses.

It didn't take long to find him since he continued to limp as he walked. When he heard them, he stopped and turned.

Relief flooded through Zipporah—at least he'd stopped, and now her father could speak with him. Moses was looking up at them, shielding his eyes from the sun with his hand.

Seeing him anew, Zipporah was struck by how this single man could have fought off all those shepherds, drawn water for their sheep, then walked them back to Midian beneath the relentless sun, and was now still walking, continuing his journey, seeming to have no thought for his own well-being.

Her father lowered his camel and slid off the animal, then crossed to Moses.

Zipporah followed suit, not wanting to miss whatever conversation they might have.

"Welcome, Moses," her father said in the Midianite dialect.

Moses certainly recognized his name and seemed surprised to be addressed as such. "Thank you," he said, but it sounded like a question.

Her father turned to her. "He speaks our language?"

"Only a few words that I taught him." Her face flushed as she spoke, feeling Moses's gaze on her. It looked as if he wanted to smile at her, but his expression remained somber.

"I'll try Egyptian, then—what little I know," her father said.

Zipporah watched as her father spoke to Moses, and his eyes changed, filling with recognition. It was plain that her father didn't know the language well, but it was enough to convince Moses to pause in his journey. For the next thing she knew, after a lot of hand gesturing and stilted conversation between the men, her father had motioned Moses onto his camel, and they were heading back toward the tents.

CHAPTER NINE
MOSES

Moses decided that some god, somewhere, was looking out for him. The fight against the shepherds had been unpleasant, but after that, only good things had happened. Atop the camel provided by the man named Jethro and his daughter, Moses had finally pieced together who exactly he'd helped at the well. All of the seven women and girls were sisters, and Jethro was their father. The flocks were usually watered with his son, Hobab, or at least one of his sons-in-law in attendance, but today they had been occupied with a caravan that had arrived and needed their services.

It was clear from the moment Moses turned at the sound of the approaching camels bearing Jethro and Zipporah that these people were full of hospitality. He hadn't wanted to impose on the women's kindness, and he had been worried about showing up as a stranger in a settlement after just fighting local tribesmen.

But with the stilted Egyptian spoken by Jethro, Moses realized that they only wanted to express their gratitude and house him for a few days while he recovered from his injuries. Moses had assented, especially now that the invitation came from the man of the household.

The Midianite tents, interspersed with a few mud houses, spread out before him in a deep valley as they approached the settlement.

The palm trees were scraggly and the grass beneath his feet picked over by various herds. The groups of tents were intermingled with small herds of goats, sheep, and camels. The sun sat in the middle of the sky, sending down its heat and making everything from people to animals lethargic. The dry wind that brushed against his skin seemed to be searching for any sign of moisture. Moses knew it was toward the end of the dry season and that the plants and earth were waiting for rain.

"You have traveled far from your home, yes?" Jethro asked.

Moses concentrated on trying to fully understand Jethro's broken Egyptian before replying. "I am looking for a new home. Egypt is part of my past."

Jethro continued to ask him more questions, and Moses answered vaguely, hoping Jethro would accept the language barrier as a deterrent. Moses wasn't ready to reveal that he'd been raised in Pharaoh's court and an edict for his capture had likely been issued.

Jethro's daughter seemed to be listening intently, although for the most part she kept her gaze forward. Ever since she had cleansed the blood from his skin at the well, he knew if he allowed himself to look at her, he wouldn't be able to look away. Thus, on their walk toward Midian, he had decided to not look at her at all. Unless he had to.

And now, with her father walking between their two camels while Moses rode, he felt even more curious about her. He'd deduced that she probably wasn't married, even though she was old enough. Besides, the way she'd looked at him told him she was looking at him as more than a passing stranger. And he didn't think she was a wanton woman.

Her expression was too guileless, her eyes too bright and inquisitive. He couldn't help but admire how she'd taken command in the aftermath of the fight in attending to his injuries. With her and her sisters' help, his pain had been diminished and his hunger and thirst staved.

"This is our home," Jethro said, pointing up ahead.

Moses recognized the women who were now gathered in front of a large tent. Young children had gathered as well, and three men stood with the women. They must be Jethro's sons or sons-in-law. Moses wasn't expecting to be greeted by so large a group.

Jethro took hold of Moses's camel's reins and brought the camel down to a sitting position. Moses climbed off, trying not to shudder in pain as he did so.

Jethro greeted his family, then turned to Moses and clapped his hand on his good shoulder. Haltingly, Jethro said, "I told them you saved my daughters from the Badrayan tribesmen. On behalf of my wife, Qurayya, and our children, I thank you. Please stay and eat with us and rest. Our home is your home."

Moses looked at all those who were watching him. Smiles and nods greeted him, and he felt his body relax. They were friendly, and they weren't looking to steal from him or enslave him. The men in the family stepped forward and gripped his hand in welcome. "Welcome," they said in turn, which Moses was able to translate.

A man who was clearly Jethro's son grasped his hand firmly. "I am Hobab. Thank you for helping my sisters." Or as least that's what Moses assumed he said. The depth of feeling in the man's dark eyes spoke his appreciation more than words could.

Jethro's wife clasped Moses's hands next, not saying anything, just looking at him with tears in her eyes. The other women bobbed their heads in acknowledgment, but it wasn't long before they and their children disappeared inside one of the tents, where it was certainly cooler.

"Come," Jethro said. "Zipporah and Qurayya will help you, and then we will eat."

"I don't want to be trouble for your family," Moses said.

Jethro boomed out a laugh. "You have brought my beautiful daughters home and increased my flocks all in one morning. There is no inconvenience in that."

Jethro's wife nodded her agreement after Jethro translated what Moses had said. Before he could protest further, Moses was led into the tent. He was surprised he could stand upright in it, and as his eyes adjusted to the cool dimness, he was even more surprised by its livability. Heavy rugs covered the ground, and the tent walls were staked high, giving the interior an open, roomy feeling.

They'd entered what looked to be the cooking room. Baskets of grains and roots and dried plants lined one side, a small fire ring was in the middle, and one of the tent sides had been rolled up to let out the smoke. They led him through the cooking area into another section lined with rugs and cushions. There was a low table with scrolls and a couple of oil lamps.

Qurayya set about lighting the oil lamps, and Zipporah arranged the cushions into a bed of sorts. She pointed to them, then motioned for him to set his things down. This seemed to be a place where Jethro must read and study scrolls. Even with all the hospitality and friendliness, Moses was reluctant to put his satchel where anyone might come and take it. So he set down his bow and arrows, along with the goatskin, but he kept hold of the satchel containing his gold and robe.

Zipporah didn't make a comment about it as they left this section of the tent and went back into the cooking area. Several family members had entered, and the women were busy preparing food while the men approached Moses and took him outside.

They stopped at the side of the tent where there was plenty of shade and where flat stones had been arranged in a circle. The men motioned for Moses to sit down, and they did as well. There was a lot of nodding and smiling, but no other communication until Jethro joined them.

He greeted Moses again and said, "You can leave all your things in my study area. No one will take them."

Moses felt chagrined sitting there with his satchel by his side, and he hoped that Jethro didn't feel offended.

"Tell us about your home," Jethro said to Moses, capturing the other men's attention as well. "I will translate."

So Moses began to talk about the land of Egypt, leaving out anything personal. As he talked, the women came and went, bringing platters of food. By now Moses was used to the food of the desert, but he determined he hadn't tasted anything quite so delicious as the food Jethro's daughters served.

He ate his fill of barley cakes, olives, spicy meat stewed in a thick sauce, and honeyed treats. The afternoon had worn on quickly while they ate and talked. As the sun settled against the western horizon,

DELIVERANCE

Hobab rose to his feet. He nodded to Moses, then said a few words to his father. As he walked away from the gathering, Jethro turned to speak to Moses. "He's taking the main body of sheep to more fertile valleys tonight. We'll not see him for a couple of weeks."

"Are the fertile valleys so far?" Moses asked.

"This time of year, they are several days' travel," Jethro said.

"How long has your family lived here?" Moses asked Jethro, looking from him to the other men.

"My father was born here, as was I," Jethro said. "My father was a temple priest, and by birthright, I am too." He drew his brows together and studied Moses anew. "What god do you worship?"

Moses was about to say Amun, but then he thought about his true heritage and how he'd left his former life behind. "I am open to new teachings and ideas."

Jethro gave a solemn nod. "It is good that you have an open mind. That will serve you well in the desert."

Zipporah arrived with a clay pot of tea. As she served the tea to the men, Moses couldn't help but glance at her once or twice.

"She's a fine woman, is she not?" Jethro said.

Moses nearly choked on the tea he was drinking. He took a moment to compose himself, then, after Zipporah moved away, he said, "You have a fine family."

"She's not married," Jethro continued as if he hadn't heard Moses. "Her younger sister Cozbi is married to the man Zipporah was promised to." He gave a laugh, and Moses was glad that the others in the group didn't understand the Egyptian Jethro was speaking.

Moses tried to keep his expression neutral, when in fact he couldn't believe this man was being so open about his family. People in the desert certainly lived with their hearts exposed. Jethro told him about how Zipporah became very ill after her betrothal to Sihon. There were no true symptoms of illness; Zipporah just refused to rise from her mat.

The daughter Jethro was describing seemed far from the Zipporah he'd encountered. Had she disliked this Sihon man so much?

"You will meet Sihon at the evening meal," Jethro said. "He is a good man; at least one of my daughters thinks so." He grinned and took a bite of the honeyed cake in his hand. Then he leaned close to Moses. "Zipporah is my most stubborn daughter, but she will make the best wife and mother."

Moses didn't know how to respond to a statement like that, so he just nodded and refocused on his tea.

CHAPTER TEN
ZIPPORAH

It didn't take much for Zipporah to discern that Jethro was telling the story about how she had refused to marry Sihon. She cleaned the platters from the meal, scrubbing extra hard with sand to get every bit of food off. Her younger sisters buzzed around her, cleaning up as quickly as possible so they could spy on Moses again. Zipporah supposed she should feel embarrassed that her father was talking about her broken betrothal, but it wasn't like everyone in Midian didn't already know. Besides, it had happened more than a year ago. A lifetime almost.

Did it matter if a strange Egyptian knew how the thought of marrying Sihon had made her so despondent that she'd rather stay hidden in a tent than spend time with him? Or how he was now happily married to her younger sister? Moses would be gone in a few days, and she'd never see him again. What did it matter if her father told him a few tales?

When the men were finished eating, her mother came to her inside the tent and said, "Father wants to show Moses all of our flocks and herds. You should accompany them." Her eyes gleamed with suggestion. And Zipporah knew that her mother was already making plans.

"He should be resting," Zipporah said, biting back what she really wanted to tell her mother. *Don't think a strange Egyptian man is going to show up in Midian and take me off your hands.*

"The Egyptian looks fine to me. Healthy in color, and he's been well fed now," her mother continued.

Her mother hadn't seen Moses fight the shepherds and then continue, while injured, filling the stone troughs with water. She hadn't seen Moses walk the women back to Midian, then turn away and continue walking, all the while with a limp but never slowing down. Yes, he'd eaten well, but Zipporah had seen how deep his wounds were, and she knew that her father's excitement could exhaust Moses.

"Here, take this with you," her mother said, handing Zipporah a goatskin of water.

"I should be checking his bandages and making sure there is no trouble with his wounds instead of following him and Father around the settlement."

Her mother's eyes narrowed, and she gave a shake of her head. "This man obviously comes from wealth and education. Did you see what his satchel contained?"

"You searched his things?"

"I have a right to know what type of guest is staying in my home."

Zipporah let out an exasperated sigh. She was curious about what her mother had found, yet she was embarrassed that her mother had searched Moses's things.

"He carries gold—Egyptian gold—and the most exquisite clothing I've ever seen." Her mother leaned close and whispered, "He might even be royalty. Maybe a banished prince or something. Or maybe he was captured and dragged into the wilderness."

Zipporah threw her hands up. "Mother, he wasn't captured and dragged into the wilderness. If that were the case, then where are his captors? And before he fought off the shepherds, he didn't have injuries." Although Zipporah couldn't be sure her statement was accurate, it seemed too wild of a tale that Moses was a kidnapped Egyptian prince.

Her mother puffed out a breath of air and folded her arms. "Regardless, he's *somebody* important. And he's not married or betrothed. Father asked him."

Zipporah's face heated. She'd wondered the same thing about Moses, but she would never admit it. Her mother and father seemed to have already decided he would be their new son-in-law. She wanted to argue, but the familiar set of her mother's jaw told her it was useless. At least for the moment. She would have to speak to her father later—he was more reasonable than her mother. The main trouble was that Zipporah actually looked forward to following her father and Moses around, if only to learn more about this strange man.

Her mother was right. With the findings in Moses's satchel, it was plain that he'd had a wealthy upbringing. But it seemed he'd lost it all. So why was her mother so adamant about pushing the two of them together? She slung the goatskin over her shoulder and left the tent before her mother could say anything more.

Once outside, Zipporah heard her mother singing a soft melody. She slowed her step—it had been a while since her mother had sung. It was a sure indication that her mother was pleased about something.

The other men had left their supper circle, and her father and Moses were already walking toward the area where they kept the goats. The sun was nearly at the horizon, and twilight was on its way. Zipporah hadn't had a chance to milk today, and in the chaos of the turn of events, it seemed that no one else had thought of it.

Fortune, the oldest and sweetest goat in the herd, came up to Zipporah, bleating her discontent. Instead of interrupting her father and Moses's conversation, Zipporah grabbed one of the empty jugs from a row she kept by the clear-water well. This well had high stone walls built up around it so that the animals couldn't get inside and soil the water. Zipporah's family used it exclusively for drinking water.

Fortune trotted after her, bleating louder and louder as she went. Zipporah bent down and scratched the goat's head and smiled at the poor thing. As soon as she started milking Fortune, the other she-goats trotted over to where she sat.

Her father and Moses glanced over at her, but then they moved off to the far side of the section, and it seemed her father was pointing out the camel herd. Her father owned more than a dozen camels. Not enough to migrate with traveling nomad families, but it was enough to be a settler in Midian. Most of her father's wealth was in sheep, then camels and goats. They were able to sustain themselves as well as trade butter, yogurt, milk, and meat for other goods with passing caravans.

Once she finished with Fortune, Zipporah patted the goat, then steered the next one toward her. Just then a shadow fell across her, and she looked up to see Moses. She glanced around, but didn't see her father anywhere.

She nodded to Moses, then returned to her milking. She didn't know what to say to him, as his mere presence was a bit distracting. He watched her closely, and from her sitting position, he simply towered over her.

When he crouched beside her, she inhaled sharply, which turned out to be a bad idea, because then she caught a full breath of his scent. Although he'd come straight from the desert, his scent was pleasing somehow—full of the desert and the wind, yet something spicy too.

He spoke to her, and she looked over at him, not understanding. Then, when he reached for the goat, she realized that he wanted her to show him how to milk the animal.

"Put your hand here," she said, moving the goat closer to him. The animal bleated at the interruption, and Moses smiled.

Zipporah couldn't help but smile as well. "Where did my father go?" she asked without realizing it was impossible for him to answer.

"Father?"

"Yes, Jethro," she said, wondering if Moses would recognize the name after all. She motioned with her hand. "Where is Jethro?"

Moses pointed back to the tents. So he did understand at least a little of what she was saying.

"All right, then." She moved slightly closer to him, the edges of their arms touching, but it couldn't be helped. "Put one hand here; the other one holds the jar." She moved his hands into position while ignoring the heat that flushed her body at touching this stranger.

Teaching him another way wasn't possible since they didn't speak the same language, but being this close to a man who wasn't related to her was something Zipporah hadn't experienced before.

It didn't take long for Moses to milk the first goat, and then Zipporah brought over a second goat for him to start on. She grabbed another jar and began working on the next goat. They milked in silence, and Zipporah caught Moses looking at her from time to time. Frustration shot through Zipporah as she wished she could talk to him, but maybe this was better after all. She somehow felt relaxed around him, and she sensed it was due to the fact that they *didn't* speak the same language.

There was less expectation, she guessed.

Every once in a while, Zipporah looked toward the tents for her father, but he was conspicuously absent. Once, she saw her mother look out of the tent for a moment, but when Zipporah caught her eye, her mother flashed a smile and quickly ducked back inside.

Zipporah shook her head, wondering if she should laugh or stomp over to the tent and tell her mother she was expecting the sun and the moon when neither was available. Regardless, her mother's soft singing floated through the desert evening.

Moses finished milking his goat, and Zipporah finished up the last one, with him watching her.

"That's all for today," Zipporah said when the final goat happily trotted away in search of a tuft of grass.

"That's all for today," Moses repeated, one side of his mouth lifted.

"Thank you for your help."

He nodded, and his full smile appeared. "Thank you."

It was the most simple of conversations, yet each word held meaning. Zipporah decided it was time to have a talk with her parents. She rose to her feet and brushed off her tunic. She felt a bit light-headed from standing up so fast, and she closed her eyes for a moment.

Moses wrapped his hand around her upper arm as if to steady her. "Zipporah?"

He'd said her name. He *knew* her name. She opened her eyes. "I'm all right. Thank you." She stepped away, and his hand dropped. The concern in his eyes spoke more than several sentences could. She touched her head. "I'm tired, I guess."

He nodded and touched his head too.

She laughed because he looked comical imitating her, but then she sobered. "You are the one who's tired. We should check those wounds again and apply more poultice to them." She moved toward him, pointing to the wraps on his arms and on his shoulder.

He looked down at the wraps, then nodded.

"Come with me," she said, motioning and starting back toward the tents. The orange glow of the setting sun splashed against the dark goat hair of the tent panels, turning them a deep honeyed color. It was Zipporah's favorite time of day. Yesterday she couldn't have imagined that a strange Egyptian man would have just helped her milk the goats and was now walking by her side.

After Zipporah had rewrapped Moses's wounds and bade him good night, she went in search of her father. She heard his rumbling tones coming from her parents' section of the tent. When she appeared in their entryway, her father turned from where he was sitting on a cushion. Her mother also looked up from where she sat stitching a piece of embroidery by the light of an oil lamp.

"We were just speaking of you," her father said.

Her mother only nodded.

Zipporah knew it had been about Moses. She clasped her hands together and walked farther into their section. "I hoped to speak to you tonight about our guest." Sinking onto the cushion next to her father, she faced him, looking him in the eye. "Father, why are you so set on putting Moses and me together at every chance?"

He lifted his dark brows. "I thought you liked him," he said.

Zipporah flushed. "I do, but he is a foreigner, and he is not even converted to our God. We know so little about him. What is his history? Who are his parents? Perhaps he already has a wife—"

"Zipporah," her father said, laying a firm hand on her arm. "Do you think I haven't considered these questions?"

"But have you asked them?" she shot back. "It's like I am the parent and you are the child."

"Zipporah!" her mother said in a sharp voice. "You will not speak to your father that way."

She exhaled and looked down at her hands, her face burning fiercely at her outburst.

"Our daughter's right," her father said, and Zipporah lifted her head in surprise to find him watching her with a half smile. "It's time I share with her what I know."

"He answered your questions?" Zipporah asked, knowing she was speaking out of turn again, but she was anxious to find out.

"He has answered them sufficiently," her father said. "In time he will open up to us more. He is learning to trust a new family and people."

Zipporah's shoulders sagged. She still didn't understand.

"Daughter," her father said in a gentle voice, "I have received confirmation from the Lord that Moses was sent to our family for a reason. He will be a blessing to all of us."

She swallowed against her suddenly dry throat. It was well and good for her father to believe that Moses was supposed to spend time with their family—but her father was acting like he wanted her to marry him.

"I know what you are thinking," her father said, placing his hand on her shoulder and squeezing lightly. "I know that it may sound like I am not judging wisely, but I do not doubt the Lord. I am not asking you to accept Moses without any questions. I think you should ask him your questions, get to know him, find out if he is a man worthy of . . ." He paused, looking over at his wife. "Worthy of you."

Zipporah brought her hand to her mouth. There was no doubt about her father's wishes now. "I—I don't . . ." She stopped, then took a deep breath. "How can you put so much faith and trust in a stranger?"

Her father's smile was soft. "Moses becomes less and less of a stranger every hour. I believe I can trust in my confirmation, but I will stand back and let you make your decisions and take your time in getting to know him."

Her mind spun until she didn't know what to think. She liked Moses. She did. But all her life, she'd been raised to believe she'd marry within her tribe and religion. Moses was so unexpected. Yet, she was always thinking about him, and the more time she spent with him, the more interesting he became.

CHAPTER ELEVEN
MOSES

Moses awakened to the sound of a bleating sheep, a noise he hadn't been used to in his former life. There had been no herds roaming by the pharaoh's palace in Mennefer. It was Moses's third day in Midian, and his bruises had started to heal. The wounds on his arms and shoulder and face felt better as well. Although he was still being careful with his movements, he'd been able to help Jethro's family with many tasks.

By the faint light coming through the slits in the tent panels above his head, he knew it was yet early morning. He also knew that Zipporah, Jethro's third daughter, rose early in the morning to milk the goats. That first day when he'd helped her, the goats had been quite miserable from being forgotten.

Moses smiled at the memory. He enjoyed it when Zipporah talked to him as if he could understand her language. Over the past few days, he'd picked up on quite a few words and then spent the nights before falling asleep repeating them in his head. It was pleasurable to try them out on Zipporah—she acted surprised and pleased each time he spoke in her language.

By far, the easiest person to talk to in this settlement was Jethro—a man Moses was quickly coming to respect. Not only did the man have a large family, but he was a true patriarch, something Moses had not seen in the fractured royal families of the Egyptian court.

Jethro knew everything about each of his children, as well as his daughter-in-law and sons-in-law. Moses had seen Jethro's children come to see him at various times for counsel, and he appeared to be generous with his time.

Jethro's wife was a bit more distant, but it was clear she had her children's best interests in mind. And it was clear they were not averse to putting Zipporah in Moses's path time and time again. Zipporah seemed to take it in stride; and more than once a day—in fact, several times a day, Moses would catch her looking his way.

Each time, she turned away quickly, but there was no denying that her gaze had sent his heart racing more than once. Now Moses felt eager to see her again, and soon. She was probably awake and with the goats right now. Without analyzing his motives, he rose from his mat and dressed in the tunic Jethro had given him. Everything around him was quiet, telling him it was still too early for the women to be starting the morning meal.

He walked quietly to a nearby section of the tent that housed a clay basin of water. He washed his face with the water, then dried his skin on a cloth that sat near the basin. He was fully awake now, and he left the tent, inhaling the crisp desert air. It was not yet sullied by the smell of cooking, smoke from fires, or the comings and goings of the family.

The sun hadn't yet tipped the horizon, but the gray dawn of the sky was quickly turning to pale blue. It would be another brilliant and cloudless day. Once the sun crested, the heat would be on its way and the coolness of the night a distant memory. As it was, Moses shivered but knew it would only be moments before wearing a robe would feel too hot.

He scanned the tent compound where Jethro's family lived, then beyond to where more tents were scattered throughout the settlement—haphazard at first glance—but as one walked through the settlement, it was clear that everything was organized for the most beneficial desert living. Shade and water were at a premium, and nothing went to waste.

He walked away from the tent compound in the direction where the goats were kept, as if moving automatically. Months ago, when he was still living in Egypt and spending his days with Ramses and

Pentu, he would never have thought he could ever exist in a small desert settlement such as Midian. He'd been betrothed to Vizier Amon's daughter Cena, an elegant and sophisticated woman. He hadn't been in love with her, but that was not uncommon with an arranged marriage. Such arrangements were the way of the royal court, and he'd wanted to do his duty and make his mother happy.

But Cena had been a woman with a wandering eye and had taken her privileges liberally. When he'd caught her in a compromising situation with another man, Moses had had enough. He'd broken the betrothal and hadn't regretted it for a moment. Cena's golden skin and wide-set eyes had been a beautiful combination, but her cunning gaze and sharp tongue had sent jolts of despair through his stomach. He'd been right to release her from their bond. And now Cena and her family and all the court intrigue seemed like another existence from another lifetime.

Moses shook his head as he realized he'd been absently watching Zipporah milk the goats. Her back was turned toward him, so she hadn't seen him at the edge of the yard. How long had he been standing there watching her? As if she sensed his thoughts, she turned her head and saw him.

The smile that lit her face warmed him straight through. She rose to her feet and waved him over.

"Coming to milk the goats?" she called out, and Moses understood most of what she was saying.

He crossed the yard and found himself smiling back. It was ridiculous, really, how much they smiled at each other, as if they didn't need to speak the same language after all.

Moses tried out his new words on her. "Good morning."

One of her dark eyebrows rose. "Good morning, Moses."

How could such a simple exchange make him so aware of her? Zipporah was the opposite of Cena in every way. There was no calculating gaze, no ulterior motives in her manner, and although she wore the simplest of tunics woven in the thick loose weave of desert dwellers, she was elegant in her own way.

With the desert sun peeking above the horizon and scattering the blues and purples of dawn and replacing them with yellow and pink, Zipporah reminded him of the first blooms of the flowers along the Nile after the annual flooding. Her long, dark-brown hair was drawn back and plaited, falling across her shoulder, and her eyes were as deep as the night. Her full lips were quirked into a half smile, and her skin was a warm brown tone.

Moses had the sudden urge to brush his fingers along her cheek. Instead, he stood there for several moments, just looking at her. He didn't know the words in her language to tell her he thought she was beautiful, and even if he did, he didn't know if she'd welcome him saying so. Typically, any woman would be pleased at such a compliment, but Moses sensed that for Zipporah, it would touch her on a more personal level.

This woman was pure and innocent, a far cry from Moses and his dark deeds back in Egypt. What if she knew he'd murdered an Egyptian taskmaster? That he'd left his mother and fled his country? That he'd lived his entire life under the false pretense of being a part of the royal family when in reality he'd been born a Hebrew slave?

Zipporah was a strong woman of the desert. She knew who she was, and she did what was expected of her. She was loyal to her family, and he couldn't picture her ever flying into a rage and harming anyone. She had lived an unblemished life, and it showed in her every action and speech.

She was speaking to him, and he recognized some of her words, such as *milk* and *goats* and *sheep*.

Her voice allowed him to finally break his focus, and he looked about him. The younger goats were playing, and the older she-goats roamed about. Whenever a goat came close to Zipporah, she reached down and scratched its head. It was clear that Zipporah loved the animals, and he understood the draw of coming out so early to do her chores. Midian was a beautiful and peaceful place this time in the morning when the harshness of the sun and heat had not yet erupted.

"There you are." Jethro's voice came from behind Moses.

He turned, startled, and wondered what Jethro's reaction would be to his being out here with his daughter before most of Midian was awake.

Before he could respond, Jethro was walking toward him, saying, "Can't keep away from the goats? Or is it Zipporah?"

Moses felt Zipporah's attention on him—she had recognized her name, though her father was speaking in Egyptian. He gripped Jethro's hand in greeting, ignoring the question. "Good morning, sir."

Jethro's eyes danced from Moses to Zipporah. Apparently Moses spending time with Zipporah didn't bother Jethro in the least.

"You haven't answered," Jethro said.

Moses hid a smile, though his pulse was racing. "I don't want to embarrass your daughter."

Jethro laughed. "She's been making eyes at you for days. And no man should take that lightly, especially coming from Zipporah."

Zipporah stepped up to her father and spoke to him, her eyes flashing. Jethro only patted her arm, then looked over at Moses. "She knows we talk about her, and she wants to know what we say. What should I tell her?"

Moses didn't hesitate. "Tell her the truth, of course."

Jethro grinned. "Of course." He looked over at Zipporah and spoke to her in Midianite.

Her face colored, and her lips thinned. Then she shook her head and turned away, refusing to look at Moses.

"What did you say?" Moses asked, his stomach twisting. Jethro was not a private man; in fact, he seemed ready to tell everyone he met—including Moses—of his family's personal matters. Moses wasn't pleased that Zipporah might be angry now.

"I told her it was a nice change to see her being sweet to a man," Jethro said in a conspiratorial whisper that wasn't a whisper at all. "I suppose I have embarrassed her after all." He released a good-natured sigh. "It seems I am forever apologizing to my wife and daughters."

Zipporah had moved away a few paces and was petting one of the goats. Moses could tell she was still upset, although she was trying not to act like she was too bothered.

Her father crossed to her and spoke to her in quiet tones. She nodded a couple of times but didn't look up at him.

Jethro turned to Moses. "This morning I have priest duties in the temple. Would you like to accompany me? You might be interested in learning more about our beliefs. I will be offering the incense after the animal sacrifices, then giving the blessings as well."

Moses felt torn between going with Jethro and trying to apologize to Zipporah. But he didn't know if he could help her understand that he did admire her, maybe more than he should, but he didn't want her to feel self-conscious either. But how would he tell her those things? And Jethro was his host, so he had to abide by his requests.

"I will come with you," Moses told Jethro. "I'm very interested in learning more about your gods."

"One God," Jethro corrected. "Like the Hebrews in your homeland, we worship one God, and He is a jealous God."

Moses nodded. It was time for him to expand his knowledge and perceptions. Amun had been quiet since Moses had left Egypt. Perhaps Amun didn't watch over people who committed serious crimes and fled the consequences. Perhaps Moses's soul had already been condemned and it was too late for salvation in this life.

He didn't know if he'd ever be able to confess his dark deeds to Jethro, but he was willing to learn more about the desert people and their beliefs. It seemed that living someplace like Midian was Moses's only hope for starting his life over again.

"How do you say farewell in Midianite?" he asked Jethro. When he told him, Moses lifted a hand in Zipporah's direction and said, "Farewell, Zipporah."

She lifted her head, and her face flushed. Was she embarrassed? Hurt? Angry? She said nothing, just nodded. Moses then turned away to follow Jethro, determined to quickly learn as much Midianite as possible.

CHAPTER TWELVE
ZIPPORAH

Zipporah's breaths came short as she tugged the dates from their branches. She had secured her tunic about her legs and was halfway up the rope ladder that had been hung from the lower branches. The shade was a welcome relief from the sun, and there was no other time she could pick dates today. She'd already experienced a setback when one of her father's camels had gotten loose from its hobble and she and Abigail had chased after it.

With her father still gone with Moses, Zipporah had to hunt down the animal herself. It wasn't that she minded, but a woman's work was never finished. Adding one more arduous task put her behind in other things. Her mother was cooking up a feast for tonight since she was inviting their entire family and closest neighbors for the evening meal. Despite the fact that all the women would be bringing platters of food, Zipporah's mother proceeded to prepare food as if she alone were feeding all of the guests.

Thus, more dates were needed. The date palm wine was low, and her mother's greatest mortification would be running out of wine for her guests. It would be a deep blemish on her hospitality. Usually, Zipporah left the tree climbing to her younger sisters, but after chasing the camel around half the settlement, Abigail had injured her foot on a sharp rock.

Zipporah tugged at the next few dates, then dropped them. They fell straight into the basket she had on the ground below her. When she heard men's voices, she paused. Through the small date palm grove, she could see two figures approaching. Her breathing quickened when she realized it was Moses walking with her father. It appeared her father was explaining some things to him about the grove.

She wished she could understand Egyptian or that Moses spoke her language. But if that were the case, maybe she wouldn't dare ask him her questions. They might give him the wrong idea—which idea that was, she didn't know. Despite her annoyance at her mother's excitement over their unmarried guest and her father's broad hints that perhaps Zipporah should entertain more serious thoughts about Moses, Zipporah remained intrigued by the stranger.

This morning she could only guess at what her father had really told Moses about her. Her father had never been one for much propriety, and usually it didn't bother Zipporah at all, but now . . . She didn't know what Moses thought of their large and chaotic family. She couldn't imagine him surrounded by a dozen siblings and a laughing father and sharp-tongued mother.

She wondered how long he would stay in Midian and why he was showing so much interest in her father. Wasn't he delayed on his journey? Perhaps he was traveling to another great city, like Jerusalem, and Midian was just a detour on the way.

What had his life been like before? Why had he left his home? Even in the plain tunic her father had given him and with his hair growing longer each day, he still stood out from the average Midianite. There was something about him that shone with intelligence and advanced thinking. He was not an ordinary man, or at least not like anyone Zipporah knew.

She refocused on her task and pulled off more dates, then climbed up another knot on the rope. Reaching for the next higher bunch of dates, she heard her father's voice growing closer. Were they coming to this side of the grove? That could mean only one thing. They'd seen her. She continued to pick, deciding that if she didn't call attention to herself, maybe they'd see she was busy.

"May I help you?" The voice that was clearly Moses's startled her.

The words startled her too because they were in accented Midianite, but she'd understood them perfectly.

She dropped the dates she'd just picked and looked over her shoulder, expecting her father and Moses to be standing there, a gleam in her father's eyes.

But it was only Moses.

"Did my father tell you to say that?" she asked.

He cocked his head, clearly not understanding her rush of words. She looked past him for any sign of her father, but he'd left the grove. Zipporah wasn't surprised her father had found a way to put the two of them together.

She climbed down the knots of the rope, and as she neared the ground, Moses held out his hand to help her land. She hesitated for a moment, then grasped his hand and dropped the last couple of steps to the earth. Moses released her hand, but the feel of his warm skin against hers lingered.

For a few breaths, she just stood there, looking up at him. His golden gaze captured hers, and she wondered what he was thinking about. They were completely alone in this grove of date palms, the breeze pushing gently through the palms above their heads the only sound. Amazingly enough, Zipporah felt completely at ease. She wasn't nervous or afraid of being alone with Moses, just curious.

Why had he stopped to help her? Was it her father's cajoling? Was it more?

Her body was growing too warm, so she pointed to the basket of dates. "When the basket is filled, we'll take it to my mother." She pointed up toward the tree. "I'm nearly finished with this tree, and then I'll start on the next one."

Moses gave a nod, then turned from her and climbed up the rope she'd just come down. Zipporah watched him climb, amazed at his easy movements. Had he harvested date palms before? She noticed he was wearing a tunic her father must have given him. Within moments, he was dropping dates from up in the branches, landing them in the basket.

With Moses busy on that tree, Zipporah moved to the next one and climbed up the rope. She collected the dates in her overtunic. There wasn't any conversation between them while they both worked. By the time Moses finished with the first palm, Zipporah had enough dates loaded in her tunic to finish filling the basket.

"Bring the basket over here," Zipporah called out.

Moses seemed to understand, for he saw that she was trying to balance a load of dates with her tunic while still holding on to the palm. He brought the basket over and held it up. Zipporah dropped her load into the basket, then climbed down the rope. Again, Moses reached for her hand as she descended the last couple of feet.

This time he didn't release it.

"Tell me of your god," he said, his eyes intent on hers.

Zipporah swallowed, her mouth dry, her thoughts racing. He knew how to ask her this question, but was he going to understand her response? And why was he still holding her hand, standing so close to her? The date palms above and the sand beneath seemed to fade away, and all she could think about was Moses's long fingers wrapped securely around hers.

She exhaled to steady her breath, then looked up at him and said, "Our God, Eloah, is over the whole earth and all people." She motioned with her free hand to include the entire grove. "He is a jealous God, and we worship no other gods but Him."

"Jethro took me to the temple," Moses said. His accent was thick, but Zipporah understood most of his words. He brought her hand up to his chest and placed it over his heart.

Zipporah felt the warmth of his chest, and her own heart rate increased in response.

"I felt warm," he said simply. He looked toward the sky. "Like the sun."

Zipporah nodded. She knew what he was trying to say. He'd felt the presence of God in the temple. The building was a sacred place, and although Zipporah had never been inside because she was a woman, she had attended festival days where she observed the sacred ceremonies outside the temple walls in which the people of Midian participated.

The reverence with which the priests worshipped, including her father, brought tears to her eyes every time. The people set aside their squabbles and short tempers, and all revered a higher being. They were kinder and softer afterward. Peace ruled, and even if it was for a short time, peace was a palpable thing.

"Our God rules the sun, the moon, and all the earth," she said.

Moses was looking at her again, his eyes searching hers for meaning to her words. He seemed content to listen to her explain, so she continued.

"Our God demands rituals and animal sacrifices," she continued. "We can repent and make amends through our sin offerings. If we live a good life, we will earn our way to a higher world."

"A higher world," Moses repeated.

"Yes, the afterlife," Zipporah said.

He released her hand. "This is heaven," he said in a clear voice, sweeping his hand and then pointing to her.

Zipporah knew she wasn't interpreting his words wrong. She also knew he wasn't talking about the grove of palms they stood in, and he wasn't talking about the settlement of Midian.

Moses was referring to the two of them, together.

But how was it possible that a stranger had appeared in their lives only days ago and somehow her heart had been wrapped up in his?

"Moses," she said, hoping she could make him understand her words. "How long will you be in Midian?"

He held still for a moment, then lifted his hand to her face and brushed at the hair next to her cheek. Warmth shuddered through her, and she felt herself flush at his touch. She had never been this alone with a man before. Yet her father had left Moses to help her.

"I am not leaving Midian," he said in a quiet voice.

His words rocked through her. They were clear and definitive. She had the urge to touch him back. To lift her hand to his face and to feel his warm skin and run her hand through the hair that curled around his ears.

He smiled at her, a questioning smile.

"Did you tell my father?" she asked. "Jethro?"

He nodded. "I told Jethro. He is happy."

Zipporah laughed. "I'm sure he is. I think my father likes you more than his son and daughters, or at least he spends the most time with you." She was speaking too fast, and she'd probably lost him in what she was saying, but he didn't seem to mind. He continued to look at her, standing close enough that if he were to lean down . . .

"Tell me of the gods of Egypt," she said in a quiet voice. If Moses had felt something significant in the temple of Midian, what did that mean for his Egyptian beliefs?

He stooped down and grabbed a thin stick, then began to draw in the sand.

Zipporah crouched next to him and watched the shape take place. Moses drew a male figure with a beard. He sketched two plumes of feathers coming from a cap on the deity's head. The god was sitting on a throne, holding an ankh in one hand and a scepter in the other.

"Amun," Moses said. "God of Egypt." He moved half a pace and began to draw another figure—what looked to be a man with a sun as part of his headdress. "Ra," Moses said. "God of the sun."

He continued to draw one figure after another until the sand around several palm trees was outlined with sketches of various gods and goddesses.

Zipporah knew the Egyptians worshipped multiple gods, but seeing Moses's handiwork made her realize how extensive their worship practices were. It seemed there was a god for everything—for the rain, the wind, the sun, the moon, the harvest . . . When Moses straightened from his sketches, Zipporah said, "Which god do you worship the most?"

Moses considered for a moment. "Amun is the favored god."

She nodded, although he hadn't completely answered her question.

He set to pushing the sand over his sketches as if he was erasing them not only from the ground but from his memory. When he finished, he brushed off his hands and crossed to the basket of dates and picked it up.

"Do you miss your home?" she asked as he turned to face her.

He met her gaze, and for a moment she saw a mixture of regret and sorrow in his eyes. Did he understand her question? His next words confirmed that he did.

"I miss my mother." He looked past her, and the line of his jaw tensed.

Zipporah took a step toward him. "Tell me about your mother, Moses. What was she like?"

He moved the basket to his other side. "My mother was beautiful, and she was kind."

They began to walk together through the grove, heading in the direction of the family tent. Moses's words were simple and sometimes intermingled with phrases Zipporah didn't recognize—phrases in Egyptian—but she caught the full meaning in the softness of his tone.

"My mother was unmarried," he said, surprising Zipporah. "She rescued me from the river."

Zipporah wasn't sure she'd understood him right. How had a baby been in a river? He would have drowned. She would have to ask her father later if Moses had told him the same story. They continued through the grove until they stepped out into the hot, late-afternoon sun.

"My mother gave up many things to raise me," Moses said. "Her father was not pleased that she chose to raise me. She adopted me."

The story was incredible. "Do you know who your true family was?"

Moses didn't answer, and Zipporah assumed it was because he didn't understand her question. Once outside of the grove, they reached the main path leading to her family's tent. He cast several glances at her, but she only looked away, pretending to retie the sash about her tunic.

If her mother saw their interest in each other, she would begin planning a wedding feast, and her father would set out the wine for a toast to their betrothal. And the truth was, Zipporah didn't know much about Moses, and he didn't know much about her. He hadn't asked her parents about marrying her either.

"I have never met my true family," Moses said, bringing Zipporah's attention back to the present. "My birth . . . is a mystery."

How could that be? Zipporah wondered. Not to know where you came from? When Moses fell silent and it seemed he wasn't going to say anything else, Zipporah asked, "Why did you leave Egypt?"

Moses stopped. She knew her father had asked him, but he hadn't given any solid answer yet. With the sun nearing the far horizon and the sky's blues turning violet, he said, "I cannot speak of it yet."

Although his voice was steady, Zipporah saw the flash of pain in his eyes, and she shuddered without realizing she did so. She wanted to ask him more questions, but he'd turned away and was walking again. His shoulders looked as if he carried a great weight on them, and Zipporah wondered what terrible thing had happened to this intelligent, strong man to make him flee a mother he loved and the land of his birth.

She caught up to him, and they walked the rest of the way with him pointing to things and asking "What is that?" and her teaching him more words of her language.

CHAPTER THIRTEEN
MOSES

Moses awakened before dawn again, as had become his habit of late. He'd been staying as a guest of Jethro's family for several weeks now. Externally, life had become routine, but internally, he was in turmoil. He was falling in love with a woman of the desert. Everywhere he turned, he saw her in his mind. Every sound had echoes of her patient voice. When he closed his eyes to sleep for the night, he could still see and hear her.

It might seem simple to another man to fall in love, then ask a woman for her hand. But Moses was a stranger, a guest, and he had nothing to offer Zipporah. Did she not deserve a man who at least owned flocks so that he might support a family? Did she not deserve a man more like herself, who'd been raised in her religion and way of life? Did she not deserve a man who knew who he was and hadn't fled justice?

Jethro's family was grateful for his help in delivering the women from the tribesmen. But the Midianites' hospitality had extended far too long, and Moses needed to create his own life. Somewhere, somehow. But when he thought of leaving Midian, something inside him ached.

Jethro had become a friend, and Moses had become fond of the large family, and he couldn't imagine saying good-bye to Zipporah. So what did that mean and what should he do?

In the gray light, Moses rose and washed his face and head, then pulled on his tunic, its weave rough and warm against his skin. At times he missed the fine, soft clothing and bands of gold he wore in Egypt, but his past seemed to grow more distant each day. This morning he opened the satchel he'd brought from Egypt and removed the golden statues. But instead of chanting words of prayer, he gazed at them for several long moments.

He couldn't imagine these statues at the Midian temple. They seemed to be from another lifetime, another place. They felt impersonal and unattainable. Slowly, Moses placed the statues back inside the satchel. Then he moved to his knees, like Jethro had taught him, and began to say his first prayer to the Midianites' God, Eloah.

When he finished, he remained on his knees, thinking and listening. He couldn't exactly explain how he felt, except for content. Peaceful. And for now that was enough. He rose to his feet and left his tent section to begin the familiar walk to the goat herd, where he knew Zipporah would be working.

As Moses walked, he was grateful to have some quiet time to himself. Once the rest of the family arose, there would be no chance for reflection in the busyness of the day. Living in the desert where one had to carve everything from the earth and work for every bit of sustenance, there was little time to be idle.

The morning air was heavy with moisture, and Moses looked up at the sky, surprised to see dark clouds gathering. Last night over the evening meal, Jethro said he'd felt the shift in temperature in his bones. Moses had felt nothing, but it appeared the old man had been right.

The rainy season was still over a month away, though it seemed they'd receive moisture today. Moses walked around the groupings of tents and headed toward the goats. Sure enough, Zipporah was already there, milking the she-goats. Moses's heart jolted the moment he saw her. She wore a light-colored tunic today, and her hair was bound with a single strap so that it still tumbled down her back. She'd pushed back her scarf, not yet needing it for protection from the sun.

Zipporah milked the goats each morning, and he'd come to look forward to this time alone with her. She was beautiful; there was no doubt about that. And on the settlement market days, Moses had seen other men notice her. She paid them no attention though, so Moses felt privileged that she'd spent so much time talking to him. But perhaps it was because he was a guest and she was merely willing to teach him the language.

As he walked to where Zipporah worked, Moses inhaled the cool air. It invigorated him, and he realized he loved this wild land. He loved caring for the flocks and attending the temple with Jethro. The Midianite worshipping practices reminded him of what he'd heard about the Hebrews. The Midianite rituals were repetitive yet sacred. And they brought comfort to Moses in their routine.

Something was changing inside of him. His discontent and questions about his youth, about being given up by a Hebrew mother, then being adopted by an Egyptian woman, didn't seem so urgent. He felt a strange sense of peace that his life had taken its winding course for a reason. That perhaps a higher being was watching over him, just as he had sensed when he prayed this morning.

Around him were a faithful and hardworking people. None of them lived lives of privilege, and they didn't spend their days in luxury. Relationships were important to these people, especially family. He had become friends with Jethro's son, Hobab, and with Jethro's sons-in-law as they shared evening meals together. Zipporah's younger sisters made him laugh with their enthusiasm.

As for Zipporah herself . . . Moses couldn't imagine leaving her. What else lay before him? More sand, more settlements, more dark-eyed women. But his heart told him that no other woman would compare to Zipporah. And he knew suddenly that he had to tell her of his past—his entire past. If there was going to be any future between them, she must know the truth about his life.

He exhaled as he neared her, and she turned to watch him approach, straightening from the goat she'd been milking.

"Good morning, Moses," she said, her eyes bright. "Do you see it might rain?"

This was what he loved—her open gaze, her friendly greeting, and the way she blushed when he touched her. She was pure and sweet, and he couldn't seem to stay away from her. But he could never expect her to leave what was important to her. To be with her was to remain in Midian, and accepting all of the things that were a part of her—her religion, her family, her home.

He came to a stop. The dark clouds in the sky were a backdrop to her radiance. She looked up at him and touched his arm. It was the first time she'd reached for him.

"Do you never sleep?" she asked, her tone teasing. "You were up late with the men around the fire." She dropped her hand. It was all too soon.

He wanted to take her hand and pull her toward him. Instead, he bent down and scratched one of the goats rubbing against his legs. "You spoil these animals," he said. His Midianite was getting better, although he knew he still had much to learn. Fortunately, they'd found a way to converse, each of them using plenty of hand gesturing.

She laughed. "You sound like my father."

Straightening, Moses said, "That is a c-compliment." He stumbled on his words, but she seemed to understand.

She peered up at him. "I am glad you are friends. He enjoys talking to you, and you've helped our family so much."

Did Zipporah think he was staying in Midian because of her father? "Are *we* not friends?"

There was that blush.

"Yes, I believe we are," she said, holding back a smile.

She was so quiet around her family, although he'd heard arguments between her and her mother more than once. They spoke in rapid, hushed whispers, so Moses wasn't able to follow. She seemed to take on the quiet-sister role when her siblings were around. The sister who was all work and duty. But with him, she softened somehow. She smiled, she laughed, she blushed.

He reached for her hand, hoping she wouldn't pull away and that he could speak the right words and not ruin their friendship. Her fingers curled around his, soft and warm, encouraging him even more. A gust of wind swirled about them, stirring his clothing and tugging at Zipporah's hair.

"Zipporah . . ." he began, and then before he could think otherwise, he leaned down and kissed her on the cheek. She didn't move and seemed to lean into him. He stayed close to her for a moment, breathing in the wildflower scent of her skin.

When he raised his head, she looked down. Her skin was tinged pink, and her quickened breathing matched his. He reached out and touched her chin, tilting it upward until her gaze met his. It would be easy to get lost in the depths of her eyes, but the time had come that he needed to confess his feelings and accept the outcome of his confession. He had been praying over the past several days that he could use the right words to make her understand.

"I have come to care for you a great deal," he said. "But I want you to know that I am not a whole man. I have done things for which I will have to pay for the rest of my life."

She was watching him closely, giving him her complete attention. "We live in a harsh land."

"There is something I need to tell you." He paused, knowing once the words were out, they could never be retrieved. "I have killed a man."

Her expression tightened. "You have had to defend yourself like all men do at some point in their lives."

He wished it had been so, but he couldn't allow her to believe a falsehood. "This was not in self-defense," he said in a low voice.

Moses could see her trying to hide her surprise, but it was impossible. Part of understanding her every word was reading her expressions as well, and she wasn't pleased with his news.

She stepped away from him, then turned until he could see only her profile.

He waited, hardly daring to breathe. Would she allow him to explain? Would she accept him even after knowing the entire story of how he'd killed an Egyptian taskmaster?

She sniffed, and Moses realized that her eyes had filled with tears. It made him feel an intense guilt again, as if he'd just left the taskmaster's side. He had done it in defense of the helpless Hebrew, but it had still been wrong. It had been vengeful, and it had set off a series of events that had completely changed his life.

Minutes passed, and still she did not look at him. Would this divide them enough that she would turn away from him permanently?

In a voice just above a whisper, he said, "I need to tell you of my past. Of why I left Egypt. Of why I can never return."

She didn't respond, and Moses took that as in indication she was allowing him to continue. He could only hope his words would be clear to her.

He began to tell her of his home. Of how he grew up in the pharaoh's palace and how the crown prince of Egypt, Ramses, was his closest friend.

"We did everything together," he said, the memories flooding in. "We learned languages, we learned art and writing, we learned to fight. We rode chariots and raced each other."

Her face turned slightly toward him. She was at least listening.

"You won the races, didn't you?" she said suddenly, although she still wasn't looking at him.

He hoped it was a good sign. "I did," he confessed. Would that bother her more? To know of his privileged life—the one he'd thrown away? "And I owned beautiful horses. My life was privileged. I didn't fully realize it until I fled my home. In Egypt, I didn't want for anything, and I was surrounded by beauty at every turn."

She looked at him fully now, her eyes narrowed, her gaze sharp. "And the women?" she asked in a harsh tone so unlike her. Moses had driven her to this anger. "Was there someone special in your life? Or many women who were special?"

Moses wanted to ease the pain in her eyes. He had put it there, and now it would only deepen. Looking back at his previous life, he realized how foolish he'd been, how ungrateful.

"I was betrothed before," he began, hoping she would hear him out. He wanted to reach for her, to reassure her, but her arms were folded tightly. "It was arranged by our parents and supported by the pharaoh. I . . . She was a woman who thought only of herself." He gave a bitter laugh and realized he wouldn't blame Zipporah for walking away from him right now.

"I wasn't much better than she at the time," he continued. "She was not true to me, and we ended the arrangement. I had never been more relieved."

Zipporah exhaled and closed her eyes. "And other women were your friends? Perhaps the women in the harem?"

"No," Moses whispered, thankful that at least in this he had not crossed the line. "I did not partake in dalliances. My cousins . . . they criticized and teased me for it."

Her eyes opened again, the pain still there. She took another step back. "Were you in love with the woman you were betrothed to?"

That answer came easily. "No. It was arranged between her father and Pharaoh for political gain. I was simply a pawn, but my mother wanted to see me settled, and I couldn't say no to Pharaoh's request."

She gave a short nod, then looked down at the ground as if she could no longer look at him. "And what does this have to do with killing a man? Did you battle over a woman?"

Moses swallowed against the tightness in his throat. "Not exactly. It did begin with a battle though."

He told her of the battle with the Libyans and how they'd commissioned the Hebrew slaves to fight with them against the Libyans when the Egyptian army was too far away to help in time. He told her of the Hebrew woman named Miriam who had fled the military camp when Ramses wanted her for his harem.

"I saw the Hebrews as tools to be used for our gain," Moses continued. "To know that a woman would flee into the wilderness and face certain death rather than live in luxury in the pharaoh's harem shocked me."

Zipporah looked at him then. "She wouldn't have ever been able to return to her people with honor."

"I realize that now," Moses said. "I was foolish not to see that before. When the battle was over, I started to see things differently. The Hebrews were no longer just slaves. They were men and women. Families. They loved and laughed and fought and worshipped. They were also severely mistreated." It was his turn to look away from Zipporah now.

But he had to continue, to tell her the entire story. "I was at one of the building sites with Ramses and Pentu when the day's work was finished for the Hebrews. An Egyptian taskmaster began beating an elderly woman who couldn't keep up with the others. A young male slave interfered and took the beating for the woman."

Zipporah's eyes widened.

"The taskmaster beat the slave to death." Moses was silent for a moment, the scene vivid in his mind. "Ramses and Pentu left, but I stayed behind. I had never felt so much rage in all my life."

He scrubbed his hand through his hair, wishing he could get the images out of his mind. In a measured tone, he told her how he fought with the taskmaster and ended up killing him. How he'd tried to hide the body by covering it with dirt and rocks. Then how he'd fled back to the palace and sneaked into his chamber. When his mother had come looking for him, he'd confessed to her, and in turn, she'd given her own confession.

"Everything I believed in was no longer valid." His voice felt raw. "The truths I had lived were all lies. I was not who I thought I was. I was one of them. A Hebrew. I should have been working as a slave, taking beatings, starving . . . Instead, I had been rescued from the river by an Egyptian princess."

Zipporah was silent for a long time. "And that's when you left Egypt?"

Moses nodded, not daring to look at her. Was she furious? Disgusted? He wasn't able to find out because moments later, she turned and walked away from him.

He lifted his head and watched her leave.

CHAPTER FOURTEEN
ZIPPORAH

Zipporah stared into the darkness of the tent and the slivers of moonlight that shone through the panels. It had been a full two days since Moses had confessed that he'd killed another man with no personal provocation. She was not naïve to the ways of the desert or the ways of men in battle one with another.

She understood disputes, battles, wars, and she even understood Moses taking out his rage on the cruel taskmaster. The more Zipporah thought about it, the more she realized he had been defending the helpless Hebrew. Moses had stood up for a defenseless person. A noble thing, perhaps, if Moses hadn't fled the consequences.

Could he not have stood before the pharaoh and explained to him, as he'd explained to her, what had happened? Could he not have told the pharaoh he didn't like the cruel treatment of the Hebrew slaves?

No, whispered through her mind, but still Zipporah was grappling with the shock of it all. The Moses she knew had valiantly defended her sisters against the Badrayans. The Moses she knew was courageous. Why then did he not stand up for himself but instead fled from his own people, those who might listen to him? What if she didn't know him at all?

Tears burned in her eyes and eventually spilled onto her cheeks as she continued to stare upward. Had Moses's sudden arrival right when she'd been given a marriage ultimatum been too convenient? Or had it been the hand of the Lord, as her father believed? And did the confirmation from the Lord extend to her marrying Moses?

Zipporah's head ached with all of her thoughts tumbling against each other. It seemed no matter which angle she considered, she kept coming back to Moses having lived an entirely different life than what she'd grown up in. What if they did marry? Would Moses soon grow discontented?

There were no palaces here or chariot races. There were no Egyptian princesses or massive stone gods. When Moses completely healed, would he grow tired of their small community and simple ways?

And how long could she avoid talking to Moses and feeling the ache in her heart intensify? Zipporah sat up and wiped her tears with the edge of her tunic. Then she rose to her feet and made her way through the family tent until she arrived at her parents' section. All was quiet, but she stepped inside anyway. Her father was sitting up in the dark.

"Zipporah?" he said.

"Yes, it's me."

"I thought I heard something." He rose to his feet and crossed to her. "What is it? Are you ready to talk?"

Her parents had noticed her silence and avoidance of Moses, but they hadn't pressed her for any information, which she had appreciated.

"Have you spoken to Moses?" she whispered, hoping her mother would stay asleep.

"Not about what transpired between the two of you," her father said. "I wanted to hear it from you. Let's go into the cooking room to talk so we don't disturb anyone."

Zipporah followed her father to the cooking room, where her father lifted the front entrance flap halfway so that more light came in. They settled on two cushions. The moonlight coming through the entrance dispelled the heaviest of shadows, and Zipporah could see her father's patient expression.

"Has Moses told you about why he fled Egypt?" she asked in a trembling voice.

"No," her father said. "He told me that he shared his story with you and was waiting for you to make a pronouncement."

"A pronouncement? I'm not his judge," Zipporah said.

"I'm afraid you are," her father said. "Especially if you are to consider marriage to him."

She bit her lip. "I don't think he'd consider marrying me now. Not after I haven't spoken to him for two days."

Her father slowly shook his head. "Moses cares for you, I know that much. That is why he shared his story with you. He trusted you with it, and now he is awaiting your decision." He paused. "Will you accept him for who he is now and what his past has been?"

"How can you even say all of this?" Zipporah said, feeling the anger burn inside her chest. "When you hear of his deeds, you will not give your blessing to a marriage between myself and Moses."

Before her father could reply, she told him everything—about Moses's privileged upbringing, about his betrothal to another woman, about his claim of not visiting the harem, and finally about his hand in the death of an Egyptian taskmaster.

When she finished, her father remained silent for a long time.

"Say something," Zipporah finally said. "I've been agonizing over this for two days now, unable to share it with anyone. And now that I've told you, there is only silence."

"Why should you agonize over it, Zipporah?"

"Because Moses killed someone. Not in a battle or to defend his life but by cold, cruel hands."

Her father merely looked at her. "So send Moses away. Tell him you will not see him again."

"Don't you see, Father? I can't!"

"Why not?" he asked, his voice soft.

Zipporah exhaled and closed her eyes. "Because I still care for him, and because I don't hold his actions against him. He was afraid, and he was trying to spare his own life. Is that so hard to understand? Everything he once thought he knew changed in an instant. Not even his mother turned out to be who he thought she was."

"So you don't blame him? You sympathize with him?"

She hung her head and whispered, "Yes."

Her father's hand grasped hers. "I have only just heard the full story, but I agree with you. I have spent a lot of time with Moses over the past few weeks, and I believe now more than ever that the Lord has brought him to Midian for a purpose."

"To marry me?" Zipporah asked.

"And much more."

Zipporah nodded. She would trust in her father, and she would trust in the Lord . . . and now she would trust in Moses. She squeezed her father's hand, and then it came. A warmth that felt light and heavy at the same time, spreading through her body and attaching to her soul. And in that moment, Zipporah knew she was making the right decision—if Moses asked to marry her, she would tell him yes.

She blinked back her new tears and asked her father, "Do you think I could speak with Moses tonight?"

He smiled. "I will tell him to meet you at the fire circle."

Zipporah leaned forward and embraced her father, then rose to her feet, too anxious to wait another moment. "Thank you, Father. I'll be waiting outside."

She hurried out of the tent and stood by the fire circle. Moonlight replaced any glowing embers or flames, but the wind had kicked up, and clouds moved steadily across the sky. With the drop in temperature, she wished she had brought her robe, but she found herself holding her breath, listening to see if she could hear Moses coming. She didn't dare watch the tent entrance.

Moments later she heard footsteps.

"Zipporah." His voice flowed through her, warming her all the way to her toes.

She turned to see Moses walking toward her. She wished it were daylight so she could see his features more clearly, but maybe this was better in case the tears came again.

"Your father woke me," he said, coming to a stop before her. "Are you sending me away?"

The mixture of hope and questioning in his eyes nearly undid her.

"No, Moses," she said, her voice unsteady. "I will never send you away. I've been thinking a lot lately."

His mouth curved into a smile. "Two days' worth."

"A woman needs time," she said, returning the smile. In a bold move, she reached for his hand. He was quick to enclose her hand in his. The wind pushed against their clothing, and the air felt heavy and moist, as if it might rain soon.

She took a breath, then said, "God had another purpose for you, Moses. He didn't want you imprisoned or put to death. He didn't want you living as a slave, either, but to be educated and taught with the royals. It's clear to me now why you were supposed to flee Egypt and the consequences of your actions."

Moses lowered his head, and Zipporah touched his face, running her fingers lightly over his cheek. He closed his eyes. "In the year that I was born, Pharaoh Seti sent an edict throughout the land of Egypt. All male slave babies born that year were to be killed."

"Yes, even in Midian we heard the tales," she said.

"I can only imagine the tragedy the Hebrews faced," Moses said, opening his eyes. "If the Hebrew mothers didn't snuff the life out of their babes, then the Egyptian soldiers came in and did it for them."

Zipporah rested her hand on his shoulder. Tears burned in her eyes as she thought about what Moses's birth mother must have felt when she'd delivered a son instead of a daughter—how the fear must have pierced her through and how she'd risked so much to save her son.

"Your life was spared more than once," Zipporah said. "You did not choose Pharaoh's actions, nor either of your mothers'. But God has preserved you for some reason and brought you to Midian. I realize that now."

He gave a slow nod. "How is it that your family would welcome a stranger so completely? A man who is not whole?"

"My father has never seen you as a stranger, and you are no longer a stranger to me," she said in a soft voice. "And you are a whole man. God meets us partway in all things."

He brushed his fingers along her cheek, then down the curve of her neck. "You forgive me of my wrongdoings?"

"It is not for me to forgive," she whispered, leaning closer to him. "You are a whole man to me."

Moses rested his forehead against hers. "Before I asked your father for your hand in marriage, I wanted you to know what kind of man you were marrying."

Tears filled her eyes, and she blinked them back. "Are you saying that you might marry me, Moses?" She moved her head back and looked up at him.

His lips curved upward, his eyes soaking her in. "What would you say if I did ask your parents?"

She rose up on her feet, her smile growing, and she kissed his cheek. The boldest she had been. "Yes," she whispered against his ear.

Moses wrapped his arms around her and pulled her close. She slid her arms around his waist and nestled her head against his chest. Closing her eyes, she felt his breathing against her, the warmth of his skin through his clothing. She didn't need an extra robe after all. Moses's past no longer troubled her. It had molded and refined him into the man he was now.

Zipporah could stay wrapped in his arms all night, but she knew her father was likely still awake, waiting to talk with her.

"Perhaps my entire life was meant to lead to this moment," Moses said, drawing away from her so he could look down at her.

"In a goat enclosure, surrounded by animals and sand," she whispered, her mouth lifting into a smile as she looked into his warm, brown eyes.

"With you . . ."

"Yes."

And then Moses lowered his face to hers and brushed his mouth against her lips as the first raindrops fell and the wind swirled around them. She tilted her head and kissed him back, melting into his strength and warmth. He pulled her even closer and kissed her again. "Zipporah," he said in a soft voice, "will you marry me?"

She drew away from him, her eyes shining. "Yes. I'll marry you."

CHAPTER FIFTEEN
ZIPPORAH

Zipporah didn't think her feet touched the ground all day. She went about her usual chores but didn't remember a single one. Rain had fallen for only a few moments, then moved on almost as quickly as it had started. Somehow the goats were milked, the flocks were watered, the dates were picked, two meals prepared, and now she was repairing a tent panel in the fading light of the day.

Moses was going to speak to her father this evening, and she couldn't think of anything else. Moses would ask for her hand in marriage, and she was certain her father would say yes. It seemed unbelievable that Moses had captured her heart and she his. She pulled a strand of thread too hard and snapped it in half. She had to rethread the bone needle and start back a few stitches.

She couldn't forget the way Moses had held her. And then kissed her. He had told her things over the past few days that should have shocked her, that should have repelled her, but she felt only compassion toward him. He'd stood up for a slave who'd been beaten, and it had cost him his family and his home. Somewhere deep inside him was a man who had to be just, who had to be compassionate.

Zipporah finished off the final stitch and created a secure knot. Then she bit down on the thread to separate it from the panel. Moses was perhaps the most courageous man she knew. Without even knowing his true heritage, he'd defended a mistreated slave. He could have ignored it and continued in his privileged life. And if he had, she would never have met him.

She wanted to stand up and shout her joy—to the sky, to the earth, to the trees, to anything and anyone who would listen. She could hardly keep herself from smiling. The passing hours had been agony as she waited for the night to fall and the moon to rise. Only then would the men gather for their nightly discussions. At some point, Moses would request to speak to her father alone.

Zipporah rose to her feet and carried the repaired panel inside the family tent, where only the women were now, preparing the evening meal.

"There you are, Zipporah," her mother said. "I need you to take this jug of stew to Cozbi and her family. She is feeling poorly today."

Guilt slid over Zipporah. She hadn't even known her sister was ailing. She'd only been thinking of her own good fortune all day.

"Where have you been?" her mother continued, watching her carefully.

Zipporah suspected she looked far too happy and that her mother had surely noticed. "Repairing the panels, like you asked."

"That was hours ago. What's going on? You look flushed."

"I—"

Abigail came running into the tent. "Mother. It's Cozbi! She's ill, and Sihon has sent for the healer."

Zipporah stared at Abigail. "What's wrong with her?"

"I don't know," Abigail said, tears spilling down her cheeks. "Her stomach has been hurting, and now she is crying in pain."

Zipporah set down the jug her mother had given her and rushed out of the tent. Her mother and Abigail ran close behind, but Zipporah had a head start. She ran past neighbors who were preparing supper near their own tents. They stared after her, but Zipporah didn't take time to explain.

It seemed to take forever to reach Cozbi's tent, and when she did, all she could hear was a baby screaming. Was something wrong with Oreb as well? Her breath came fast as she pushed her way into the tent to see Cozbi lying on her mat, curled up and looking pale, her eyes closed. Her husband, Sihon, was walking with the baby, who was crying incessantly.

Zipporah reached for the baby, and Sihon gladly handed him over, but the baby only started screaming louder. "Has he been fed?" she asked over his wails.

Sihon shook his head. "Cozbi is only getting worse. She can't even get up."

Zipporah wanted to check on her sister, but it was hard to focus on anything besides the hysterical baby. "Wait outside," she told Sihon. "My mother will be here soon."

When Sihon left, Zipporah tried to console the baby, but he kept crying. When her mother arrived, breathing heavily, Zipporah had never been so glad to see her.

"Cozbi can't feed him," Zipporah told her mother immediately. "Where can I take him?"

"Tema," her mother said, barely glancing at the child and heading toward Cozbi. She knelt beside her and smoothed the tangled hair from her face. "Tema is still nursing her baby. She'll have to take on Oreb until Cozbi is better."

"What do you think is wrong with her?" Zipporah asked, watching her ministrations.

"I'm not sure yet," her mother said. "Take the baby."

Zipporah hurried outside, then passed tent after tent until she reached her older sister's place. Everyone stared after her as she carried a crying Oreb past them. A few times he briefly settled down but then would start crying again.

She let herself into Tema's tent without calling out a welcome. Tema looked up from where she was grinding barley. Her three-year-old daughter sat close by. Tema had two daughters, a three-year-old and a baby a few months old. Tema rose to her feet, and Zipporah practically shoved Oreb toward her. "He's starving," she said over his crying. "Cozbi is very ill."

Tema took the baby and settled onto a cushion, then put his rooting mouth to her breast. When he quieted and was feeding, Tema looked up at Zipporah. "What's wrong with Cozbi?"

"She can't keep any food down. She's too weak to even sit up. When I arrived at her tent, she was curled up on her mat, not moving, and Oreb was screaming."

Tema nodded. "I can feed him for now, but I don't have enough for both babies unless I want to be a goat."

Zipporah hoped Cozbi's illness would pass soon, but if not . . . "Would he drink goat's milk, do you think?"

Tema shrugged. "It's been done. It depends on the child—some of them will reject it." She wiped her forehead. "My baby is asleep right now, but when she awakes, she'll be hungry too."

"I understand," Zipporah said. "I don't know what else we can do."

Tema finished feeding the baby and handed him back to Zipporah. She didn't want to take him in case he started screaming again, and she had no way to feed him. "Can't you keep him tonight?"

"I don't know how I'd manage it," Tema said. "If Cozbi can't feed him in a few hours, then maybe try the goat's milk." Her three-year-old started to tug on her mother's tunic, and Tema's attention was diverted.

Zipporah left the tent, grateful to be carrying a contented baby, but that could change at any moment. On the walk back to Cozbi's tent, Oreb fell asleep in her arms, and Zipporah wished she had the power to make the child happy. But without his mother and without nourishment, he'd start crying again soon enough.

When Cozbi's tent came into sight, Zipporah saw her mother pacing outside the entrance. "There you are. Cozbi has the desert fever," her mother said, her face pale. "I should have never sent you to your other sister. Oreb may have the fever as well, and it's very contagious."

Zipporah looked down at the sleeping child in her arms, then back to her mother. She couldn't very well hand over the baby now. If he had it, that meant Zipporah might be susceptible too. She took a couple of steps away from the tent. Desert fever could be fatal; it could also spread rapidly if they weren't careful.

"What about you, Mother?" she asked. "Is it safe for you to go into her tent?"

"I had the desert fever when you were small, remember? No one has ever had it twice. Besides, I've already touched your sister, so I'll remain here and watch over her." Her gaze flicked away but then returned to Zipporah, more determined than ever. "Tell Father. I've sent Abigail to warn neighbors."

Zipporah wanted to stay and help her mother, but there was no way to know yet if the baby had the disease, and it was best to keep him separated from his mother. Zipporah's mother was a strong woman, but whenever the desert fever swept through Midian, the young and the old were the most susceptible. Her sister had a good chance of recovery, but if her child had it, he might not be so fortunate.

Zipporah looked down at Oreb's peaceful face, his smooth baby skin and soft dark curls. "I'll take him back to our tent and find a way to keep him separated from everyone else." The unspoken words were that Zipporah would have to stay with the child. She walked as fast as she dared while being careful not to disturb Oreb's sleep. But as she moved around the neighboring tents, word was already starting to spread that Cozbi had desert fever.

Mothers were gathering their children close, and people watched Zipporah with wariness. By the time she neared her home, Zipporah had no idea what she was going to do. How was she going to keep the baby separated from the rest of her family? She couldn't risk anyone else being exposed. If the desert fever spread through Midian, there would certainly be deaths as a result.

It was dangerous for Zipporah to be holding the child, but she couldn't imagine not caring for him. She had to find a way to keep him fed and happy while separated from others, until she knew if he had the fever. The sun was low on the horizon by the time she reached her family's tent.

Her father was standing outside with Moses and Sihon. They turned as Zipporah approached. Before they could cross to her, she said, "The baby might be contagious with desert fever. Mother says that Cozbi has it."

Sihon visibly started. "No, it can't be," he said. "How can your mother be sure? Maybe it's a simple stomach ailment and the healer can give her special tea."

Her father put a hand on his shoulder, and Moses took a step toward Zipporah, then paused.

Zipporah tightened her hold on the baby and looked at all the men, finally meeting Sihon's panicked eyes. "Mother's seen it many times," she said in a quiet, steady voice, even though she felt anything but calm. "We can only be vigilant and wait it out."

Sihon's face seemed to pale even further as he looked over at his son. "What about Oreb?" His voice was just above a whisper. "Does he need to be quarantined?"

"I'm already touching him, so I'll do it," Zipporah said. She looked from Sihon to her father and Moses. "Can you set up a tent for us? I'll sleep out here with him."

"Are you sure?" her father asked. "We could find a place within the tent and tell everyone else to stay out."

"The risk would be too high," Zipporah said. "I need my tent to be completely separated."

"I can stay with her," Moses cut in. Everyone looked at him in surprise. "Not inside the tent with her, but I'll sleep outside, in case they need anything."

Her father nodded, gratitude evident in his face. Zipporah wanted to turn Moses down because she didn't know how she was going to manage keeping the child fed and happy—there might be a lot of crying. But Moses's offer warmed her through. It would be comforting to have someone close by. And if it turned out that Oreb did have the desert fever . . . well, Zipporah wasn't going to dwell on that right now.

Sihon had turned away, his jaw clenched in emotion, and Jethro put his arm around his shoulders.

"I'll set up the tent," Moses said in a quiet voice, respecting the other men's grief and shock. "And then you can get the child settled."

As her father and Sihon moved away, speaking to each other in hushed tones, Zipporah let out a breath. She was getting help with the tent, but her main concern was feeding Oreb.

"What else do you need?" Moses asked, stepping toward her.

"You might not want to stand so close to the child," Zipporah said.

Moses halted and looked down at the sleeping baby. "It's hard to imagine that he's sick right now. He looks so peaceful. What are the symptoms of desert fever?"

Zipporah turned and walked a few paces away. She didn't want to be overheard by Sihon. He was distressed enough. "It starts out like a stomach ailment—as if someone has eaten something diseased or rotten. But, then, after everything is purged from the body, the body heats up, and the person isn't able to keep anything down. Other fluids are lost, and . . ." Her voice cracked.

"I've heard of it, then," Moses said, speaking when she couldn't continue. "What is the healer doing for her?"

"In the past, the healer tried to get the person to drink. Sometimes . . . the person would starve . . ." Her voice choked off, and she blinked back hot tears.

"Zipporah," he said, touching her arm.

She flinched and moved away. "If Oreb has it, I'm susceptible as well." She wiped at the tears on her cheeks. "Diseases such as this can spread rapidly in desert communities. Two years ago, it ravaged the Badrayan tribe. They lost nearly half of their people."

Moses scrubbed a hand through his short hair. "We will stop the spread of the disease. What else do you need besides that tent?"

Zipporah's eyes filled with tears again. For a moment, she remembered that tonight was when Moses was going to speak to her father about marriage. And now this had happened. She looked into his gold-brown eyes. "I need a goat."

"I can get you a goat, and then I'll get started on the tent. We'll set up over by the pomegranate tree." He waved her in that direction.

Zipporah walked to the pomegranate tree. She didn't need the shade or protection of it since twilight was fast approaching. Nothing was as it should be. She and her mother should be preparing a large meal, then serving the men. The men should be speaking in jovial tones, discussing their herds and the latest passing caravan. The women should be minding their children and sharing the latest news about their neighbors.

Not this quiet stillness. Not her father and Sihon starting off to her sister's and not knowing what they'd be facing.

And not Moses setting up a quarantine tent for her.

CHAPTER SIXTEEN
MOSES

"He's hungry again?" Moses said as Zipporah came out of the tent. It had been two days since she'd kept Oreb in the small tent.

Moses wasn't sure who'd slept less: the child, Zipporah, or himself. Not only did Moses not sleep when the child was crying, but he didn't sleep when all was quiet, as fear of the unknown kept his pulse throbbing and his mind full of worries.

Zipporah looked exhausted. Her golden skin had paled, and there were deep violet circles beneath her eyes. "He doesn't like the goat's milk," she said, her voice scratchy from the early morning.

The sun had barely tipped the horizon, and normally Zipporah would be out milking all the goats. But Moses had taken over that chore as Zipporah struggled to care for the child. So far, there hadn't been any signs of the desert fever in Oreb, and Moses frequently asked Zipporah how she was feeling herself.

"Any word on Cozbi?" Zipporah asked, wariness and hope showing in her eyes.

"I spoke to your father about an hour ago when he came back from checking on your mother," Moses said. It seemed no one was sleeping. "She still isn't drinking anything, but your mother continues to soak cloths with tea to put into her mouth."

Zipporah gave a slow nod. "That's all that can be done, then," she said. "Did he say how my mother is doing?"

"She shows no signs yet," he said.

A flash of relief crossed Zipporah's face. "Good." She moved to the she-goat they had tethered, and Moses rose to his feet.

"I'll do the milking."

Zipporah stood and watched as Moses bent down and milked the goat. He was finished quickly, and he handed the clay jug to Zipporah. Just as she took it, Oreb's cries intensified. Zipporah gripped the jug and rushed into the tent, calling out soothing words to the baby.

He wanted to follow but knew she wouldn't allow him inside.

"Moses!" Zipporah called out. "He's thrown up."

Moses had crossed to the tent entrance by the time Zipporah finished speaking. He ducked and stepped into the small tent.

"Don't come in," Zipporah said, looking up at Moses from the mat where she was trying to soothe the crying child. The fear in her expression hammered right through him.

With one hand, she dug at the edge of the tent where there was a patch of sand exposed beneath one of the rugs. She scooped it up and dribbled it over where the baby had been sick.

The poor thing kept jerking his legs as if he were in pain. Was it the goat's milk? Or did he have desert fever?

Moses entered and knelt beside Zipporah. "Let me see him."

"No," Zipporah said, her eyes wide. "You shouldn't be in here."

Moses reached for the child and wrapped his arms around the small body, pulling the child from Zipporah. Her hands fell away in defeat.

"Hand me the cloth," he said.

Zipporah soaked a small cloth in the jug of goat's milk, then handed over the dripping cloth. Moses adjusted the crying child in his arms so that he was supporting Oreb's head better, then he rocked the baby as he held the edge of the cloth in the child's mouth. Oreb immediately began sucking. For a moment he was quiet.

"You shouldn't be in here," Zipporah said, but there was no force behind her words. She continued to clean up where the baby had been sick, then looked over at Moses. "You will have to remain quarantined yourself."

He glanced over at her, then looked back down at the child. "I guess we can all be stuck together."

Zipporah let out a sigh and settled with her knees pulled up to her chest. She rested her chin on her knees and watched Moses feed the baby. After a moment, she whispered, "Do you think he's in the first stages of the desert fever?"

Moses hoped not, but as he looked down at the baby, he couldn't know for sure. "He's eating now, let's be grateful for that. Let's hope that it's the goat's milk irritating his stomach and not the fever. We need to find a woman who will feed him as her own until your sister is better."

"No woman wants to take the risk," Zipporah said.

Moses let out a breath. "If only Midian had Hebrew slaves," he said in irony. "My mother—my Egyptian mother—told me she brought in a Hebrew slave to feed me as a babe." He shook his head. "I wonder what's going through Oreb's mind."

Zipporah gave a half smile. "I think he just wants to sleep without an aching stomach." Her voice faltered. "At least I hope that's all—that, and missing his mother."

"I wonder what I was like as a baby," Moses said. "Being taken from one mother and given to another."

"I'm sure you were well taken care of and well loved," she said in a quiet voice.

Oreb's breathing steadied, and Moses realized the child had fallen asleep. "Look," he whispered. "He seems to be feeling better now."

Zipporah moved to Moses's side, and together they looked down at the child.

It was an intimate moment. Even though Oreb wasn't their child and they weren't married, Moses felt this could be what their marriage was like. Both looking down at their child, concerned for his well-being.

"Zipporah," he said, and she lifted her head. He wished he could clear away the exhaustion on her face. "I'm sorry about your sister, and I'm sorry I haven't been able to speak to your father yet."

Her eyes fluttered shut for a moment. "It's all right. I am not so worried about you changing your mind."

Moses raised his brows. "You aren't? Some men might run after spending the last two days and nights doing what I've done."

"That's exactly true," she said. "They wouldn't have lasted through the first night. When you told me you . . . wanted to marry me . . . I wondered what type of husband and father you might be." Her face flushed, and she looked away for a moment. Then her eyes were back on him. "I didn't doubt that you'd be wonderful, mind you, but a woman does think about such things."

He tried to read her expression. "And what did you decide?"

"That even if you wanted to change your mind, I wouldn't let you," she said, a smile growing on her face. "What do you think about that?"

Moses felt his own smile form. It was good to hear her tease him after all the worry. "I think I'd better obey you." He leaned toward her, pleased to see when her skin flushed again. They were nearly alone, secluded in a tent, with no one around. He was grateful that the child gave them propriety, but that didn't mean he couldn't kiss her, did it?

She was leaning toward him now, and it was as if they were being pulled together by a rope. "What if I'm contagious?" she whispered.

"It's too late for that now." Moses kissed her softly, gently, not wanting to wake the baby in his arms. Zipporah wrapped one hand around his neck, kissing him back and holding him in place as she did so.

"She's well!" a voice called from somewhere outside the tent.

Moses drew away from Zipporah and turned just as Jethro pulled aside the tent door. "Cozbi's fever has broken, and she is clear eyed and asking for her child." He looked at the baby now stirring in Moses's arms. It was as if Oreb understood the news about his mother.

Jethro grinned. "He understood me. Let me see the child."

"He was sick a short time ago," Zipporah cut in. "Only I should carry him to Cozbi."

"All right, then," Jethro said, frowning in concern, although he couldn't hide the elation the news of his daughter had brought.

He looked from Moses to Zipporah. "If you are both exposed, you must stay away from the others for another day or two."

Moses rose to his feet. "I'll carry the child," he said, looking at Zipporah. "I've been exposed too."

They said good-bye to Jethro and walked together along the quiet paths of Midian. He held the baby in his right arm, and with his left hand, he reached for Zipporah's hand and squeezed it. Moses felt secure, whole. Even if one of them came down with the desert fever, he had never felt so grateful as he did at this moment.

They said nothing to each other, both content to walk in silence while holding hands. It was peaceful to walk through Midian when all was quiet. Even the animals were sleeping. Once the sun started to warm the air, children would awaken, women would start cooking, and men would begin their day of labor.

"This is their tent," Zipporah said in a low voice. She released his hand and parted the tent opening. "Mother? Cozbi?"

Moses heard a murmur of voices reply. Zipporah turned to him and reached for Oreb. Taking the baby in her arms, she said to Moses, "Come in."

He hesitated, unsure whether he should go into the private home, but Zipporah gave him a smile and tilted her head. So he stepped inside after her, and the tent panel closed behind him. The interior was dim, and it took a moment for his eyes to adjust. The tent was divided into two sections, rugs spread across the ground, and cushions and jars and baskets lined up along the edges.

Sihon rose from the section on the left; it seemed he'd been preparing a tea. He nodded at Moses, relief in his eyes.

"How is the child?" Sihon asked, stepping forward.

Zipporah lifted a hand. "We don't know if he has the desert fever or not."

"Bring him to me," a thin voice spoke from the other section of the tent.

Cozbi was in the corner, sitting up and draped in a robe. Her face was much thinner than Moses remembered it, and her large eyes dominated her pale face. But her gaze was alert as she stretched out her arms. Next to her sat Zipporah's mother. She looked almost as pale as her daughter, but there was joy in her expression as well.

Oreb stirred and opened his eyes. He'd recognized his mother's voice and started fussing.

Zipporah gave a light laugh and carried him over to Cozbi. Moses watched the tender exchange between sisters and felt a sudden longing. He'd never had siblings; it had always been only his Egyptian mother and him. He turned from the scene and followed Sihon into the left section of the tent to give the women some privacy in their reunion.

"Do you want some tea?" Sihon asked.

Moses shook his head. "I may have been exposed, and I don't want to get too close to anyone."

Sihon nodded, then went about steeping dried leaves in the steaming water. "We are grateful for your help to our family."

Moses let out a breath. "I am pleased your wife has recovered."

"Our prayers to God were answered. We have been blessed."

Moses watched as Sihon stirred the tea in slow strokes with a wooden utensil. In this harsh land of heat and sand and illness, God was indeed watching over the humble settlement. The women's voices from the next section rose and fell, mixed with exclamations and soft laughter. Moses's heart swelled at the sounds of the sweet reunion. He was grateful that Zipporah's sister had recovered, for Zipporah's sake as well. The sisters were close, and Moses wanted Zipporah to be happy in all things.

"Moses," a woman's voice said, and he turned to see Zipporah's mother.

She crossed to him and wrapped her arms around him, pulling him into an embrace.

Moses was stunned—Zipporah's mother had always seemed so stern, and he'd never before seen her display affection.

"You have sacrificed so much to help our family," she said. "Thank you, thank you." She pulled away and looked up at him, her smile transforming her normally drawn face. "You are always welcome in our home—until the end of your days."

It had been a long time since Moses had had a motherly hug, and he never thought he would feel this way around a woman he hadn't even known a month before.

"You are a treasure, and I hope Zipporah knows it," she said, patting his cheek. Her eyes filled with moisture.

Moses felt his eyes burn. His own mother had often called him a treasure. Now wasn't the time to argue with his personal thoughts on that statement, but the words from Zipporah's mother had brought back the sharp pain of forgotten memories.

"You hope I know what?" Zipporah had shown up, and her mother turned to look at her.

"Moses is a good man," she said, her voice firm yet soft.

Zipporah's face flushed. It was clear she hadn't shared the fact that he was intending on asking Jethro for permission to marry. And now he knew that Zipporah's mother would approve.

"I know, Mother," she said, her eyes flitting to Moses, then away again. "We must go. We're still under quarantine." She looked at Sihon. "You take care, brother."

He nodded, and Zipporah moved toward the tent entrance.

"Thank you, Zipporah," her mother called out. "Thank you for watching over the baby."

She smiled, nodded, and lifted the flap. "Coming?" she said, glancing back at Moses.

"Yes," he said, then offered his good-byes to Sihon and Zipporah's mother.

Zipporah was waiting for him outside, and he wanted to take her into his arms and hold her close. No one was about, but Moses didn't want to make her feel uncomfortable. So he leaned down, grabbed her hand, and kissed her cheek.

"Moses," she said, protesting, although it wasn't a very strong protest. She squeezed his hand. "If my mother sees you, she'll announce our marriage herself."

"I wouldn't complain," he said, lingering close so that he could breathe her in.

Zipporah drew away, unlinking their hands. Now she led him along the path back toward her family home.

"You'd better be speaking with my father soon," she said.

Moses laughed. "The next time I see him."

CHAPTER SEVENTEEN
ZIPPORAH

ZIPPORAH SAT QUIETLY, HER KNEES pulled to her chest, as she listened to the conversation on the other side of the tent. Moses was speaking to her father, but they spoke in Egyptian, and Zipporah couldn't make out a single word. Except for her name.

She smiled and hugged her knees tighter. Moses was speaking to her father about marrying her, and her father's voice sounded pleased. The sound of Moses's voice sent a warm shiver across her skin.

It had been a week since Cozbi's desert fever, and only one other woman in Midian had contracted it—a friend of Cozbi.

Moses hadn't fallen ill, nor had Oreb. And Zipporah was fine. She's spent another night in the quarantine tent, with Moses sleeping outside it. She'd felt secure, and every moment that she'd been awake, she'd prayed that the illness wouldn't find her or any more of her loved ones. And she counted Moses among her loved ones.

The voices changed, were less hushed, and it sounded like her father had risen to his feet and was telling Moses good-bye.

Zipporah rose as well, staying absolutely silent. She had to move before her father came inside the tent and saw where she'd been waiting. But it was too late. Her father stepped inside just as Zipporah made it to her feet.

He raised his brows, but he was smiling. "I have given Moses my blessing."

Zipporah didn't know whether to laugh and collapse or run to her father and throw her arms about his neck.

He crossed to her first and pulled her into his arms. Zipporah squeezed him tightly. "It's really done, Father? He really asked?"

Her father chuckled and patted her back. "You are to be a married woman, and your mother won't wish for any type of delay."

Zipporah pulled away from her father, her heart soaring. "When?"

"I am sure your mother will have a say in that. As for Moses, he can tell you himself." His smile was broad, and he touched her cheek. "My stubborn daughter, having found her love at last. Moses has been a blessing to our lives."

It was true. And the knowledge made Zipporah realize how much his Egyptian mother must miss him. And his Hebrew family who had to give him up. Zipporah felt like the most fortunate woman in all of Midian to have such a man ask for her hand in marriage.

"He has made the request, then?" her mother said, coming into the tent, her eyes full of anticipation.

When Moses had formally requested an audience with Jethro, Zipporah's mother had pursed her lips but said nothing. Her expression had told Zipporah she'd guessed, and Zipporah didn't want to say anything more about what promises Moses had made to her until he'd spoken to her father.

Jethro faced his wife and kissed her cheek. "Moses has asked for Zipporah's hand in marriage, and I have agreed."

She didn't even try to hold back a smile. She looked past Jethro to Zipporah. "You have been holding out on me. When did you decide that Moses was good enough for you?" The words might have been cutting on another occasion, but her mother was still smiling. It was a rare thing for her mother to tease.

"He . . . we . . . Perhaps it was all the goat milking we did together," she said at last.

Her mother moved to Zipporah's side. "Perhaps we can give the goats an extra treat today." She grasped Zipporah's hands. "I am pleased for you, daughter. It seems that a man could capture your heart after all—even though it had to be a stranger from another land."

Her father laughed. "Zipporah would never settle for the conventional Midianite anyway."

Her mother laughed with her father, another rare event. When she sobered, she said, "Well, are you going to go to him or not? You need to accept him still, you know, and set the date. Preferably before I grow any more gray hair."

Zipporah flushed. She did want to see Moses. But her pulse was hammering so hard it vibrated throughout the rest of her body. She took a deep breath, then turned from her parents, who were now whispering together.

She found him by the evening fire. The other men had long since left, and her younger sisters had already gone to bed. When she approached Moses, he didn't look up. The reflection of the fire's low flames danced along his profile.

She settled across the fire from him, on the other side. She wasn't sure why she didn't sit by him, but perhaps she wanted him to speak first. The night had cooled, though Zipporah was far from cold. She felt as if she were wearing several layers of clothing when in fact she wore only a single tunic. Moses raised his head slowly and met her eyes, and she was left with no doubt of his attachment to her.

He rose to his feet and walked around the fire until he stood above her. Then he held out his hand. She placed her hand in his. Waves of warmth shot through her as his hand closed around hers. They'd held hands many times, but each time the meaning grew deeper. She let him draw her to her feet.

"Your father agreed," he said in a low voice, still holding her hand.

"He told me," Zipporah whispered. "And I'm so happy he did." The corners of his mouth lifted slowly, and Zipporah wanted to kiss him, but she waited for him.

"Did you think he might not?" he asked.

"I suppose I was pretty confident he'd agree to your request," she said. His other hand slid around her waist and she found herself leaning closer, turning her face toward his.

"Zipporah," he said, his breath warm on her face. "Will you be my wife?"

Every part of her nearly melted. His question wasn't a surprise, but coming from his lips, it was the most beautiful Midianite question she'd ever heard.

"Yes, Moses, I will marry you." She was surprised that she could speak so clearly when she felt as if her soul had separated from her body.

He released her hand and slipped his other arm around her. She lifted her own arms and wrapped them around his neck, pulling him close at the same time he drew her against him.

"Thank you," he whispered.

She smiled. "Thank you, Moses. Thank you for rescuing our sheep and for helping me every day." She ran her fingers along his cheek just as he bent down and kissed her.

His kiss was warm and caring, saying things that combined both of their languages into a single understanding. Zipporah wished she could remain here all night in his arms, and her body tingled when she thought that the day would soon come when she could do just that after their marriage.

"You will not be sorry that you settled for a foreigner?" he asked when he drew away.

She moved her hands along his shoulders. "I will never be sorry, no matter where our lives take us." She brushed a hand against his cheek. "What about you, Moses? Will you be sorry that your home is the desert settlement of Midian when you were raised in one of the most elegant courts of the world?"

His mouth softened into a smile. "You are more elegant than any treasure or person I've ever seen." He reached for her hair and wrapped a finger around a curl that had fallen from her plait.

Moses's tender gesture went straight to Zipporah's heart. "Will you say that when I'm big with child?" She couldn't believe what she'd spoken aloud, and she blushed furiously.

Moses only laughed. "I will still love you when we're both bent over with age and wrinkled from years of desert wind and heat." He pulled her against him and leaned down, burying his face against her neck.

Again, Zipporah wished they could stay like this forever, that the sun wouldn't rise on a new day, and that chores didn't face her every waking moment. "My mother will be wondering why it's taking me so long to return to the tent; and if I return without a date settled on, then she'll send me back out here."

"Mmm," Moses mumbled against her skin. "Tomorrow?"

"Too soon," she said with a laugh. "My mother needs time to prepare the feast and invite the entire settlement. There will be dancing and singing, you know." She drew back so she could look at Moses, and he lifted his head. "Have you ever been to a Midianite wedding?" Of course he hadn't, but Zipporah liked to tease him.

He shook his head. "Tell me what they are like."

"You will see," she said with a smile. "I don't want to spoil any surprises." She paused, linking her hands with his. "What are the weddings like in Egypt?"

He seemed to consider, and after a moment, he said, "I don't know what they're like in the Hebrew slave camps, but I'd assume they are very religious-centered."

"And at the palace? Among the Egyptian royalty?"

His mouth thinned as he drew it down. "Elaborate. Long. If there is any excuse for a celebration, Pharaoh will embrace it. He and his queen are the perfect leaders of a wealthy kingdom. Viziers and dignitaries come from all corners of the land of Egypt, and foreign ambassadors are invited as well. If only for Pharaoh to show off his wealth." He paused, and his gaze moved past Zipporah as if he were remembering a particular wedding.

"Just the betrothal event is surrounded by celebrations and banquets. Entertainers and dancers are brought in. The platters of food seem endless, as are the wines and teas. And the gifts are immense. From live animals to priceless pearls to trinkets of gold and silver."

Zipporah smiled. "We'll have live animals too—just nothing exotic. You'll have to settle for goats and sheep."

CHAPTER EIGHTEEN
MOSES

"We need your help," the voice said, sounding far away. And then someone was shaking Moses's shoulder and repeating the request.

It took Moses a moment to realize what was happening. He was in Jethro's family tent, and the man himself was trying to awaken him. Whatever Moses had been dreaming about, all thoughts fled as he sat up.

"What's wrong?" Moses asked, his voice hoarse from sleep.

"The Badrayans have attacked our settlement," Jethro said, his face coming into focus in the dimness of the tent.

Moses climbed to his feet and reached for the bow and arrows he kept near his mat. "Where? How bad?" he asked, securing his dagger in the waist of his kilt. He would not need a robe—not if he was to be fighting. His thoughts conjured up all sorts of devastations. "Your family?" he said before Jethro had a chance to speak.

"My family is fine; none of them have been harmed," Jethro said in a hushed voice as if he was trying not to wake any of the women in the other tent sections.

Relief should have replaced Moses's angst, but it didn't.

"They attacked the tents to the north of us," Jethro said. "Two women are dead; one of them was with child. And an older man is seriously injured."

Angered heat pulsed through Moses. Midian had become his home. The Midianites his people. He was to marry Zipporah in a matter of days, and there was no way he'd let a warring tribe bring harm to her or her family.

Jethro continued. "The Badrayans' attack was swift and unexpected, but they must have been scouting the outlying tents for days. They picked the most vulnerable one. The younger men of the family are out with their sheep. Even my own son is away with our flocks, and my oldest grandson with him. The timing couldn't have been worse."

Moses shook his head, trying to comprehend the brutal deaths of two innocent women and the attack on an older man. "Where are those Badrayans now? Have they been captured?"

"That's what I need your help with," Jethro said, his eyes wide in the dimness. "We need to track the tribesmen and make sure they learn to stay away for good."

Moses was more than ready. "Let's go." He followed Jethro out of the tent and saw that Sihon and his younger brother Peor were waiting for them. They gave each other silent nods of acknowledgment; no verbal greetings were necessary. The moon was low and halved, not casting much light. But the stars mapped the sky with millions of dots of lights. Dawn was near. The air was cool and sharp, though Moses knew he was far from feeling any of the cold.

It reminded him of the night he slept in the grove near the well, although then he had his robe to cover him. He turned to Jethro and said, "Do you think this is revenge for what I did to them at the well? Could they be the same men?"

Jethro's expression said it all. But before he could respond, a woman rushed out of the tent. She wore only her sleeping tunic, and her hair tumbled wildly about her shoulders.

Zipporah. She ran to Moses and grasped his hands.

"Be careful, Moses," she said, then released him and turned away. She hurried back to the tent and disappeared almost as quickly as she'd appeared. If there hadn't been others to witness what had just happened, Moses might have doubted it.

"She woke up when the messenger came to deliver the news," Jethro said. "But I agree with her. Be careful." His gaze shifted to the other men. "All of you. I will not have my daughters grieving."

Sihon stepped forward and clasped Jethro's hand; Peor did the same.

"You're not coming?" Moses asked Jethro amidst the farewells.

"I will only slow you down. Besides, I'll not let my wife and daughters out of my sight. And they will want to be part of the funerals." He rubbed a hand across his face, and his voice trembled at his next words. "May God light your way and grant blessings for a swift return. I will not sleep until you are back in Midian." He clapped Moses on the back and added, "Be well, son."

Jethro turned from the men and headed toward the tent entrance. Moses stared after him for a moment. He'd never been called *son* by a man before. He had never had a father.

"We brought you a goatskin of water," Sihon said, holding it out, interrupting Moses's reflections. "Hopefully we'll be back before the sun rises."

Moses shouldered the goatskin and nodded. "I have done little desert tracking, but I can be an additional man if it comes to a fight."

Sihon gave a soft chuckle. "Oh, it will come to a fight, my friend." He motioned with his hand for Moses to follow them. "The wind is picking up. We must make haste before their tracks are blown away."

Moses set off with Sihon and Peor in a light run along the hard-packed paths that wound through Midian. They headed north, and when they reached the edge of the last collection of tents, they stopped to talk to a gathering of men.

"We're going to find them," Sihon said to a man who separated from the group. "We have the Egyptian with us."

The group of men turned their dark eyes on Moses, not knowing what to do but trusting him.

"Do you have enough weapons?" one of them asked.

Moses nodded, and Sihon said, "Watch for any more activity."

"We'll be here until you return," the first man said. "May God light your way." He stepped back with the others.

As they continued at a jog through the desert, Moses thought about what Jethro and the other man had said about God lighting their way. Their belief in a higher being was simple, uncomplicated. They spoke of God as if He were a revered leader, possibly even a friend, and not an ancient, remote being who existed in another sphere.

"Here," Sihon said, stopping and crouching by some scraggly grass that shot up from the desert floor. Just beyond, visible in the growing light, sat a wadi that led up the slope of the Sarawat mountain range, a line of jutting mountains rising out of the earth like new plants.

Moses settled next to Sihon and watched as he pointed out the visibly bent grass, and just beyond, tracks that were discernable along the undulating desert floor.

"Did they go up one of the mountains?" Moses asked quietly, looking up at the looming range. A shape moved. It wasn't a rock. He dropped to his stomach. "Get down! I saw movement on the ridge."

Sihon and Peor joined him on the ground just as an arrow sailed above them.

"They're shooting this way," Peor squeaked out as if it weren't obvious. But Moses understood his nerves, especially if the young man hadn't faced many battle situations.

"Move to the left and take cover behind those bushes," Moses said, half crawling toward the scraggly bushes that would have to act as a barrier for now.

Once they were settled, a man on each side of him, Moses exhaled, his own nerves settling as he studied the positions of the three—no four—men. Perhaps even more. A shallow valley separated them from the rise at the foot of the mountain where the arrow had come from. Large boulders that had tumbled down from the higher ridge created a great hiding place for the Badrayans.

"Get your weapons ready, very slowly," Moses whispered. "We'll wait until one of them relaxes or makes another movement."

Slowly, Moses slid the bow off his shoulder and brought it in front of him, then he nocked the first arrow. Peor moved his bow and arrow into position as well, his breathing coming fast. Sihon gripped his spear and looked ready to spring up like a large cat at the slightest movement from above. Moses wondered why Sihon hadn't brought a bow, but perhaps he wasn't skilled at using one.

Since Moses wore no tunic, he hoped the color of his skin blended with the desert floor. Both Sihon and Peor wore brown tunics and dark headdresses. For now, they melded with the waning night, but when the sun rose, they'd be easily visible.

DELIVERANCE

The Badrayans wore lighter-colored tunics, but they were well concealed behind an outcropping of rocks right now. They would have the advantage when the sun came up, and Moses hoped this standoff wouldn't take that long.

Peor's breathing hadn't slowed, so Moses whispered, "The last battle I fought in was against a ferocious army—the Libyans." Moses spoke slowly, choosing his words carefully so that Peor could get the most out of the story. "We rode in chariots and fought against them for an entire day."

"Chariots with one horse or two horses?" Peor asked.

"Two. You should try to shoot a bow and arrow while riding on a chariot," Moses said with a soft chuckle. "It's a wonder we didn't stab our own legs or feet."

Peor's breathing relaxed as he continued to ask questions about the Libyan battle. He had to repeat himself a few times so that Moses could fully understand.

In the middle of one of his questions, Moses cut him off. "One of them is moving."

Another arrow came sailing toward them, and it was clear that the Badrayans didn't know their exact location, for it took a wild path.

In the intervening moments when the tribesmen were watching where the arrow would land, Moses stood up and sent his own arrows in their direction. While the Badrayan's arrow had missed its mark, Moses made his target.

A scream traveled across the shallow valley dividing the two groups of warriors. Moses felt the impact of the painful scream echo in his stomach.

"You—" Peor started to say in a trembling voice, then cut off when the rest of the Badrayans came out from behind the boulders and started to shoot arrows.

Five. There are five of them. Which means there had been six. Moses rose as well, nocking the next arrow and releasing it. Peor and Sihon joined him, but Peor's fingers slipped as he tried to nock his arrow. Sihon grabbed it from him and started to smoothly send one arrow after another. Obviously he *was* skilled in this form of combat.

The Badrayans screamed war cries as they ran down their ridge, heading straight for Moses and the two brothers. Moses continued to aim and shoot, along with Sihon. Another tribesman fell, tumbling down the slope. Now there were only four. How many did they have to strike before the men surrendered? Moses nocked the next arrow and released it.

Peor stood with his spear ready, and Moses was hoping that the young man wouldn't have to use it. Moses feared that the trembling Peor would easily be outsmarted by a more experienced fighter.

The tribesmen kept running toward them, screaming and yelling what could only be their revenge. These men were on a path of personal destruction. Another fell. Now the numbers were even. Three against three, and it occurred to Moses that the Badrayans were not going to stop. They weren't going to retreat, and they'd rather die avenging their fallen comrades than return to their settlement to tell of their loss.

"Hold your positions," Moses said as another arrow sailed past them. "Continue shooting until they pass the wadi, then we'll prepare to fight them with our daggers." He nocked another arrow. As he sent it toward the running tribesmen, he said to Peor, "Crouch down. If one of them charges you, use the strength of your legs to aid you in thrusting the spear into him."

"All right," Peor said, his voice faint.

If there had only been two tribesmen left, Moses would have told Peor to fall back, but with three ferocious men who apparently weren't stopping for any reason, they needed Peor, no matter how inexperienced he was. Moses only hoped that the young man wouldn't meet an unfortunate fate tonight.

The three Badrayans were close enough that Moses could make out their facial features—their heavy brows, long noses, and camel-colored headdresses flapping behind them. Recognition passed through Moses—two of them looked familiar, confirming that these were the same shepherds who'd scattered Jethro's flocks at the well. Their piercing war cries vibrated against Moses's ears. The three of them leapt over the wadi and charged up the slope.

"Drop your bow now," Moses called out to Sihon. Both of them dropped their bows and reached for their daggers. "Spread out—move a few paces away from me—we need to separate them."

Moses barely noticed the sweat that covered his body despite the cool night air. He focused on the man heading straight toward him. It looked like an even match, and Moses already knew the desert men were scrappy fighters. Moses's height was to his advantage, but during the last few weeks he had been milking goats, watering flocks, and picking dates, not practicing for combat.

Adrenaline and anticipation surged together, and Moses knew he was ready. He'd make sure he defended Midian properly, even if it cost him his own life. He wouldn't let these Badrayans who picked on women at the well and attacked families in the dead of night defeat him. He would worry about the cost later.

Without telling the brothers of his plan, Moses leapt forward and charged at the three tribesmen, letting out his own war scream. His sudden movements took the Badrayans off guard, which was what Moses had intended, and the first contact he had with the middle tribesman was on the angle of the slope. Since Moses was at a higher elevation, he was able to loom over him.

Swinging wide with his right hand, Moses switched the dagger to his left, then lunged. The tribesman staggered back and lost his balance without Moses even touching him. But the other two men had redirected their charge, and both of them lunged for Moses.

As Moses was thrown to the ground in a tangle of arms and fists and legs and feet, he hoped that Sihon and Peor would reach him soon. One dagger to the chest would finish him off, no matter how much more battle experience he'd had compared to the Badrayans. His blood would run just as red.

Moses twisted hard to the right and avoided a dagger that had been aiming toward his face. As he rotated, he grabbed one of the men's arms and bent it with all his strength. The man cried out, and Moses again had the advantage if only he could shake off the other man clawing at his legs.

He pushed himself to his knees and took hold of the first man's long hair that had uncoiled from his headscarf. Yanking his head back and shoving him to the ground, Moses held his dagger against his throat. "Speak your mercy," he yelled in Midianite, not sure if the tribesman would understand.

The tribesman spat in Moses's face, and Moses said again, "Speak your mercy or you will die this moment." He delivered a kick to the other man who had latched onto his legs and was trying to drag him away. The second man suddenly released Moses, and Moses glanced over in surprise to see Peor kneeling there, staring down at the man who had Peor's dagger stuck in his back.

Time slowed, and Moses felt the horror and victory of Peor's hammering heart as if it were his own. Down the slope, Sihon was battling with the third man, who'd recovered from his fall and was fighting against Sihon's spear. The tribesman whom Moses was still holding down closed his eyes.

"Kill me," he said, his voice thick and guttural, defeated.

"You will return to your settlement and tell them we've given you mercy," Moses said. "You will not attack the people of Midian again, and if you do, there will be a battle like you've never seen before."

"Kill me," the man said again, "for I cannot return dishonored."

"You *will* return dishonored," Moses countered. "It is your deserved fate. Everything that happened tonight to you and your tribesmen was brought upon you by your own hands."

Sihon cried out, and Moses looked up. He was holding his arm, but the man beneath him on the ground was still. Sihon scurried up the slope, still cradling his arm. He looked over at the man Peor had killed. "They are all dead," he said to Moses. "Only this one remains."

Sihon kicked sand into the man's face, and the man sputtered for breath. "You have been foolish tonight," Sihon said. "You should be grateful you are being spared, but only because you will deliver our message."

The man shook his head. "Kill me."

Sihon gave a dark chuckle. "We will not do you the service. You'll live the rest of your days knowing that all of your comrades died and you could not save them. In Midian, we will do whatever it takes to protect our families."

The man let out a choking sob.

Moses released him and rose to his feet, keeping his dagger at the ready should the man suddenly leap. But the man only turned to the side and covered his face with his hands.

"It is finished," Moses said, looking about them. Peor was still on his knees, a stunned look on his face. Two men were dead at their feet, and the other three were somewhere on the ridge across the gully, arrows in their bodies.

Moses crossed to Peor and laid a hand on his shoulder. "Come. We must return to Midian and report. We have done difficult things tonight, but we have also saved many lives."

Peor nodded and grasped Moses's outstretched hand, then climbed to his feet.

Sihon crossed to his brother and slung an arm around his shoulders. "You did well tonight. We couldn't have done it without you."

Peor only gave another nod. They reached their original hiding place, and with trembling hands, Peor picked up the bow and arrows Sihon had dropped. Moses did the same with his own weapons, and Sihon dug his spear into the sand. "This will mark our place of victory so that all will know it."

"You're bleeding," Peor told Moses.

He looked down and saw that his shoulder had been cut—not the same one that had been injured previously. Peor took off his headdress and tore it into strips. Moses was impressed with the young man's deftness at bandaging his shoulder. Peor might be nervous and inexperienced in battle, but he could confidently bind a wound. When Peor finished wrapping Moses's shoulder, Moses thanked him. There were other smaller cuts on his legs, but they didn't warrant bandaging.

"You too, Sihon," Peor said, turning to his brother.

Sihon scanned his body. Two deep cuts were on his calves, and his forehead was bleeding. Peor bandaged Sihon's cuts using Sihon's own headdress for bandaging as well. Despite all of the fighting they'd done, Peor had only scrapes and no deep cuts.

They set off, the moon faint in the sky, the stars providing only a dim scattering of lights. In Moses's mind, the last hour had been precarious, and a few times he hadn't been sure if he'd come out of the battle alive, let alone all three of them. But now they were safe.

Sihon, with one arm draped over Peor's shoulders, moved closer to Moses and draped his other arm across Moses's shoulders.

The gesture reminded Moses of another time, another place, and another life in which he had two close friends—Ramses and Pentu. They had hunted, fought, debated, and raced each other. Now that life was gone, and Moses would never see the two of them again. But here, under the Midianite sky, Moses had two other friends who'd become close comrades through battle and their common goal of protecting their families—and Moses's new family.

CHAPTER NINETEEN
ZIPPORAH

Zipporah pulled her robe tightly across her body, warding off the chill of the morning wind. She stood with her mother and Cozbi, who held Oreb as they paced outside the family tent and awaited the return of the men.

It seemed like days since Zipporah had hurried out of her tent and said good-bye to Moses, but it had only been hours—hours that made up the longest night of her life. Zipporah had imagined both the good and bad. How had the men fared? Were they on their way back now? Or had they met a terrible fate? Perhaps it would take days to track down the Badrayans who'd attacked the settlement.

Zipporah ached as she thought of the family who'd been attacked. They'd been innocents caught in the crossfire of hatred. She'd heard Moses and her father talk about how the attackers were most likely the shepherds who'd scattered their flocks at the well. Which meant they had been planning revenge for weeks.

"You should take the baby inside the tent and let him nap," her mother said to Cozbi.

"I don't want to miss a moment," Cozbi said. "What if they return while I'm inside?"

"Then let me take him," her mother offered.

Cozbi shook her head. "You know he's too particular. He won't let anyone put him down but me or Zipporah."

Zipporah would have offered, but she didn't want to miss any sighting of the men either.

Her mother sighed and said, "Very well, then. I'll start the morning meal." She went into the tent, and since it was still early, Zipporah wondered if her mother just needed some time alone. They were all on edge. None of them had answers.

Zipporah's father had already built up the fire and was sitting next to it with Tema's husband. Throughout the night, men had come and gone, speaking to Jethro in hushed tones and drinking the tea that was continually provided by the women. It seemed no one in Midian was sleeping.

Zipporah watched the sky turn from black to indigo, then fade to a murky gray. Every moment she wondered what Moses was doing, saying, or feeling. Was he fighting? Was he running? Was he exhausted? Was he alive?

She couldn't relax, couldn't sit by the fire and talk with the men and hear their worries echoing her own thoughts. She had to be doing something. "I'm going to milk the goats," she told Cozbi. Although it was early yet, she didn't think the goats would mind.

She walked to the goat enclosure. Her father's gaze followed her, and when he realized where she was going, he gave a nod of approval. Fortune was the first to trot over to Zipporah. She bent down and scratched the goat's head. "There you are, old girl. How did you sleep?"

The goat bleated in response.

"I didn't sleep either," Zipporah continued. She grabbed one of the waiting jugs and positioned the goat for milking. As she worked, she thought of the many times Moses had come out early in the morning to help her. Only when he'd stayed somewhere overnight with the sheep had he missed their morning ritual.

Zipporah missed Moses, and before she knew it, she was whispering a prayer for his safe return. By the time Zipporah finished with all the she-goats, the sun had spilled over the horizon. The sky's deep blue was quickly fading, and the knot of worry in Zipporah's stomach tightened. It would be a hot day, and who knew how far Moses and the other men had traveled scouting the tribesmen.

As she walked back toward the tent, her father motioned for Zipporah to join him by the fire. He rose to his feet as she approached. "I'm going to the northern tents to see if there has been any news." His eyes were red, and he had new worry lines on his forehead. "They should be returning soon."

Zipporah could only pray it was true. The men hadn't taken enough water to last more than a day or two out there, and if one of them was injured, it would take a lot of stamina to bring back the wounded man.

She made up her mind. "I'm coming with you."

Jethro shook his head. "Mother will need you here."

"It's barely dawn," she said. She looked over at Tema's husband; his head was bowed and he looked half asleep. "Wake him up, and he can keep watch."

Jethro's mouth thinned as he considered. Finally, he said, "All right. You may come, but when I tell you to return, you must do so immediately. There's no telling what may happen. The Badrayans could have sent more men to our settlement."

"I will be safe," Zipporah said. "I'll be with you, and all the settlement is on alert."

With her father's assent, she went to tell her mother. Before her mother could protest, Zipporah grabbed a goatskin and hurried out of the tent and headed in her father's direction. They moved quickly on the paths through Midian, stopping only occasionally to confirm that no one had any new information.

Everyone was eager to learn the outcome of Sihon, Peor, and Moses's trek. Was it just another step toward a real battle? Midian had been in battles before, but Zipporah had never felt she had so much at stake. Her sister's husband and her betrothed were both directly involved. In the past, even when her father had gone out to fight, her mother had been able to keep the worst of the worries away. But then, Zipporah had been a child and hadn't understood the full danger.

Now Zipporah understood.

When they reached the edge of the settlement, she was surprised to see such a large assembly of armed men. It appeared that all the young men in Midian, with the exception of those who were not out in distant valleys with flocks, had gathered, drawing together to defend themselves. The men were organized into groups of ten, and they were quiet and still, watching the desert for any signs. They carried a conglomeration of weapons, from bows and arrows to spears and even some simple shepherd staffs.

One group of men was practicing shooting arrows at a fleece target. The atmosphere was hushed and tense. Zipporah's pulse raced as she thought of the reality of what would happen if there were a battle. She followed her father as he spoke to various men, asking for any updates. No one had heard or seen anything since Moses, Peor, and Sihon had taken off in the middle of the night.

When they moved away from the man who'd given them the latest information, Jethro looked out over the desert, and Zipporah followed his gaze. "They probably headed straight north, looking for tracks along the way."

Zipporah knew the Badrayan tribe lived on the other side of Jabal al-Lawz. She'd never traveled that far before, but she knew the mountain itself was pretty desolate. "Do you think they went up the mountain?"

"Possibly," Jethro said. "It would certainly provide shelter and more places to hide." He adjusted his headdress so that his eyes remained shadowed from the rising sun. "Sihon is an excellent tracker, and Moses, Peor, and Sihon are skilled warriors."

Zipporah nodded—this she knew, but it didn't bring her much ease. When weapons were involved, the battle skills were made more level, although she had witnessed Moses defeating five men by himself.

"Do we know how many tribesmen attacked?"

"The estimates are anywhere between five to ten," Jethro said with a grimace. "The number keeps growing."

Just like any good desert tale. This time, though, Zipporah hoped the number ten was an exaggeration. "I worry for all the men," she said. "But Peor is the youngest, and while his combat skills are excellent, he is the most inexperienced. What if one of them gets injured? Will the other two be able to cope?"

"Peor is strong and fast, like a gazelle," Jethro said. "He is in the best of hands with his brother, and Moses will do what it takes to protect him as well. I would be hard-pressed to say that Moses isn't one of us now. He has served our family unceasingly."

Her father was right. "Moses has done so much," Zipporah agreed. "Our settlement has invested a great deal of trust in him by sending him with Sihon and Peor."

"Look at the men who have gathered," Jethro said. "Do you see any who would be more skilled than Moses?"

Zipporah shook her head, not able to imagine that any of the Midianites could defeat Moses one-on-one.

"He has more than satisfactorily proven himself, and he will be a fierce contender with any tribesmen, even if the numbers are five against one again." Jethro wrapped his arm around Zipporah's shoulders, and she leaned her head against his shoulder. "They will return to us, my daughter," he continued in a quiet voice. "You will see. The Lord will preserve them."

"How can you know?" Zipporah said before she could think better of it. It wasn't that she doubted her father's beliefs, for she wanted to believe as well. But right now she wanted sure knowledge, as impossible as it might seem.

"We can only have faith," Jethro said, his voice barely audible. "It's all we can hold on to right now or else none of us would be able to withstand the uncertainty. This is why the priests have kept the incense burning in the temple all night. We must take comfort knowing the entire settlement of Midian is behind this."

Zipporah knew her father was right, but that didn't stop the fear and doubt. She hoped she could feel peace as she tried to put her trust in a being who was all-knowing and all-powerful. There was literally nothing she could do at this moment that would affect the outcome of what was going on between the Badrayans and Moses.

She closed her eyes, offering up what must be her hundredth prayer. She knew that with the rising sun, Moses and the men would be more exposed and more susceptible to the elements. Each passing hour without their appearance increased the odds against them.

Zipporah and her father found a place to sit under a worn-out pomegranate tree—too old and weathered to bear fruit any longer. While Zipporah kept watch on the span of wilderness, her father visited with various men.

The wind blew gently across the sand and rocks, and as the sun warmed the air, the bugs skittered around looking for a cool, shady place to hide. Zipporah didn't pay much attention to the men who came and went, speaking to her father. She looked out over the desert hills toward the distant Jabal al-Lawz. It was nearly midmorning when she saw something dark that hadn't been there before—a dark shape that was moving, hundreds of paces out.

The shape seemed to undulate with the heat shimmering from the sand. Then the shape divided, becoming two, and then three.

Zipporah scrambled to her feet and hurried forward, raising her hand to shield her eyes from the sun above. "It's them," she whispered to herself. Then louder, "Father, it's them!" She couldn't take her eyes off the approaching figures, even though they were still quite a distance away. She heard murmurings around her and felt, rather than saw, the waiting Midianites realize what was happening.

The men had returned. And there were three of them—which meant Sihon, Peor, and Moses were all coming back. The man on the right side of the group was Moses—who else would have a bare torso and short hair? Zipporah clasped her hands together. Elation surged through her, and joyful tears filled her eyes.

They were walking slowly, but they were walking, and that told her that they were all fine. Injured perhaps, but well enough to walk back to Midian. Voices rose around her as the men exclaimed and spoke among themselves. Her father came to stand by her side and pulled her into his embrace.

Her father's tunic was rough against her cheek. Even so, she squeezed him back. "They're alive!" Jethro said, his voice thick with emotion.

Zipporah only nodded. Her throat was too tight to speak. When she pulled away from her father, he kept his arm about her shoulder as they watched the three men continue walking toward their settlement.

They were still a good distance away, but the men had seen the group waiting for them. Sihon raised his hand in greeting, and Zipporah wished her sister could be here to see the triumphant return of her husband.

"I'm going to them," Zipporah said.

Instead of protesting like she thought he might, Jethro said, "I'm coming too."

They started walking toward the three men. The sun blazed down on them, and Zipporah pulled her scarf up to keep the heat off her skin.

"Do you think they were successful?" Zipporah asked her father as they trudged through the sand.

"By the looks of them, yes," her father said. "They appear as if they've been through battle."

They were closer now, and Zipporah could make out the men's faces. The men's clothing was stained and dirty, their bodies were perspiring, and it looked as if Sihon and Peor had used their headdresses to create bandages to wrap about their wounds. Sihon's head was wrapped in a bandage, and Moses's shoulder was bandaged as well—it was the shoulder opposite the one he'd injured in the shepherd fight. Peor looked unharmed for the most part. Zipporah felt as if she were witnessing the aftermath of Moses fighting off the shepherds at the well.

As the men neared and Zipporah and Jethro continued walking toward them, she caught Moses's gaze. He'd seen her, and she felt pulled toward him as if there weren't a hundred paces of sand between them. Zipporah wanted to run and throw her arms around him and never let go. But there were too many people who would be watching. She stayed at the side of her father, and as the last paces were crossed, she kept her hands to her side and steeled herself against running.

CHAPTER TWENTY
ZIPPORAH

The sand between Zipporah and Moses stretched out hot and too far. She adjusted her scarf over her head, wishing a breeze would kick up. Regardless, she knew she was better off than the three men walking toward them.

"You are well?" Jethro shouted when Sihon, Peor, and Moses were within hearing distance.

Sihon grinned through the dirt and sweat on his face despite his head bandage. "We are only roughed up, but the Badrayans met a more dire fate."

Peor was grinning as well, but beneath his happy expression, Zipporah noticed trepidation as well. What had happened out there?

Next, Zipporah looked at Moses, gazing long enough to see the soberness of his eyes. A chill brushed over her skin as if the air had suddenly turned cool.

"We caught up with them in a matter of hours," Sihon was saying as they came to a stop in front of Zipporah and Jethro.

Jethro reached out and clasped each of the men's hands. "We are glad you are home safe."

Up close, Zipporah saw the bandages in more detail. Moses's shoulder was bleeding through its wrapping, and Sihon had bandages around both of his calves. The one around his head looked well wrapped, but a blood spot had appeared.

Peor didn't have any bandaging, but the side of his face was scraped, and he had small cuts and bruises along his arms.

Zipporah wanted to clean their wounds and redo their bandages, but it would have to wait. Everyone would want to hear their story. She kept all of her instincts contained and walked alongside her father as they escorted the men back to the first Midian tents.

The Midianites surrounded the three men as they reached the settlement, and congratulations and cheers reverberated around Zipporah. She hung back, watching the good wishes and listening to the questions being fired at the men.

Finally, Sihon raised his hands, and the congratulators fell quiet. "We will tell you all a tale that will make you want to run and hide in your tents."

Laughter erupted, and Sihon grinned, enjoying the attention and the chance to boast of their defeat of the Badrayans. "Imagine a large leopard, proud of his spots and determined to sneak around in the middle of the night to catch his prey."

The Midianites were captivated, leaning closer and listening to each word.

"This leopard thinks it can flee and not be discovered," Sihon continued, his voice loud and clear. "It thinks that because it is so stealthy, no one will be able to find it."

He waited until the murmurs from the men settled down, and Sihon said, "What this leopard didn't know is that the men of Midian have a greater weapon with them—the lion."

A few men whistled and others clapped while all eyes turned to Moses. His expression didn't change, just remained rigid.

Another chill spread across Zipporah's skin.

Sihon continued, despite Moses's lack of emotion. "The leopard tried to pounce, gave us its best shot, but the leopard was an inferior beast. It could never match up to the mighty Egyptian lion. Although the leopard roared and leapt at us with all of its teeth bared, the lion cut it down."

Silence gripped the Midianites for a moment, then they let out a loud cheer. Sihon was laughing, and next to him, Peor wore a wide grin.

Zipporah was struck again by the soberness in Moses's eyes. She wondered what had really transpired in the wilderness between the two different tribes versus the entertaining story Sihon was telling.

"Wait..." Sihon held up a hand. His voice was now sober. "We did let one of the Badrayans go so that he could take our message back to his people."

Conversation erupted among the Midianites, and it was clear to Zipporah that there were mixed feelings about this revelation.

Moses stepped forward, and for the first time, he spoke. His language had become smoother, but he still spoke in a measured way. "The Badrayan asked for us to kill him. He told us he would be disgraced were he to return to his tribe with only a report of defeat."

Heads bobbed, and the hushed whispers were fierce.

"This is why we need to patrol all of Midian's outer reaches night and day," Moses said. "Not just the north, but all sides. The patrol needs to be rigorous." He glanced over at Sihon, who looked less triumphant now. "We did exact our revenge, and the Badrayans paid for it with their lives, but this is not over yet. Yes, they attacked first, but we retaliated in a manner that won't soon be forgiven."

As the tribesmen discussed how a patrol should be organized, Zipporah swallowed against the swelling lump in her throat. She didn't like the charged atmosphere. Moses had returned safely—her many prayers had been answered—but now more dangerous things might lie ahead.

She looked at Sihon, Peor, and Moses—all different but men who had joined together in the common cause of protecting Midian. She was proud of them; she recognized how much they'd put their lives in jeopardy for their people. Would even more be required of them? It was a new thing, this deep fear. As a child and young woman, she hadn't known how much it was possible to hurt while just anticipating the worst.

"Sihon!" A voice broke through the crowd. Cozbi ran toward him holding Oreb, and the couple embraced each other. "You're safe!" she cried out.

Zipporah felt her own tears start. Perhaps she should just focus on this moment and be grateful for the safe return of the men.

It was some time before the patrol rotations were worked out, and most of the men returned to their tents to catch up on missed sleep.

Sihon and Peor left with a happy Cozbi, and Jethro and Zipporah walked with Moses back to the family tent. Along the way, as they passed other homes, men congratulated Moses. Children also ran alongside them, asking Moses all about "fighting the Badrayans." He was kind to the children and talked with them easily. But the closer they drew to the tent, the more quiet he became.

Jethro had noticed as well. "Is there more to what Sihon told us, Moses?"

He let out a heavy sigh. "There is." He glanced over at Zipporah, then took her hand in his, which only made her more nervous about what he might say.

"Come," Jethro said. "Let us sit under this group of trees and rest for a moment before returning to the family and their many questions."

They were on the other side of their goat herd, and when they sat down, a few goats wandered over. Moses reached out and scratched the top of one of their heads. He looked exhausted, and Zipporah knew his shoulder wound should be cleaned up and rebandaged.

She and her father were silent, waiting for him to tell the story in his own way.

"There were six of them," Moses said in a quiet voice. "We had reached the base of Jabal al-Lawz when they shot the first arrow." He shook his head as if he could see the image in his mind. "We dropped to the ground, and when one of them next came into view, I shot an arrow."

Moses clasped his hands together and stared down at them. "The arrow hit its mark." His voice fell to a whisper. "The Badrayans charged, and Sihon and I kept sending our arrows until only three were left."

Zipporah reached over and put her hand on top of his. "We sent you to do a hard thing," she said in a quiet voice.

Moses shook his head. "It was my honor to find the Badrayans and to avenge the lives they took from Midian." He looked up, directly into Zipporah's eyes. His eyes were reddened with exhaustion and possibly regret. "But you should have seen the harsh looks in their eyes and heard their screams of hate."

His attention shifted to Jethro, his hands gripping Zipporah's now. "It is far from over. If the other Badrayans are like those six tribesmen, they will not rest for long; they will not wait to retaliate." He blew out a breath. "Even now, as we enjoy the shade of this tree, there is no doubt in my mind that they are planning to attack anew."

Zipporah lowered her head, letting the information sink in.

"Perhaps I erred when fighting the shepherds at the well," Moses said.

Zipporah snapped her head up, startled at his words. "You think you should have let them run over the well with their flocks?"

"No," Moses said. "They were in the wrong, and it would have happened again if they had gotten away with it the first time. But perhaps because I lived, they did not have their revenge. If I had been killed, they would have stayed in their own lands, fearful of a Midianite retaliation."

"You're wrong," Jethro said. "Your life is more valuable to us than a thousand Badrayan men." He grasped Moses's arm. "If you hadn't done what you did at the well, they would have grown in bravery and continued to strike."

Zipporah nodded. "Do not take this tragedy upon yourself, Moses. You have not erred in the least." She looked past the trees they sat beneath toward the milling goats beyond. Their life was harsh at times but also beautiful.

"You are one of us now, Moses," Jethro said. "In every way that's important. Perhaps your life was more comfortable and civilized in Egypt, but we are honored to have you with our family."

"Life in Egypt isn't necessarily more civilized," Moses said in a distant tone. "If anything, the politics are more complicated. You might live in a palace, but if you had any sort of power or influence, your life was in danger from your own relatives and friends. Their armies might have been larger and better outfitted with weapons, but it was essentially the same. Man against man—both fighting for what the other has."

"Do you think man will ever feel that he has enough?" Zipporah asked quietly.

Jethro scrubbed a hand over his beard. "Some men, no. Some men will never find contentment in whatever lot God has dealt them. They will always be unhappy unless they have more than their neighbor, and sometimes even beyond that."

Moses met Zipporah's gaze. "Yes, I think a man can feel he has enough." He paused. "Like me. I have enough. Right here."

Her heart was full—completely full.

"Even if this Badrayan battle continues?" she asked. "And even if you have to herd sheep the rest of your life?"

He smiled, and it was beautiful on his battle-weary face. "Even then." They stared at each other for a charged moment.

Jethro cleared his throat. "We should be getting you back to the tent, Moses, to clean you up and let you get some rest. We will invite our family and friends over for supper, and you can tell them your story."

The three of them rose and continued through the grazing goats, and when they reached the family tent, Zipporah's mother was there, waiting with open arms. Her mother only demonstrated affection on rare occasions, so it was with surprise that Zipporah watched her mother rush to embrace Moses. Next, she embraced Jethro. And finally, Zipporah.

"You're all back safe," her mother said. "Praise God." Tears welled in her eyes, and she brushed them away. She looked at Moses. "Come, come inside. We'll get you cleaned up with new bandaging."

Zipporah didn't need to be asked to help Moses. She went inside the tent with him, and before he entered his section, she said, "I'll bring water and fresh cloth in a few moments."

"Thank you," he said, his eyes dark in the dimness of the tent.

She forced herself to hurry back to the cooking area. She felt exhausted from staying up all night and worrying about the men tracking the Badrayans, but she knew Moses's needs had to be attended to before she'd be able to rest.

In the cooking area, her mother had already filled a jug with warm water. Zipporah crossed to the baskets of dried herbs and selected a mild herb. Crushing it with a round stone, she mixed it with warm water and a dab of honey. When the poultice was the right consistency, she turned to her mother.

"Here are some clean bandages," her mother said. "You go on and attend to him. I'll start the supper preparations, and after we've both had a rest, we can finish up the meal."

Zipporah had never seen her mother so conciliatory. It seemed that this event with the Badrayans had put everyone on alert, and families had become so much more important. Her mother had to be as tired as Zipporah, yet she was still up and working.

She carried the jug of warm water, the bandages, and the poultice to the section where Moses slept and kept his things.

"Moses, are you ready?" she called out in a soft voice to make sure he wasn't in the middle of changing his clothes.

"I am. Come in," he said.

Zipporah entered. Moses had changed into a clean kilt, and he'd washed up with the jug of water her mother must have already taken in. His hair and torso were wet, and the evidence of the desert dirt had been washed away. He looked up at her from where he was unwinding the bandages around his shoulder.

"Here, let me do that," she said, setting her things on the ground. "Sit down."

Moses sat on his mat and leaned against the cushions, closing his eyes. Zipporah worked carefully, being careful not to add to his pain. When she removed all of the wrapping, she winced. There was more than one cut, and they were all deep. Bruising had also formed around the cuts.

"What happened?" she asked.

"The man we let go had a fairly sharp dagger," Moses said, one side of his mouth lifting into a smile. His eyes fluttered open, and Zipporah realized how close she was to him. There was nothing between them now. "You don't know how glad I was to see you waiting for me."

Zipporah let out the breath she hadn't realized she'd been holding. "You don't know how good it was to see you walking back, alive, on your two feet, with only this single bandage." Her voice had started to tremble, and she cut off her words before tears could pool in her eyes.

But they did anyway. Hot, fast tears formed, and there was no time to brush them away. Moses straightened. Reaching up, he brushed the tears from her face, absorbing them with his fingers.

"Don't cry," he said, his voice low.

"I'm not crying." Zipporah inhaled sharply, trying to hold back her emotions. She was exhausted; waiting to hear the outcome of Moses's group had been almost unbearable. And now it was all catching up to her.

She blinked rapidly. "Hold still," she said, trying not to let Moses's closeness and the intimacy that surrounded them overwhelm her. "I need to clean these cuts."

He dropped his hand, which Zipporah immediately regretted, but it allowed her to set to work. Dipping a square of cloth into the warm water, she washed the dried blood and dirt from his shoulder. The cuts started bleeding again, and she pressed a new dry cloth against his shoulder. Moses exhaled at the pressure.

"Does it hurt?"

"Not as much anymore," Moses said, his eyes closing, and Zipporah continued to staunch the bleeding.

She wished she could take the pain away; she wished the Badrayans would stay out of Midian forever. She didn't want to have to say good-bye to Moses again. What if something happened to him?

Rewrapping his shoulder, Zipporah tried to be careful, but she could tell by the paleness of Moses's face that it was hurting him more than he admitted.

"If there is one thing I'm certain of," Moses said unexpectedly, "it is that you and your father were right. God was with us in the desert this morning. The Badrayans are fierce and skilled fighters. We could have easily been defeated."

"Three against six is steep odds," she said.

"It was more like two against six," he said. "I need to train Peor to fight under pressure. He almost cost us our lives with his hesitation." His gaze held hers. "I can only thank God for our preservation."

"I was surprised he was uninjured," she said. "What happened?"

"He helped me when I was being attacked, but he was useless with his bow and arrow," Moses said.

"I've seen him practice many times with the other men," she said. It wasn't like she was an expert on bows and arrows, but surely he couldn't have been that horrible if he'd returned unscathed with Sihon and Moses.

"It wasn't so much his fighting skills; knowing how to nock an arrow and release it is only part of battle training." Moses exhaled, his face gaining a bit of color again. "Control of fear is the most essential part of battle training. He was shaking so much that Sihon took the bow and arrow from him."

Zipporah tried to imagine the scene—and the panic going through Peor at being faced with ruthless tribesmen running at him with their weapons.

"So what happened? How did he fight?"

"He didn't at first," Moses said. "When I was in hand-to-hand battle with the final man, he was able to collect his senses enough to use his dagger on the man who'd toppled me."

Zipporah's breath caught. "So he did kill one of the tribesmen?"

"Yes," Moses said in a sober tone. "It shook him to the core; I know the feeling well. But at least I'd been through training; and in *my* first battles, I had other Egyptian warriors surrounding me and fighting alongside me."

"Then train him," she said. "Especially if we think the Badrayans will be back."

Moses captured her hand in his. "They will be back, Zipporah. And I fear that many lives may be lost. It's not only Peor who needs battle training, it's most of the men in Midian. And we will need all of them."

CHAPTER TWENTY-ONE
MOSES

As he stood outside his tent section, Moses watched as the sun rose, replacing the violet shadows on the Sarawat Mountains with golden streaks. Today was his wedding day. In moments, the air would warm and the settlement of Midian would stir. A fortnight had passed since he had tracked down the Badrayans with Sihon and Peor. A fortnight of peace. A fortnight of some of the greatest anxiety Moses had ever experienced in his life.

With each passing day, Moses knew they were a day closer to battle. Under the approval of Jethro and the elders of Midian, Moses had organized training for the men. Not only was he teaching Egyptian strategy to Peor and Sihon—who were proving to be very adept—but he was training young and old men alike.

It seemed that every man in Midian wanted to be trained in Egyptian strategy in addition to their desert fighting skills. These men were strong and fierce and ready to fight for their homes and their families, not for some auspicious ruler or governing body. A loss to the Badrayans would mean a loss of Midianite homes and women and children. It would mean a loss of their way of life.

But for the moment, Moses tried to push the impending battle to the back of his mind. Today would be unlike anything he could have predicted or even imagined. His marriage to Zipporah would be the first step for Moses in becoming a new man. He was taking on a completely new life and identity. And he had God to thank for it. Far from home, and far from any wedding celebration that would have accompanied Moses if he hadn't killed the Egyptian taskmaster and fled the country, Moses felt that a higher being had watched over him.

Was it possible that Midian and Zipporah had been his fate? That everything in his life had led to this moment? It was hard to reconcile the two lives and their vast differences, but Moses recognized that he'd never been more content. Even though he missed his Egyptian mother, and even though the desire to know his birth family still burned deep within, it was as if God had handed him this new fulfillment.

He and Zipporah had settled on a month-long betrothal, which turned out to be too short, at least according to Zipporah's mother. There was much to be done, including weaving tent panels for the new couple's home. It had been a welcome distraction during the battle preparations.

Moses had long grown used to living in a tent, but there were times when the sand and wind and bugs made him recall more luxurious times of living. Yet one look at Zipporah and he completely forgot about tubs filled with scented water for daily bathing, servants to shave his head, and feasts and entertainment every night.

The desert life had proved to be full and lively, more than Moses could have ever predicted, especially with the battle preparations. Even with the wedding today, Moses was confident that Midian would be well protected. They had also worked out an alert system if any Badrayan tribesmen were spotted.

Voices rose from within the tent, and Moses knew the family had awakened and preparations would soon be underway. He looked toward the goat enclosure, half expecting to see Zipporah there with the animals. But he knew she'd be going about other duties for the wedding instead and that one of her younger sisters would be taking over the milking.

"Moses, you're awake early." Jethro's voice sounded behind him.

Moses turned to see his almost father-in-law exit the tent. The man was smiling at him, and Moses smiled back.

It was a new thing for him to have a father, and Jethro had been nothing but generous to Moses.

"Are you ready to get married today?" Jethro asked, clapping Moses's good shoulder.

Moses's injured shoulder was mostly healed. The scarring would run deep, but it only reminded him of the sacrifices he was happy to make in behalf of his new family.

"I am ready," Moses said. "I feel as if I've been waiting for this day . . . for a long time."

"I felt the same way when I married my wife," Jethro said. "Our mothers are cousins, and we grew up together in the same group of children who ran around Midian. I noticed her long before she noticed me. But once she did notice me, I knew life would never be the same, and nothing I ever did would be more important than the family I created with Qurayya."

Moses nodded in agreement while at the same time a lump constricted his throat. He wondered if his Egyptian mother, Bithiah, would ever have a man devoted to her like Jethro was to his wife. Bithiah had been a single mother since she'd adopted Moses, and she'd made all decisions on her own. All her cares and worries about raising a young son had to be kept quiet as she protected her great secret.

"The Lord has blessed my family time and time again," Jethro said, his voice humble. "When you showed up on that day many weeks ago, I had no idea what a blessing you'd be to us."

"And I had no idea how much your family would come to mean to me," Moses said. He grasped Jethro's hand, and the man pulled him into an embrace. Even with the desert wind blowing around him and the sound of the flies rising with the warming day, Moses truly felt at home.

"Come," Jethro said. "It is tradition to go to the temple and make your offerings before the wedding. Then we'll return and set up the marriage tent."

Moses and Jethro set off in the early-morning light along the winding paths of Midian, leading a kid goat. The temple was situated on the eastern end of the settlement. Moses's step was light as he walked alongside Jethro. The man would be performing the marriage ceremony as well since he was a priest.

At the temple, Jethro directed the sacrifice of the kid goat and performed the ritual for several other temple-goers.

When they returned from the temple, the settlement had fully awakened. Moses found himself looking for the stationed guards who manned each lookout point. He recognized many of the men now and greeted them as they passed. Moses might not know them by name, but he was familiar with their family clans. It seemed everyone was connected in one way or another, even if it was by a previous generation or two.

By the time they reached the family compound, the women were arranging rugs and cushions outside the tent.

"There you are," Jethro's wife said, coming forward to greet them. She had a harried expression, but Moses could tell she was excited for the marriage of her daughter. "We need the wedding canopy built before you set up the wedding tent. I don't want the sun to bake down on the cushions and rugs."

"All right," Jethro said. "We'll get started." He leaned down and kissed her cheek.

"Oh, get to work," his wife said, batting him away, but the pleased look in her eyes was unmistakable.

Moses watched the interchange between husband and wife, thinking about how they were such hardworking people. They didn't live in palaces or have extensive servants, yet they found happiness in each other.

Moses helped Jethro with the canopy, and then they started on the marriage tent. It was bad luck to fix it before the day of the wedding. Moses also assumed that Zipporah was staying inside the tent, out of sight, since they also considered it bad luck for the bride and groom to see each other on their wedding day before the marriage ceremony.

Jethro and Moses worked to set up the marriage tent between the main family tent and the goat enclosure. Moses wondered if this meant he'd be listening to the goats all night. If he was with Zipporah, maybe he wouldn't mind so much.

"Does this have to be the final place of our tent?" Moses asked as they cleared the ground to make it smooth.

"It is not a permanent home, if that's what you mean," Jethro said. "You will inherit a portion of my flocks as part of Zipporah's dowry, and then you can decide where you want to live and raise your family."

"You have been generous enough already," Moses said.

"Ah, you may think so," Jethro said. "But if Zipporah is anything like her mother, they will get along better living apart after she is married. And you will definitely want a happy wife."

Moses grinned, then turned as he saw a group of women walking toward the family tent. He recognized Zipporah's older sisters and children. Other women walked with them as well.

"It's just getting started," Jethro said, sounding pleased. "Soon this entire place will be invaded with helpers, and you won't recognize it when the women are finished."

Jethro's words proved to be right when, hours later, just as the afternoon sun started to melt the sky into evening shadows, the family compound looked fit for any visiting royal guest.

The wedding canopy had been decorated with palm fronds and desert flowers. Endless platters of food had been set out, covered for now, on top of low wooden tables. A group of children was in charge of shooing the flies away.

Moses still hadn't seen any sign of Zipporah. With all of his tasks completed, he went to his tent section and washed in the basin of fresh water someone had brought in. He wondered if it had been Zipporah herself. He scrubbed his hair. It had grown past his ears and jawline now. He pulled it back and tied it with a strip of leather. Then he used a small dagger to trim his beard. Many of the men of Midian wore their beards quite long, but Moses preferred his short. He used the polished copper plate to study his reflection.

If he ran into his mother or someone like Ramses now, Moses knew they wouldn't recognize him. His skin was darkened by the sun, his hair had grown out, he was leaner and stronger, and scars stood out on both shoulders.

He'd been trained as an Egyptian warrior, but there was nothing like tracking down tribesmen in the middle of the night and fighting for your life without the luxury of a horse-drawn chariot and fine bows and arrows. The bow and arrows that Moses now used were carved from desert trees—hardy and strong and straight yet rough and dirty.

He dressed in his cleanest kilt, then pulled out the robe he'd carried across the desert with him. The one his mother had sewn for him. Bithiah's image flashed through his mind as he held up the red and indigo robe with its interspersing of yellow threads, its length falling softly to the rug. He imagined her head bent over the sewing, the beads of her Nubian wig clicking together as she made the neat and tiny stitching. In the dim light of the tent, the robe looked darker than it really was, almost a deep purple, but he knew that once he was outside the sun would catch the robe's fine weave and make it shine like silk.

What would Zipporah think of the robe? He'd never shown it to her, but he wanted to look his best. He was now a Midianite, but he would have never come to this place if it hadn't been for his Egyptian upbringing. He would have never had the warrior training to defeat so many shepherds at the well and deliver Zipporah and her sisters from harm.

The elegant robe symbolized the linking of his past as a royal Egyptian and his future as a desert Midianite.

Laughter and music floated from outside into Moses's tent section. It was time to join the wedding party and to await his bride. He marveled that he was finally marrying Zipporah. A few short months ago, he couldn't have even imagined he'd find happiness in the wilderness.

Moses knelt in his small tent section, closed his eyes, and clasped his hands together. He offered a prayer of gratitude to God. Praying in this manner was still new to Moses, but life had become precious out in the desert, and he took every opportunity to offer up gratitude.

Moses exited the tent. The sun was just starting to set, and the heat of the day had faded. It seemed all of Midian had assembled for the ceremony. Sihon came up and greeted him. "We were wondering if you were going to come out," he teased.

Peor was next. "We will be related now," he said.

Jethro motioned for Moses to join him beneath the canopy. "We are ready—Zipporah will be coming out soon."

Moses smiled to himself. He moved through the gathering, greeting people as he went, not processing everyone's names. Several commented on his robe, but he only nodded in acknowledgment and continued toward Jethro.

The crowd hushed, and Moses knew it was because Zipporah must have come out of the tent. He turned to look for her, and his breath caught at the sight.

She was veiled, so it wasn't that he could admire her beauty, which he knew lay beneath the veil she wore. He could well imagine her dark, lively eyes, her dark, lustrous hair, and the softness of her skin. But his breath caught because he realized he was about to take Zipporah as his wife and commit to her in front of God and many witnesses.

Just the fact that she had accepted his hand in marriage and was now walking toward him, ready to make the sacred oaths as husband and wife, sent his soul soaring. Yes, he'd chosen her, but she'd also chosen him.

She looked like a heavenly apparition as she walked toward him. Then she stopped about a pace away, and he could see her smiling.

He reached for her hand, and her soft skin touched his, sending bumps along his arm. He wished that everyone could melt away and that it could be just the two of them, alone, in the desert settlement he'd come to love so much.

Flowers had been woven along the edges of her veil and repeated at the hem of her long, ivory-colored tunic. The scent made Moses feel heady, or was it Zipporah's presence? He held on to her hand and tried to absorb the fact that this was really happening. Was it possible to feel so much happiness at once?

Jethro began the ceremony with a prayer, and Moses bowed his head and closed his eyes, keeping hold of Zipporah's hands.

When the prayer ended, Jethro continued talking about the promises of the marriage covenant, and then he turned to Moses to ask, "Will you honor Zipporah as your wife and be faithful all the days of your life?"

"I will," Moses said. It was the easiest promise he'd ever made.

Jethro then turned to his daughter. "Zipporah, will you honor Moses as your husband and be faithful all the days of your life?"

"I will," she said in a soft voice.

Jethro wrapped a silk scarf around their joined hands, securing them together. Then he lifted their hands and said to the gathering, "The Lord has joined Moses of Egypt and Zipporah of Midian together as man and wife." He looked at Moses. "You may raise the veil to reveal your new wife."

With his free hand, Moses reached for the hem of her veil and lifted it.

Her face was dewy from being hidden beneath her veil, and her eyes were wide and luminescent. "Hello, wife," Moses said in Egyptian. He knew she didn't understand him, but he still leaned down and whispered, "You have my heart."

He brushed his lips against hers, perhaps startling her, but she didn't pull away. The people clapped and cheered around them, and Moses grinned as he drew away.

Zipporah's smile was answer enough.

CHAPTER TWENTY-TWO
ZIPPORAH

Zipporah's wedding day had seemed to last for months, yet it was over in what seemed like a mere moment. Had it all been a dream? She turned to look at Moses, who was sitting next to her at the wedding feast, and assured herself that this was real. She was married now. To Moses.

Torchlights surrounded the low tables, and the guests lingered, eating the food her mother and sisters had spent a week preparing and drinking the sweet date wine. Zipporah was surrounded by everything and everyone she loved. Was it possible to love this much and to feel this much love in return?

Moses was speaking to her father, and they laughed over something. The sound of their happiness and friendship made her smile. As the night deepened and the torches started to burn out, final blessings were intoned by Jethro and the other priests of the settlement.

Zipporah could barely soak it all in. She was elated but exhausted. Sleeping little the night before made her feel light-headed as the night wore on, and she'd barely had any wine. Then the procession music started, signaling that the guests would escort the bride and groom to their marriage tent.

Moses rose and extended his hand to help Zipporah to her feet. His eyes were warm, and she smiled at him. She'd smiled so much tonight that her cheeks had started to ache.

Moses led her through the gathering as people clapped and sang, and then they turned in the direction of the marriage tent. The gathering followed them, throwing out final farewells and blessings along the way.

When they came to a stop at the entrance, her father and mother both kissed her on the cheek, then Moses lifted the tent flap, and Zipporah stepped inside.

Her mother had decorated the small space beautifully, and there were rugs spread across the ground, with cushions lining the sides. A small table had been set with a jug of wine and a platter of ripe dates and a mound of goat cheese and flatbread. An oil lamp burned, casting its dancing glow about the tent.

Moses stepped into the tent behind her and closed the tent flap. And then they were alone, at last. Sounds of singing and laughing still came through the tent's walls, but when Moses turned to Zipporah and took her hands in his, all sounds faded away.

"How are you, my wife?" he said in a quiet voice.

She looked into his eyes, feeling the warmth in them touch her. "Happy, my husband," she whispered.

His smile was slow. "That's all I can hope for." He pulled her into his arms, and she nestled against his broad, strong chest.

The voices outside grew fainter, replaced by the sounds of the desert wind.

Zipporah was no longer tired or light-headed. She wasn't hungry or thirsty. She only wanted to be in Moses's arms and wished that the night would stretch out into eternity. That the chores of tomorrow, the interactions with everyone else, Moses's work in training the Midianites for battle could all wait.

"Tell me of your robe," Zipporah said, turning her face up to look at her new husband.

He gave a nod and then slipped it off his shoulders. He shook it out, then put it onto Zipporah's shoulders. The touch of the cloth was soft and airy, unlike anything she had felt before. "It's beautiful."

"My mother sewed it," Moses said in a reverent tone. "I won't have much occasion to wear it here in the desert, but I took my opportunity today."

"All of the other young women surely envied me my groom," Zipporah said, touching the edges of the robe. The stitching was neat and even, smaller than she'd ever seen.

"Because of this robe?" he said, his tone teasing.

"Because you are an amazing man," she said, reaching up to touch his cheek.

He captured her hand in his and pressed his lips against her palm. "I love you, Zipporah."

"I love you too," she whispered.

The robe about her shoulders slipped to the ground as she wrapped her arms about her husband and kissed him. She'd soon be Moses's wife in every way. She couldn't have picked a better man to give her heart and soul to.

* * *

Zipporah didn't want to move. She lay on her marriage mat with Moses's arm slung around her waist. His breathing was slow and steady in sleep. It was strange and new and wonderful to have this man at her side all night, their bodies intertwined, fitting each other's curves perfectly.

It was still quite dark outside, but she could hear one of the goats bleating from its field. Perhaps it was ill or had been injured. She really didn't want to get up or wake Moses, but the longer she waited, the more she worried.

Finally, she slid from beneath Moses's arm, pausing when he stirred. When he settled back to sleep, she rose to her feet and reached for her shawl. Slipping out of the tent, Zipporah saw that the sky was still a deep black; dawn was still more than an hour away. It was all the better. She wanted to continue to sleep beside Moses and didn't care if the sun took forever to rise, although it looked as if rain might be coming with the clouds stirring against the sky.

The soft bleating came again, and Zipporah tilted her head, realizing that the sound hadn't come from the direction of the goat enclosure after all. Had one of the younger goats strayed? She walked in the direction of the sound, away from the marriage tent. The bleating seemed to move farther away, so she continued. When she'd gone farther then she intended, she stopped, feeling a chill touch her skin.

She suddenly felt very alone and very far from the marriage tent. Even the stars seemed dim and the moon darker. Zipporah was torn between continuing after the goat and returning to the security of the tent. She knew Midian guards patrolled all of the settlement's edges, but the vast space between her family's land and the outskirts was enough to make her feel utterly alone.

The goat hadn't made a sound for several moments, and Zipporah decided she could hunt it down in the morning with Moses at her side. She hoped the poor thing wouldn't stray too far and that it would perhaps get tired and lay down to sleep. As she turned back toward the marriage tent, she sensed that someone was watching her. Her pulse jumped, and she started to run toward the tent, hoping not to trip or fall in the darkness.

She was halfway to the tent when something sprang up in front of her, and a shape darker than the night reached for her. Zipporah opened her mouth to scream, but a hand clamped over her nose and mouth, cutting off all sound.

Zipporah hoped it was Moses—that he'd awakened and come looking for her. But the strong, thick arms that enclosed her were not friendly.

She struggled wildly as another man joined the first and wrenched her arms behind her back, tying them swiftly and tightly with a rough rope. The first man wrapped a heavy cloth about her mouth, nearly cutting off her ability to breathe. She inhaled sharply through her nose, gasping for air.

Twisting against the two men, she let her knees buckle so that she became dead weight. But they let her collapse to the ground, face-first, and one of the men propped his foot on top of her back, keeping pressure there so she couldn't move. Her only focus was to get away from these men, to not let them defeat her. She tried to wriggle away, but the second man grabbed her hair and wrenched her head back.

"Stop moving," he hissed.

Zipporah froze. His language was Midian's cousin—Badrayan. These men had infiltrated Midian, and now they would kill her.

They had stopped at nothing when they'd first attacked a few weeks ago and killed two women.

That didn't bode well for her. She was furious now. If she was to die, she wouldn't let them take her without a fight. Twisting wildly, she loosened one of her arms from the man's grip, but he quickly grabbed her again. Sand scraped against her face as she continued to strain against his grasp. One of the men chuckled under his breath, and within moments they'd tied her ankles together so she could hardly move.

She wanted to scream at them, ask them what they were doing and what they wanted. Would they drag her someplace and leave her for dead? Would they demand payment from her father? They were whispering to each other in harsh, guttural words.

Please, Lord, O God, she silently prayed. *Send Moses. Send my father. Anyone.*

She could only imagine what Moses would do if he were to awake and discover what was happening only a few dozen paces away from the tent. He'd use his bow and arrow. Yet she wondered if he even had his bow in the marriage tent.

One of the men hoisted her off the ground and, with the other man's help, slung her over his shoulder. She wouldn't have thought it possible, but apparently it was. She cried out at the sharp pain in her stomach, but the sound came out as a muffled moan.

The tribesman carrying her began to walk away from her tent. She wondered why he was carrying her and not forcing her to walk. And then she knew. He didn't want her tracks to be found. Her breath left her body at the realization. She felt sick. What was going to happen to her? Why hadn't they killed her yet? Where were they taking her?

With each jolting step, Zipporah was carried farther and farther away from her home and what had been, only a short time ago, her almost perfect life.

CHAPTER TWENTY-THREE
MOSES

It wasn't the absence of Zipporah's soft body next to his that awakened Moses. Nor was it the faraway bleating of a goat. It was the instinct that Moses had refined in his months of living as a fugitive from Egyptian law.

His eyes opened, and at first he could see only darkness. That Zipporah had left the tent was seared into his mind. If he took the time to dwell on it, it had almost been like a dream. Had he felt her move? Had he heard her nearly silent footsteps? And why had he not arisen immediately?

He knew. He'd been drunk with the contentment of the physical love of his wife. He'd thought she'd be back within moments. He'd thought that with the blessings raining down on him so generously the day before, none of them could possibly be taken away so soon.

Moses rose swiftly, and without fully thinking of the reasoning behind his actions, he grabbed his bow and sheath of arrows. Every woman in the settlement of Midian had been warned against traveling even to her neighbor's tent alone, let alone to the edge of their settlements in the middle of the night.

He stepped out of the tent and turned in every direction, searching for his wife beneath the waning moon. The silence was too great.

Had Zipporah gone into her family's tent for something? He looked toward the main tent structure but didn't see any evidence of an oil lamp burning, although she could make her way around in the dark easily enough.

A cool wind brushed against Moses's skin, and he involuntarily shuddered. He hurried toward the main tent and stepped inside the cooking area. "Zipporah?" he called in a soft voice. There wasn't a sound. Dread pulsed through him.

Moses didn't hesitate and made his way to the section where Jethro and his wife slept. He hated to wake them, but he hated worse that Zipporah wasn't where she should be.

"Jethro?" he called quietly as he stood at the entrance of the tent section.

"What?" The man's voice was raspy with exhaustion. He sat and rubbed his face. "Moses? What is it?"

"Zipporah left the tent for something, and she never returned," Moses said, the words jolting through him as he spoke.

"Did..." Jethro's wife was speaking now. "How was she after..."

Moses face heated. He hadn't even considered what Qurayya was suggesting. But deep down he knew that wasn't why she'd left. The important thing right now was to find her. "She was fine."

Jethro rose to his feet. "How long has she been gone?"

"I'm not sure," Moses said with regret. "I awakened with the sense that she was gone. It could have been only a few moments by the time I was aware. Did either of you hear her come back to this tent?"

"No. Perhaps she's returned now," Qurayya said.

"Yes," Jethro said. "I'll come with you though." It was too dark to see Qurayya, but Moses heard the worry in her voice. Jethro pulled on a robe and grabbed his sturdy staff, which could also be used as a spear if needed.

"I will search the other sections of the tent to see if she's somewhere inside," Qurayya said.

The concern in her voice only made Moses's worry increase. He hoped this search would all be for naught and Zipporah hadn't been able to sleep and had gone somewhere to do... what?

It didn't make sense, and for that reason Moses hurried out of the tent, his feeling of urgency growing. Jethro kept pace with him; it seemed their thoughts were the same.

"Did you check the goats?" Jethro asked in a low voice.

"I looked over there and didn't see her," Moses said. They went to the marriage tent first, Moses hoping she'd be back inside—perhaps wondering where he'd gone.

But the tent was empty. This time Moses noticed that her shawl was missing, the one that was a mixture of the colors indigo and pale sand. He had seen it in the tent, hadn't he? "Her shawl is gone," he told Jethro, who was scanning the tent, his brows drawn together.

"Has she ever disappeared like this at night before?" Moses asked, hoping there might be something Jethro knew.

"No," Jethro said. "She's an early riser, as you know, but not when it's still so dark out. Dawn must be at least an hour away."

They exited the marriage tent, Moses hardly able to comprehend that Zipporah was gone. It wasn't long ago that they'd been sleeping, his arm around her . . . How much time had passed?

"Jethro," a woman's voice called, and both men turned to see Qurayya hurrying toward them. "She's not inside the tent." She was breathless by the time she reached them. "But I forgot to tell you something in the midst of all the celebrations yesterday. My friend Reba from the north border gave me a message to pass along to you." Her voice cracked. "There was a sighting of a couple of shepherds not of our tribe past the northern tents."

Moses felt a chill run through him. "Badrayans?" he and Jethro said at the same time.

"Reba said no," Qurayya said, "but the guards are still watching the shepherds with interest." She put a trembling hand on her husband's arm. "That's why I didn't tell you at the wedding. Everything was going so well, and I didn't want to—" Her voice choked off, and she fell into Jethro's arms.

Moses cursed the night and the inability to see any sort of tracks that Zipporah would have made. He was faintly aware that Jethro was comforting his wife and that she was crying. Moses's stomach turned to stone, and his mind was numb. He couldn't comprehend what might have happened to Zipporah if she had been captured by the Badrayans, what might be happening now. She had been in his arms, sleeping next to him, less than an hour ago. And now she was gone. Living through hell—unless they'd already killed her.

He started walking swiftly toward the goat enclosure, calling out for Zipporah. The only sound in return was the bleating of sleepy animals. He turned and headed toward the edge of the settlement, looking for any human shape. Perhaps she'd fallen; perhaps she was sick and couldn't walk back. But why would she be out here in the first place? The questions pounded through his head.

The moon had chosen this night to be a dull yellow, and the stars seemed stubborn in their light. "Zipporah!" he called out again. He didn't know how many times he'd yelled her name, but his throat felt dry and rough.

And then he stopped. There, on the ground in front of him, was a flat shape of multi-colors, a piece of cloth. Before even picking it up, Moses knew that it was Zipporah's shawl. "No," he whispered to himself. "Zipporah!" he yelled.

Shaking, he crouched and picked up the shawl. For a moment, he held it against his nose, breathing in her scent with disbelief. She'd been here—farther out than any errand should have taken her. There were still a couple of hundred paces to the first ridge, and from this position Moses couldn't see any guards standing or sitting, whiling the time away.

He rose, holding the shawl against him and scanning the graying horizon. Which direction had they taken her? Every moment that passed was another moment that they could be mistreating her. With the vast sky above and the desert sand stretching out in its infinitude, Moses knew that he alone couldn't find her. He needed an army.

He noted the exact location of where he'd found the shawl, then hurried back to Jethro and Qurayya.

When she recognized the shawl Moses carried, Qurayya burst into hysterics.

"We need three runners," Moses said over her lamenting. She fell quiet for a blessed moment as he spoke. "We need the guards alerted and for all women and children to stay inside their tents. For those living near any of Midian's outer edges, they need to move toward the center of the settlement."

Jethro clapped his hand on Moses's shoulder, but Moses barely felt the pressure. He continued giving orders as if his mind had to work through every instruction before he could take any action himself. "Every boy and man, age twelve and up, needs to choose a weapon and be prepared to defend Midian with their life. We are now at war with the Badrayans."

"I'll go alert the guards and send out the runners," Jethro said in a voice filled with determination and emotion. He turned to his wife. "Gather the girls and take them to Cozbi's tent. You'll be closer to the center of the settlement there. When there is any word about Zipporah, I will come there."

Qurayya hurried away toward the tent, her hand to her mouth as she tried to rein in her emotions.

"I'll fetch Hobab," Jethro said, turning to Moses. "Go find Sihon and Peor. We need to start tracking at first light. I'll meet you back here before the sun rises," Jethro continued. "This time I'm coming with you. I must find my daughter."

As Moses hurried along the path to Sihon's tent, he hoped this was some terrible dream or some horrible event happening to another person. But the rocks and sand beneath his feet and the wind tugging at his kilt were all too real. Zipporah had been abducted. Was she alive? Would Moses be able to sense if she'd been killed? Would he be able to feel her absence?

He felt nothing, yet he felt everything. His emotions were in a fierce battle, one side trying to convince him to turn and keep running to where he'd found Zipporah's shawl, to run past Midian until he found her. The other side of his mind was trying to convince him to march every able boy and man toward Badraya and take revenge before the sun was high in the sky because it was already too late for Zipporah.

Moses focused on calming his thoughts and keeping his actions rational. Zipporah could still be alive. She might be able to escape. More lives didn't need to be lost.

"Sihon," Moses called out as he approached his newest brother-in-law's tent. He didn't care if he woke those in the neighboring tents. Soon enough, the morning would dawn with a new reality—of Midian on the warpath.

Sihon stumbled out of the tent, blinking open his bleary eyes. It had only been a few hours since the wedding celebration had ended.

The moment Sihon saw Moses, his expression became alert. "What—?"

"Zipporah's been abducted by the Badrayans," he said, interrupting Sihon.

The man's mouth fell open. "How? Where?"

Moses told Sihon all that had transpired, as well as the instructions he'd given to Jethro.

"So we are to track her down while the men of Midian prepare for battle?"

"Yes," Moses said. "I want a dozen of Midian's best men to come on our search. We also need able men to prepare the others for the impending battle."

"What do you want Peor to do?" Sihon said.

The young man had excelled in his training over the past weeks, and Moses trusted him with his life. "He comes with us. Tell your wife to prepare for her mother and sisters' arrival at your tent. We must leave immediately."

Sihon nodded and ducked inside his tent.

Moses closed his eyes as he waited. His heart made a dull thud in his chest as if it were beating reluctantly. Too much time had already passed. He opened his eyes, scanning the sky and the heavy clouds hovering above. Despite the clouds, the sky was finally starting to melt into gray, with dawn now being less than an hour away.

Sounds came from inside the tent: a quiet conversation, then a woman crying.

"I told my wife," Sihon said, stepping outside a few moments later. He carried his bow and arrows, and a goatskin was slung over his shoulder. The lines on his face had deepened. "Let's fetch Peor, and then I know where to find the other men."

"Moses!" a woman's voice shrieked from inside the tent. Cozbi came out of the tent, tears streaming down her face. She grabbed Moses, tugging on his arms. "Find my sister! Bring her back!"

"Cozbi," Sihon said in a stern voice, pulling her from Moses. "We need to prepare immediately. Every delay is a delay in finding Zipporah."

Cozbi choked back another sob and turned away, her body trembling as Sihon led her inside. After more murmured words,

Sihon came outside again. "Let's hurry before the entire settlement is in hysterics."

Moses followed Sihon to his parents' tent, where Peor lived, and once Peor heard what had happened, he was ready to depart within moments.

By the time they made it back to Jethro's homestead, Hobab and Sihon had collected a dozen other men, bringing their total to fifteen. Camels had been gathered to give the traveling group more speed. The sight of Jethro standing by the marriage tent with several armed men was a relief to Moses.

They greeted each other solemnly, and Jethro said, "Everything is in motion. Our job is to find Zipporah." Hobab stepped forward and clasped Moses's shoulder, a determined understanding passing between them. Then Moses turned and studied the gathered men. Their features were becoming more distinct against the lightening sky. Moses recognized all of them, although he didn't know them by name. They'd all taken part in his training sessions.

His eyes burned with gratitude at these men's willingness to help him on his mission. They looked nothing like the Egyptian soldiers Moses had trained with, but they would fight without mercy.

"We'll start at the place where I found Zipporah's shawl," Moses said, feeling his voice shake as he spoke his new wife's name. "Then Sihon will examine the area for tracks and determine which direction we will take. Do not travel ahead of Sihon; we don't want any footprints or the terrain disturbed."

Moses turned to Sihon. "Follow me. I'll show you where we'll begin."

The men guided their camels and followed Moses as he led his own camel toward the place where he had found his wife's shawl. He wouldn't let the shawl go until he found the woman it belonged to.

CHAPTER TWENTY-FOUR
ZIPPORAH

Zipporah's head pounded, she had sand in her mouth and eyes, and her scalp itched. At least the two men were letting her walk now. They'd carried her a good distance, well past the set of ridges, until they reached the hills of Jabal al-Lawz. Even a man as strong as her husband wouldn't be able to carry her up the mountainside.

Were they truly going to climb the whole mountain? Zipporah wondered as she stumbled along the incline. She'd tried to ask for water once through the cloth they'd tied around her mouth, but they'd only shoved her. What she wouldn't give for a drink now, though she knew there were other things to worry about. Why had these men let her live? Why hadn't they killed and discarded her? Where were they taking her?

The Badrayan tribe lived to the north, not west.

O Lord, my God, Zipporah silently prayed. *Preserve me. Return me to my family. Soften the hearts of these men. Don't let them harm me.* Hot tears formed in her eyes as despair overwhelmed her. She knew what happened to women captured by enemy tribesmen. Worst case, she'd be killed; best case, she'd be forced to marry. Although Zipporah wasn't sure which would be worse. There were other terrible possibilities between those two scenarios, but she didn't want to consider them.

Zipporah stumbled yet again, and the strong hand gripping her arm tightened. She'd been able to discern that the taller man with the long hair tied back was named Zur. The shorter man with shoulders as wide as an ox was named Rekel.

It was Rekel who kept her upright now with his stone-like hands. And then, instead of going up the slope, they cut across it, Rekel half pushing Zipporah ahead of him. The men were increasing their pace, and she wondered why the change. Then she realized that dawn was breaking, and even with the cloud cover, if they were on this particular slope, they would be easier to spot if the Midianites pursued.

Hope surged through her. Was Moses coming after her? She thought of his skill with an arrow and how he could easily target these men. If he didn't come, she would find a way—no matter how long it took—to escape. Even if it meant losing her life. Still, Zipporah did the only thing she could think of and deliberately tried to leave evidence of their travel by stepping on small bushes as they walked.

Ahead of her, Zur called back to Rekel, "Don't let her fall." The path had narrowed until it wasn't even a path at all—perhaps it was a goat trail, steep and treacherous. She looked down at the sharp dropoff. One misstep and it would be easy to fall.

Rekel tightened his grip on her arm, if that were even possible. If Zipporah didn't think Moses was coming after her, she might have been tempted to twist away from Rekel and let herself fall off the edge.

The path became more rocky until it could barely be seen. As the night faded and the sky turned to a pale gray, Zipporah stumbled along, climbing over rocks and walking through narrow crevices. She'd never been this deep into the Sarawat range before, and with each step, her discouragement and sense of foreboding increased.

Then the men came to a sudden stop, and Zur held up his hand as if he were waiting for something or listening. Zipporah finally got a good look at him in the growing light. He might have once been handsome, but his nose was crooked—likely from being broken more than once—and his dark eyes seemed to cut right through her with their wrath. Plainly this man didn't have a gentle thought in his head. His penetrating gaze on her seemed to dare her to move or try to escape. Zur brought his fingers to his lips and let out a long, low whistle. Moments later, a whistle sounded from somewhere up ahead.

Her heart plunged. They were connecting with another tribesman.

Zur grinned. "Almost there," he said, scanning her face. "I can't wait to get the scarf off your mouth so I can get a proper look at you." He reached out and touched the tips of her hair that fell against her shoulders.

Zipporah jerked back, only to slam against Rekel, who stood behind her.

"Skittish . . . like a goat," Zur said with a laugh. "I can tame that easily enough." His eyes narrowed. "Let's go."

Rekel propelled her forward, unrelenting in his grip, and she was sure her arm would be bruised for weeks. They walked through a narrow passageway, then came out onto a rocky plateau. Several men waited for them, and it was clear they'd set up a camp.

A tent had been erected on one side, and in the center of the area were the remains of a cooking fire. Two thin and malnourished goats were tied to a scraggly tree.

Zipporah looked at the gathering of men, and they stared back at her. They were Badrayans, all right, their tunics the color of the desert sand, and their skin browned almost to black by the sun. Zur began to speak rapidly, and the men cheered. Zipporah took a step back, but Rekel was right behind her again. She tried to pull away from him, but he clamped his hand on her other arm.

"We have brought our prize," Zur said, his voice filled with pride. "She is our reward for our loss of men."

This was why they'd spared her life? So that she might entertain these men? She shivered at the thought of what that might mean. It might have been better had she propelled herself off the steep slope.

There were at least a dozen men in this camp, and they were all grinning at her, their eyes watchful. Was there one man in this group whom Zipporah could influence? She looked desperately from one to another, but they were all the same—eyes wild, and not a bit of compassion in any of them.

"We will remove the covering from your mouth," Zur said, turning to her, his eyes dark on hers. "But if you scream, I will use this on your throat." The dagger he held at her throat looked well used, and Zur's threat didn't seem idle.

"Do you understand?" he ground out.

Zipporah could only nod. Zur reached up and untied the cloth behind her head. The rush of air against her mouth was a relief. She could finally breathe freely.

"What do you want with me?" she asked, her hoarse voice barely above a whisper.

Behind her, Rekel chuckled, his breath hot on her neck.

But Zur only narrowed his eyes as he studied her. "We were going to capture you before your marriage, but we knew the Egyptian would be more angry if we did it after the wedding."

Zipporah's face grew hot with indignation. Her legs felt as if they might give out. If Rekel hadn't been holding her so tightly, they would have. This had all been planned. They had been watching her.

Hot and cold tremors passed through her body at the thought.

"Get her some water," Zur said, calling to one of the men in the crowd.

A short, thin man stepped forward. Zipporah knew better than to think he was weak. All of these men were hardened by wilderness living. She wasn't dumb enough to reject the water, although it was tepid and sour, as if it had come from a soiled well. She choked on the water, hoping it would stay down.

The few swallows she was allowed to take brought blessed relief. Her head felt clearer, and she was able to breathe easier.

"How many hours has it been since you captured her?" one of the men asked.

Zur glanced at the sky and the churning clouds. "Three hours. They should be on their way by now—as soon as the sky lightened enough to see the shawl she left behind."

Zipporah was startled. The shawl had fallen off her shoulders when they'd captured her, but she hadn't realized they'd noticed it.

Zur was watching her, a half smile on his face. "You didn't think we'd forget your clothing, did you?" he said amongst laughter from the other men. "We knew it would be easier to track you if they found the shawl in plain sight."

"You . . ." Zipporah took a ragged breath. "You planned this? You want my people to come after you?"

Rekel chuckled. He folded his muscled arms across this chest. "I want the Egyptian to come after us. Only his death will avenge the deaths of our brother and our friends."

The tribesmen murmured their agreement, and one of them called out, "Should we enjoy his wife while we are waiting?"

Zur spun and knocked the man to the ground. Standing above the fallen man holding his bleeding nose, Zur growled, "No one touches her. When her husband is dead at my feet and she is a widow, I'll marry her. Then none of you will ever have claim to her." He turned to face Zipporah, and the intensity of his gaze made her wish she'd found a way to escape, even if it cost her life.

"See, woman? I'm not the barbarian you think I am."

The man on the ground groaned and turned to his side, attempting to get up.

Zur slammed his foot into the man's side, resulting in the man curling up in pain. "It may depend on who you ask though."

Rekel laughed and moved Zipporah forward. "Where do you want her until you can claim her?"

"The tent," Zur said. "I'm tired of everyone staring at my future wife."

CHAPTER TWENTY-FIVE
MOSES

As soon as Sihon directed the group toward the western slopes of Jabal al-Lawz, Moses knew. The Badrayans were setting a trap. If they'd taken Zipporah to their settlement, they would have continued north. Moses had been pushing his camel as fast as it would go, and he was glad that all of the camels were strong and rested. Jethro had no trouble keeping pace; he was just as motivated as anyone else.

Even though all of the men didn't know Zipporah personally, everyone knew Jethro, and they could well imagine how they'd feel if it had been their own daughter or wife who'd been abducted.

Sihon rode in the lead, Peor next to him. Moses stayed to the right of them, keeping pace and looking for any signs of the tribesmen. Hobab rode at the rear of the group, keeping a lookout for anyone who might be following them.

"Do you think she's alive?" Peor asked Sihon.

Sihon hushed his brother, but Moses had overheard. "She's alive," Moses said with confidence.

Peor looked chagrined, yet he was bold enough to ask, "How can you be certain?"

Moses waved his hand toward the rising hills just ahead of them. "Their trail is leading us west instead of toward their settlement, where they'd have the benefit of increased security."

"So they don't want security?" Peor asked.

"I don't know exactly," Moses said. "But they left Zipporah's shawl behind . . . I believe it was intentional, as if they wanted us to follow them."

Peor's eyes widened. "Have they set a trap?"

Moses scanned the rising rock formations, looking for any sign of movement or coloring that didn't belong. "I believe they have. And we are walking right into it."

"What should we do?" Peor's voice dropped to a whisper.

"Continue following their tracks," Moses said. "And pray."

Peor swallowed visibly, then ran his hand across his forehead. The sun had stayed behind the clouds as it rose, but with their exertion, the men were already sweating.

Moses urged his camel on. It was hard to believe that just hours ago he'd been nestled in his marriage tent with his new bride. He would have never dreamed that shortly he'd be trekking through the wilderness to find her. His mind churned with worst-case scenarios, which only made him more determined to find Zipporah as soon as possible.

If the Badrayans harmed her, it would take many lives to avenge her.

As they neared the first outcroppings of the mount, Moses moved his camel closer to Sihon's. "What do you think?" he asked.

Sihon used his headscarf to wipe the sweat from his face. "I think they'll see us soon enough if they haven't seen us yet." He cast a sideways glance at Moses. "But I assume that won't stop us or slow us down."

"You're right." Moses looked back at the men who rode with them, Jethro included. They might each be perspiring, but none of them had slowed one bit. Each had determination in their expressions—these men were ready to fight.

Gazing forward again, Moses said, "This is too familiar. Too planned."

"I agree," Sihon said. "It was only a few weeks ago we were out here tracking down the six Badrayans."

Moses was silent for a moment. "Perhaps we shouldn't have let one live."

Sihon released a sigh. "I thought of that too, but it was too late. Each death would have been marked anyway, and revenge would have come sooner or later."

"Revenge, yes," Moses said. "That's what this is. I believe it's personal."

Sihon snapped his head toward Moses. "You mean they captured Zipporah because of you?"

"Yes," Moses said. "One of them knew I was the one at the well . . . and when I was involved in the last skirmish . . . it's now revenge against me personally."

Sihon drew his camel to a stop, then climbed down and crouched to inspect a bush. He fingered a broken twig, then rose to his feet again. Angling to the right, he started walking again. "It's possible," Sihon said, picking up the conversation again. "But it could have been any of us."

He waved his hand in the direction of the men in their group. "All of these men are defending Midian as a whole—our families and our homes—whether it was your wife or my wife, we'd be out here doing the same thing."

"I hope you're right," Moses said. He agreed with Sihon, yet he felt that he was being specifically targeted. Was it his fault all of this was happening in the first place? Had he unwittingly brought this danger to an innocent people?

"I can assure you that you're one of us now," Sihon said, mounting his camel again. "You have been since that day at the well."

Moses nodded, although his stomach was still knotted. Perhaps the shepherds would have left the women in peace after having a bit of fun and Zipporah would be safe at home now.

"You can't go back and change anything, Moses," Sihon said, keeping his voice low. "Regrets only eat at your soul. I believe God is with us and that we'll find Zipporah."

Moses had to trust in Sihon's words—it was the only way he could stay sane at this point. But in what condition would they find her? How were they treating her? He wanted to run up the slopes and inspect every crevice. He wanted to scream for justice. But mostly he wanted to find Zipporah and bring her home.

"Another broken bush," Sihon said, slowing his camel to point at a bush with snapped twigs. He shook his head. "It's almost as if . . ."

"As if Zipporah created a trail for us to follow," Moses said, drawing his camel to a stop to see the bush better. There was evidence of three people walking now instead of the two earlier—in which case, Sihon explained, they'd carried Zipporah earlier.

Moses had been relieved when three were in evidence—it meant that Zipporah was well enough to walk on her own. The fact that the Badrayans hadn't used camels told him that they planned to travel through the mountains. He looked up at the rising slopes of the mountain. There were dozens of places they could have traveled. Hundreds. They could be very close, or they could still be far ahead. Moses looked down at the broken twigs and the continuance of the tracks they'd been following. He took comfort knowing that at this very moment they were on the right path. Moses studied the rock terrain as it rose and twisted and then broke off and rose again.

Jethro drew his camel up next to Moses's. "They could be anywhere. We must pray," he said in an urgent voice. "There is no time to waste. One wrong turn could make things worse for my daughter."

"Gather close, everyone," Sihon called out, and the Midianites drew their camels together in a half circle. Moses bowed his head. All around them, the Midianites bowed their heads as well.

"O Lord, O God," Jethro began, his voice trembling. He stopped and opened his eyes, looking to his son. "Will you offer the prayer?"

Hobab nodded and started to speak, his voice low and reverent. "O Lord, O God. Thou art magnificent in Thine ever-seeing guidance. Watch over our Zipporah and protect her from harm. Guide us to find her and deliver her from evil. O God, we are ever grateful for Thy mercy. Amen."

"Amen," Moses said, the word echoed a dozen times over by the other men. He scanned the ground in front of him. Just a few paces away was another trampled bush. Sihon saw it at the same time.

"We will need to couch our camels and begin our climb," Sihon said. He assigned two men to remain with the camels.

Moses slipped off his camel and tied Zipporah's shawl around his waist. Then he shouldered his bow and sheaf of arrows. The rest of the men climbed off their camels and followed Sihon and Moses as they began to ascend the rocky slope, one step at a time.

Moses should have been exhausted from a night of little sleep, but his strength had been renewed by the words of Hobab's prayer. He recognized the power and comfort it gave him to know he wasn't alone. Not only was he with Jethro, Hobab, Sihon, Peor, and the other Midianite men, but God was with them. Moses felt it as sure as he felt the solid ground beneath his feet.

The clouds had lowered and darkened. And even though the sun was hidden, its heat could still be felt, mixed now with the moisture in the air. The combination seemed to soak heat into Moses's skin, right through his clothing.

He trudged on, and the men were mostly silent, each lost in his own thoughts and determination. Sihon paused again, crouching next to a ledge. "This rock slide looks fresh," he said, pointing down the slope above which they stood. "There is no growth, nor are there any snake holes."

Moses scanned the area ahead of them. There was a passageway through a crop of rocks. "Could they have gone through there?"

Sihon straightened. "It's narrow, and I'm not sure where it leads."

Moses held up a hand for him to stop speaking. The men surrounding them stopped their quiet conversations as well. "It's too quiet," he said in a hushed tone. "Listen."

And the men did. They didn't move, didn't speak, but only listened, each of them looking around, waiting. They stood on a ledge; behind them lay a gradual slope back to the desert floor; ahead of them lay a narrow passage leading upward to another part of the mountain.

A drop of rain fell, then another, splashing on the dry earth. Moses continued holding up his hand for silence, and the men didn't move as the rain slowly dripped onto their heads and clothing. Then Moses brought his fingers to his lips and gave a low whistle. Several moments passed. Then Moses gave the whistle again.

Sihon looked at him with an arched brow, but Moses didn't explain. The rain increased its tempo, driving harder and faster. Moses turned his face upward, closing his eyes, listening above the rain. Still no return whistle. It could mean that he was wrong about there being a signal for the Badrayans or that he'd just alerted them to the Midianites' presence.

And apparently the rainy season was starting today.

A shower of rocks tumbled down the slope up ahead of them, and Moses's first instinct was to nock one of his arrows. He flew into action and had the arrow ready to shoot before he even had time to see what had caused the rocks to fall.

Someone was above them, but he scrambled out of sight before Moses could take aim.

"There!" Sihon called out, and instantly the other men readied their weapons.

Moses peered through the pelting rain, scanning the rocks above, looking for any sign of life. It was impossible to know how many men might be hiding in these rocks, but it was clear the man who'd alerted them hadn't meant to. Perhaps he was a watchman? Had he heard Moses's whistle?

Moses looked at the passageway ahead, then the rocks towering over it. They'd be at a disadvantage if they became stuck in the passageway when the Badrayans attacked from above. Or the tribesmen could cut off both entrances to the passages.

But here on the ledge they were completely exposed.

He turned to Jethro. "We need to split up. Half of us will remain here, the other half will go through the passageway. When I give the signal, come through after us. If there is no signal for twenty minutes, head back down the mountainside."

Jethro's face paled. "We'll wait here for your signal, then."

Moses wiped the rain from his face, then gave Sihon and Peor a nod. He motioned for a few others to follow them, then Moses stepped into the passageway. He walked slowly, keeping an eye on the rocks above and watching for any signs of falling dirt or rock. An attack could come at any moment, and he didn't know how long the passageway was.

The rain was lighter in the passageway since it was blocked by the boulders, but everything was becoming wet and slippery. The sky rumbled above, quickening Moses's heartbeat, and the hairs on his arm prickled. And then he saw it. A piece of cloth, a movement from above. He aimed his arrow and let it fly.

Then everything seemed to happen at once. Several men appeared above and arrows soared down while the Midianites tried to take cover as best they could.

Moses stayed in his place, nocking arrow after arrow, sending them as fast as he could, hitting as many targets as possible. Peor went down first, and Sihon rushed to his side, crying out for his brother.

Then Hobab fell with a cry, clutching his arm, but Moses kept shooting, keeping his mind focused on one thing—the Badrayans.

He didn't know how many of the tribesmen were felled, but when the arrows stopped coming toward the Midianites, Moses went back to check on Hobab and Peor, maneuvering through the narrow passageway.

Sihon had removed his headscarf and tied it around Peor's leg. An arrow had struck Peor's thigh and was still protruding out of his flesh. Hobab was sitting up, leaning against a rock, gripping his bleeding arm. His face was as pale as alabaster. He'd pulled out the arrow that had entered his shoulder, but at least he was conscious and sitting up.

Moses called to one of the Midianites and told him to tie a cloth around Hobab's wound, then he turned to Sihon. "Hold Peor still, and give him something to bite on." He looked around for help from another Midianite. "We'll need two of us to hold him down."

One of the men stepped forward to help Sihon, and when Peor was secured, Moses pulled out his dagger. "Look at me, Peor."

The young man's eyes focused on Moses, but only barely. His face was as pale as the moon. "I'm going to get the arrow out so that it won't fester. We need to act fast because any moment the Badrayans will be back with more men. The sooner the arrow is out, the sooner you can get out of this passageway."

Peor nodded, tears mixing with the rain on his face.

Moses retied the scarf around Peor's leg, then nodded to Sihon and the other Midianite. He made a small cut next to where the arrow had entered Peor's thigh, and Peor's face went absolutely red with the strain of trying not to scream in pain.

"Almost done," Moses said, then set to working out the arrow. He kept his thoughts away from what Peor's pain might be. Finally the arrow was out, and Moses quickly bound the wound, then looked at Sihon. "Take Hobab and your brother to Jethro, and tell Jethro to keep them hidden while they recover their strength."

"I'm staying here with you," Sihon said, his jaw clenched. He looked to the other Midianite. "Help the injured men out of the passageway."

The man half carried Peor back toward where Jethro was waiting. Hobab followed, taking measured steps and steadying himself against the rocks as he walked. Moses hoped Peor would be fine—as long as the wound didn't fester and as long as he sustained no further injuries, he should stand a good chance of survival.

Sihon studied the rocks above. "How long do you think we—"

Moses clamped a hand on his shoulder and motioned for him to crouch down. He waved the other men down as well until they were all crouched and pressed against the rock. They would not be completely hidden from above, but their vital body parts would be protected.

"They know how many of us there are by now," he said in a quiet voice. "Though two have left us, they will probably have enough men to overpower us. And their desire for revenge will be even stronger now that we've felled some of their tribesmen."

Sihon nodded, his face grave. "I'm ready."

CHAPTER TWENTY-SIX
ZIPPORAH

Zipporah stayed as small as she could in the crooked tent by pulling her knees to her chest and wrapping her arms around them, then lowering her head to her knees. "Please, Lord," she whispered in prayer. "I pray Thee, O God, please deliver me from these men."

The Badrayans had been laughing only moments before, and she'd smelled a cooking fire, although it had started to rain. But then the laughter had stopped abruptly, and Zipporah had lifted her head, straining to hear what was going on.

Zur or one of the other men had ordered everyone to be quiet. Then she heard it.

A whistle—low and long.

The hairs on the back of her neck had stood on end; she knew it was a signal. Someone had arrived. More Badrayans?

Then chaos had erupted, and Zipporah could only listen to the sounds coming from outside and imagine the worst.

Was it Moses? The Midianites? Zur issued urgent commands, and men were calling to each other, talking about weapons and fighting and—

The worst came when she heard the cries of pain coming from farther away. A tribesman poked his head inside her tent, and with sharp words told her not to move.

"What's happening?" Zipporah had asked in a fearful voice. "Is it—?"

But the tribesman had disappeared again.

She couldn't just wait anymore, sitting there, not knowing what was happening. She rose gingerly to her tied feet and hopped to the tent wall. More cries. Shouts. Cursing. Someone called out, "He's dead!" Another shouted, "Watch out!"

Then a heavy silence descended with the now rapidly falling rain. Drops of water leaked through the tent panels above, dripping onto Zipporah. She looked up at the tent ceiling. How had she come to this place? Why was this happening to her?

And then Zur burst into the tent, his eyes wild, his mouth working in rage. Why was he screaming at her?

"Get down!" he yelled. "They've come for you, but you're mine. Do not forget that."

"I'm not yours," she yelled back, instinct taking over.

But Zur slapped her cheek, stunning Zipporah so much that she was thrown off balance. Her legs crumpled, giving out once and for all.

Zur was on top of her, his weight nearly crushing her as he grabbed her arms and lashed them together.

Zipporah cried out as the lashing bit into her skin, likely drawing blood.

"What's happening out there?" she managed to ask.

"You will obey everything I tell you," Zur growled out. "If you don't, you will die this hour."

Her pulse pounded so hard she felt it thud from her head to her feet. Zur's hands moved down her body, and she tried to twist away, but his weight was too much. Then he relashed her ankles together, and she knew she was completely at his mercy.

She squeezed her eyes shut, hot tears burning against her lids. Had Moses really come? Was he fighting now? Had he killed one of the Badrayans? Were they retaliating now? Had her prayers only put her husband in grave danger?

Zur touched her face, and Zipporah's eyes flew open. He was staring intently at her, like an animal stalking its prey. She was still on her back, hopelessly tied, and Zur hovered over her.

"Don't hurt my husband," she said in a cracked whisper. "Take me, but spare him." Her prayers changed then, no longer for her own rescue; they were now for Moses and the preservation of his life.

Zur chuckled, his face so close to hers that she felt his hot breath on her skin. "Don't worry about your husband—he won't be around for long. He won't be able to resist coming to rescue his love."

Zipporah wanted to spit at Zur, but her mouth and throat were so dry that even if she tried, she wouldn't be able to.

Zur produced a dagger with his left hand, then ran his right hand along her cheek and down her neck. She wanted to scream at his touch, but the dagger was cold against her skin. "You are a prize," Zur said. "But your husband might be a bigger prize. After all, what can a woman do for the good of a settlement? Tempt a man? Have a baby?"

She turned her face away from his, wanting to gag from inhaling his foul scent.

"Don't you look away," he said, clenching her jaw in his strong fingers. He moved her chin so that she was looking directly at him again.

Outside the tent, there was more shouting, and one man was crying out as if he were in pain. "They're coming through the passageway," someone shouted. "Be ready."

Zur's eyes flicked to the tent entrance, then back to Zipporah. "We'll finish this later, but I will leave you with this to think about." He suddenly lowered his head and pressed his mouth against hers.

Zipporah reeled back and tried to twist her head again.

Zur only laughed, and then he was on his feet, dragging her with him until she was half standing, half leaning on him for support. "Come on, woman," he said, his grip tight on her arm. It felt as if he were cutting her to the bone as he grasped the tender bruised skin she'd gotten from Rekel.

"You're about to meet your fate," Zur said, pushing her through the tent flap.

The ground was wet enough that the dirt had started to turn to mud, and the rocks surrounding the area were slick with rain. The heavens had decided to open up after months of unrelenting drought.

The Badrayans were spread out through the enclosure, braced against the walls, their weapons drawn, their eyes trained on the passageway opening.

Zipporah was pushed forward. Touching a large rock with her hands, she caught her balance, trying to stay upright. Would Moses appear at any moment? A tribesman whimpered under an alcove to her right. He was bleeding from his arm, and instead of trying to bind it with a headscarf, he merely rocked back and forth clutching at the bleeding wound.

"Kneel!" Zur commanded, shoving her downward.

It didn't take much for her knees to bend and her legs to give way. With her tied ankles, she had no sense of balance. The rain continued to come down, soaking her clothing and hair. She thought if she were given a chance, she could wriggle out of the lashings because her skin was wet and slippery. But as she moved her wrists, the lashings only seemed to tighten.

"Don't try to escape," Zur growled. He stood behind her and pulled her against him so that her head was locked against his legs.

It was impossible to imagine a scenario in which she could escape. Zur grabbed her shoulder and pulled her back even tighter, then he brought the dagger to her neck. The blade was cold and hard, and Zipporah imagined that she could taste the metal in her mouth. Sharp and bitter.

And then she felt Zur's hands tense even more. She looked up to see a man coming through the passageway. It was a Midianite—she could tell right away. She peered through the rain until she realized it was Moses.

She wanted to sag with relief, to cry out, to run to him. But Zur had her bound and the dagger pressed firmly against her skin. Her emotions battled within. *Moses, you came*, she thought. *O Lord, thank you for sending my husband. O Lord, preserve him. Don't let him die.*

CHAPTER TWENTY-SEVEN
MOSES

"Let's get through this passage and see what's on the other side," Moses had said. He had a feeling the Badrayans were hiding close by. He was on his feet in a moment, other men following behind at intervals. By spreading out, they were able to cover more area and defend themselves better.

With every step, Moses expected a Badrayan to appear above on a rock or ahead of him in the passageway. But as it opened up, he realized he should be expecting something worse. Perhaps there would be a whole army of them waiting.

The sound of crying reached him, and Moses stilled. Was that a woman? Zipporah? He looked back at Sihon, whose face had frozen. Then it relaxed and he said, "Goats."

Moses didn't feel a speck of relief. Wild goats lived in the mountains, but they didn't bleat as if they weren't used to the harsh terrain. What was going on? Moses stopped as the passage widened into a large area that looked like it had been a camp—perhaps abandoned moments ago.

A tent stood at the far side, and two goats were tied to a tree, straining against their ropes and bleating in the rain. But what caught Moses's attention was the woman kneeling in the rain and the tall Badrayan holding a dagger to her throat.

"Zipporah," Moses whispered, staring through the rain at his wife.

Her eyes were on him, dark and soulful.

She was alive. *Alive.* He let the word settle into his mind until he could fully comprehend it. He wanted to tell Jethro that his daughter was here—living, breathing. Desperation shot through Moses—he'd come this far, and Zipporah had made it this far—but what had she endured? He had to rescue her, get her away from all of this, from all of these men.

As he met her gaze, his stomach dropped. The image before him was difficult to believe, yet the pelting rain on his face and the muddied ground below his feet confirmed that this nightmare was real. Zipporah, his wife, was kneeling in the moist earth, her hands lashed together in front of her. A tribesman was holding a dagger to her delicate throat.

He looked at the Badrayan, and Moses realized it was the same man he'd let go free—the man he hoped to never face again. And in the man's eyes was unadulterated hatred.

"O God, have mercy on us," Sihon said, coming through the passageway and stopping next to Moses.

As the Midianites appeared in the clearing one by one, Moses began assessing his options. There were seven other tribesmen, all situated on the outskirts, pressed up against rocks, a couple with bows at the ready and others with spears and daggers.

Moses exhaled, thinking fast. The numbers were nearly even, and Moses had confidence his men could defeat the tribesmen. But what would the cost be? Peor and Hobab were already injured, and some of the Badrayans had been killed.

"Who are you and what do you want?" Moses called out, directing his question to the man restraining Zipporah. He wanted to run and dive into the man's body, knocking him away from Zipporah, then get her out of this place.

"I am Zur," the man said, then spat out of the side of his mouth as if he was trying to get rid of a poisonous leaf. "But you wouldn't know that, would you, *Egyptian?*"

Moses flinched at the man's sneering tone.

"We have not been introduced, it seems," Moses called back. "Primarily because each time we've met, you've been trying to kill me."

Zur's laugh was harsh. "No wonder you charmed this woman into marrying you." He grabbed Zipporah's hair and twisted it tightly. She cried out, and he laughed again.

Rage pulsed through Moses, and it was all he could do to stop himself from launching toward Zur. "Stop hurting her," he said through gritted teeth. "She has nothing to do with what's between us."

The other tribesmen stepped forward.

Zipporah's eyes focused on Moses again, and he wanted to scoop her up in his arms and carry her back down the mountain. Rain had soaked her clothing, and she was shivering.

Moses sensed Sihon behind him signaling to the others. They were making plans to attack, but Moses didn't like the look in Zur's eyes. The tribesman wasn't averse to using Zipporah to his advantage.

"Let her go, and we can both go our own ways," Moses said. "We will each accept our losses and return to our homes and families. Many lives will be saved if we call a truce."

Nothing in Zur's eyes changed, nothing softened. "Once you killed my brother in the desert, all negotiations ended."

Cold anger shot through Moses. "This argument is between men and should not involve women and children."

"Women and children have always been the spoils of war," Zur said. "No one will ever change that, not even if we live to be a thousand years old."

Moses took a step forward, his hand gripping his now-wet bow.

"One more step and I'll slice her throat," Zur growled.

Moses clenched his bow tighter. The other tribesmen had moved closer as well; behind him the Midianites crowded against the entrance of the passageway. They were all locked in together. One lost temper or misdirected move could lead to nearly everyone's deaths.

"What do you want in exchange for my wife's freedom?" Moses asked.

Zipporah's eyes closed, and she bent her head forward. Moses couldn't stand seeing her so helpless. The fire and the intensity of her gaze had been destroyed, and all that knelt on the ground before him was a weak and exhausted woman. *Don't give up*, he wanted to say.

Zur's face slid into a smile. "I'm glad you inquired, because I have a trade in mind."

Moses inhaled sharply. He didn't care for the tone of Zur's voice, and he almost guessed Zur's demand before he spoke again.

"We'll trade the woman for . . . *you*," Zur said, his grin widening in triumph.

Moses didn't even need to think about it. He slid the sheaf of arrows from his shoulder and let it drop to the ground. Then he released his bow, and it landed next to the arrows.

He raised his hands and strode toward Zur. "Release her," he said. "I will come with you."

"Moses, what are you doing?" Zipporah whispered, looking up at him.

He clenched his jaw, trying to stop himself from fighting Zur right then and there, initiating a battle that would end in many deaths.

Zur scoffed, then jerked Zipporah to her feet. She groaned in pain but held still as he sliced the lashings about her wrists, then her ankles. With the Badrayans and Midianites both staring each other down, Moses untied the shawl about his waist and handed it to Zipporah.

But she shook her head. "Keep it until I see you again," she said, her voice ragged.

Just as Moses finished refastening the shawl about his waist, Zur stepped forward and tugged Moses's arms behind him, then lashed them together. Both men were nearly the same height and stood eye to eye. "You will be a most prized slave in Badraya," Zur said. "I doubt you'll be given a moment's rest."

"Moses," Zipporah said, standing close, watching him being bound.

He met her eyes but only briefly. It was too painful to think of their separation. "Your father is waiting on the other side of the passage. Go to him."

She reached out, but Moses shook his head.

"Go now, Zipporah," he said, hoping she'd understand that Zur and the Badrayans could change their minds at any moment. The sooner she was out of sight, the better.

She finally nodded. He watched as Zipporah half ran, half stumbled toward the Midianites. Sihon took hold of her arm and moved her behind him, shielding her from the other Badrayans. Sihon looked to Moses for confirmation.

"Go," Moses said. "Take her home and return her to her family."

Sihon nodded, then motioned for the rest of the Midianites to retreat through the passageway. Moses's last glimpse of Zipporah was of her watching him as Sihon led her toward the passageway.

Once they were gone, Moses turned back to Zur. The tribesman was already calling out orders to the other men.

"We will put the Egyptian to work right now," Zur said, nodding to a couple of his men. "Start him collecting rocks for burying the men he killed. Get the bodies and bring them down here. We will bury them before we leave."

He turned his scowling face toward Moses. "You will clean up your own mess. When we arrive in Badraya, I will let the families of the men you killed do with you what they will."

He called over a couple of men who carried spears. "Watch the Egyptian as he gathers rocks. If he doesn't obey every instruction, you may kill him."

The two men nodded, hefting their spears. One of them used his spear to cut the lashings from Moses's hands and feet. "We'll retie you when you are finished with your work."

While the rain drummed all around him, Moses worked at collecting rocks and stacking them together. After each body was brought down from the cliff above, Moses set to work covering the bodies with rocks to prevent animals from carrying away the remains.

With the rain washing off the dirt and filth of the dead men's faces, Moses was struck by how young they were. They looked to be around Peor's age. Moses didn't know if his arrows had been the ones to kill the three men, but he suddenly thought back to the evening he'd killed the Egyptian taskmaster and how he'd tried to hide what he'd done.

It seemed that death and conflict had followed him ever since. Was this God's way of punishing Moses for what he'd done? When he'd finished piling the rocks onto the third man, his head ached from exhaustion. Yesterday had been the greatest day of his life; today was possibly the worst.

But he'd do anything if it meant keeping Zipporah and her family safe. He hoped they were well on their way to Midian by now.

Zur approached Moses again, eyeing him up and down. "Your day is only beginning, Egyptian." He looked over at the men who were guarding him with spears. "Tie his hands together again. We leave now."

"Which way are we traveling?" one of the tribesmen asked.

"Over those rocks. We'll make our way down the other side of the mountain." He scoffed, looking back at Moses. "You aren't much of a replacement for a beautiful woman, but you'll bring great sport for my friends."

Moses stood in the driving rain as Zur ordered the tribesmen to break down what was left of their camp. It seemed to amount to only a single tent, a few bundles of supplies, and the two miserable goats. When the Badrayans had their supplies slung over their shoulders in satchels, Zur steered Moses through another narrow passageway, this one leading in a different direction from the one where Moses had arrived. It had rained so much by now that rivulets of water ran down the rocks.

Moses was completely soaked, his wrists ached from the ropes, and he had no idea what lay ahead of him. But at least Zipporah was safe with her father and the others. She'd be home within hours and surrounded by her family. He focused on that alone. It didn't matter what happened to him as long as his wife was safe.

The path wound down, past rocks and through growing streams of water. And then they started up an incline that was steep enough the men needed to use both their hands and feet to climb. It was difficult for Moses to balance with the limited use of his hands.

"There," one of the men up ahead of them said, coming to a stop. He was on a ledge several paces ahead of Moses, and he was looking back the way they had come.

"What is it, Rekel?" Zur asked.

Rekel shook his head. "They aren't leaving. They've taken shelter from the rain."

Zur forced Moses upward until all three of them were on the ledge. From this position, Moses could see the area the Midianites had first climbed. Rekel was right. The Midianites had traveled to the base of the mountain where they'd couched the camels, and now it looked like they had set up canopies. Apparently they were taking shelter to wait out the rain.

Moses wondered what their plans were. *Don't do anything foolish*, he thought. *Take Zipporah back home.* Having her this far from the settlement worried him—he didn't like the way Zur had treated her, and there was no telling what else he might be capable of.

"Fools," Zur muttered. "Perhaps the Egyptian's wife wants to return for another kiss."

Hot anger pulsed through Moses, and before he could consider what he was doing, he slammed his body into Zur's.

Everyone burst into action, and Moses was dragged off of Zur, Rekel lifting up Moses's arms until they burned in pain.

Zur rubbed the back of his head as he got to his feet. "Perhaps we should fight each other now, right here, Egyptian," he sneered. "Do you have a preferred method of dying?"

Moses didn't say a word; he just kept his focus on Zur's face. "What did you do to her?"

"Not enough," Zur said, his lips curling. "We were rudely interrupted by the Midianites."

Moses struggled against Rekel's grasp, but two other men grabbed his arms as well.

"Either you come with us nicely," Zur said in a sharp tone, "or we toss you off the next cliff. Your death will be slow, and when this rain ends, your body will be baked beyond recognition."

Rekel hauled Moses to his feet. "What's your decision, Egyptian?"

"I choose to live so that I can one day have my revenge," Moses spat out.

Zur laughed. "You will have your revenge when you're dead. We can fight again in heaven."

CHAPTER TWENTY-EIGHT
ZIPPORAH

The rain beat down on the canopy over Zipporah's head. She didn't know if she'd ever feel dry again. She sat huddled next to her father, with her brother and Sihon and Peor across from her. Peor's leg was bandaged, and the paleness of his face had given way to some color. Hobab had more color in his face, but his arm appeared to be totally useless for the time being. The men were discussing their next strategy—after they returned Zipporah home.

Her body trembled, not from cold but from seeing Moses captured and tied up by Zur. The man was pure evil. Over and over again, she felt his mouth on hers—his hot, disgusting breath, his calloused hands. And it made her sick. More, it made her angry.

She realized she'd lived a blessed life for many years. Midian had been relatively peaceful, and the men treated their women well. Children grew up in safety, learning to live off the land and to care for their herds. Disease was sparse, and they only feared the desert fever and the occasional childbirth gone wrong.

She tried to concentrate on what her father was talking about with the others, but her mind kept clouding with the events of the night before. Being captured and carried away by Rekel and Zur. Being forced to stay in that tent. Listening to the sounds of battle and death surrounding her while she was helpless to do anything. Watching Moses, her new husband, give himself up to the Badrayans.

A silent scream traveled up her throat, but nothing came out. She was too exhausted to even speak. When her father asked her what had happened, she hadn't been able to tell him. She knew she was fortunate, that most women would have been killed or assaulted. Even so, she felt that something irretrievable had been taken from her.

"We need a small group of men to infiltrate the Badrayan settlement," Sihon was saying. "Men who are very skilled—"

"Like Moses," Peor said. He thumped the ground. "What about the Munnah brothers?"

"Sihon is a better tracker than either of them," Jethro said.

"Agreed," Hobab said. He shifted, then winced in pain. "We can't waste time; we need to start tracking them right away."

Zipporah looked up at Sihon, whose face was grave.

"I would be happy to go," he said. "I'd even go alone, but if Moses is injured, it will be difficult to get him back by myself."

"I'll go too," Peor said, but Sihon shook his head. "If we're caught, there will be no mercy. Mother can't lose both of her sons."

"We came out here, and I went on the first tracking expedition," Peor complained.

Sihon nodded, but his expression remained grave. "Moses was with us both times. It's because of his skills that none of us was killed."

"Even with Moses's capture and trading for Zipporah, this is not over," Jethro said in a quiet voice. He clasped his hands together and looked down at them. "The Badrayans are stronger than we are, and they aren't afraid to steal from others. They've stolen from both the Hur tribe and the Baal tribe."

The men fell silent for a moment, and Zipporah stared out at the rain falling around the canopy. "Didn't Moses say he lived with the Hur tribe for a while? Before coming to Midian?"

"You're right," Jethro said.

"I remember now," Hobab said. "Moses said that a man named Asif taught him about being a shepherd and that he made him a bow and arrows."

"That's where his bow and arrows came from," Jethro finished. "They are skilled weapon makers and excellent hunters."

Zipporah looked at her father. Their gazes connected, and she saw that her father was thinking the same thing she was. "What if someone from the Hur tribe could help us?" she said.

Jethro was already nodding. "Asif." He looked at Sihon and Peor.

"It would be rare for another tribesman to risk his life for one of us," Sihon said.

"But we should try anyway," Zipporah said. "I'll come with you and beg them to help us save my husband's life."

"Zipporah," Jethro began. "You need to stay safe. Think of your mother's grief—and mine—if something were to happen to you. Hobab is too injured to continue traveling with us. He'll return you safely home."

"I know Mother will worry," she said in a quiet voice. "But don't you see, if there's any way to help Moses, I must."

Jethro rubbed her hand. Even the warmth and strength of her father's hand wasn't enough to dispel the chill in her body. "You are my daughter, and you will always have a home with me."

"I know that," Zipporah said, her eyes burning with unshed tears. "But when I married Moses yesterday, he became my home. I belong where he is."

Jethro squeezed her hand. "We will decide in the morning," he said. "We are all exhausted and will rest through the night. Tomorrow we will continue to Midian and then put together a plan."

Zipporah saw Sihon and Peor exchange looks, and she thought she understood their concern. "The longer we wait," she said, "the more chance the Badrayans will harm Moses. We can't wait until the morning." Although as she spoke, she knew that the rain made it impossible for them to travel, especially with Peor's injury. And it wasn't wise to split the group since a larger number of men would protect them from another attack.

Jethro looked to Sihon, who spread his hands. "I agree with your daughter," Sihon said. "The three of us could travel to the Hur territory and ask for help. I know they are not friendly with the Badrayans."

Jethro rubbed his face and closed his eyes for a moment. He paused so long that Zipporah wondered if he was praying. When he opened his eyes, his expression was determined. "All right. We leave immediately. Peor and Hobab will stay here and rest until the morning, then the others will return with them and continue to fortify Midian."

"Father, let me go with Zipporah," Hobab said. "My arm is getting stronger by the hour." But everyone could see that it was quite useless.

"Go home and recover, Hobab," Jethro said. We need you strong again to defend Midian's borders."

Peor tried to get to his feet. "I'm coming." His face crumpled in pain as he put weight on his injured leg. "I can ride a camel," he gasped.

Jethro grabbed Peor's arm and helped him back down onto the mat. "You need to heal so you can help us upon the return of Moses. The Badrayans won't be happy and will surely retaliate." His gaze went from Peor to Hobab. "Both of you need to be prepared."

Peor squeezed his eyes shut and nodded.

Jethro looked at Zipporah. "Are you sure you have the strength to come with us?"

"Yes," she said in a voice stronger than what she felt inside. But it would be worse to wait while the others worked out a plan. If there was any way she could help save Moses, she'd do it.

She placed a hand on Peor's and Hobab's shoulders. "Thank you for your sacrifice in coming to rescue me." She met her father's and Sihon's eyes. "Thank you both. I have never prayed so hard in my life." Her voice broke as her emotions surfaced. "But I didn't mean for Moses to be traded for me."

"We know," Jethro said, pulling her into an embrace. "I don't think anything could have stopped him from trading places if it meant your safety."

Zipporah blinked back tears. "Let's go petition the Hur tribe."

Her father and Sihon stepped out of the tent and collected the three fastest camels. Sihon procured a robe from one of the men and handed it over to Zipporah. She pulled it over her shoulders, knowing the dryness of the robe would only be temporary. The rain continued to drive down, soaking everything in sight.

Zipporah hadn't spent a lot of time riding camels any great distance, since her chores were more domestic, but she didn't let her trepidation hold her back. She climbed onto the camel that had been made ready for her and hung on tightly as it rose to its feet, rocking steeply frontward, then back. The bridle was attached to a thin leather strap she wrapped around her hand a couple of times. She then grabbed on to the long, light stick with which to touch the camel's cheeks to guide it.

"Let's go," Jethro said, urging his camel forward, slowly at first, then faster.

Zipporah mimicked everything her father and Sihon were doing, although her heart was pounding like mad. The leather strap was slick with rain, and the camel's wet fur was hard to balance on.

She hugged her knees against the camel and lowered her torso until she was practically lying on top of the camel. She tried to relax and move with the camel as it loped along the desert terrain, rain pelting them. She didn't ask her father how far the Hur settlement was; it didn't matter. She'd ride day and night if that was what it took.

So she was surprised when, a few hours later, Jethro's camel slowed.

Zipporah slowed hers as well and rose from her prone position, acutely feeling every ache in her body. The rain had tapered off, but the clouds still hung low.

"We are near their settlement now," Jethro said.

"I'm surprised no one has come to confront us yet," Sihon said.

The desert was beautiful here, perhaps due to the rain, Zipporah thought. Desert flowers grew in clumps near rocks, and their group had passed more than one grove of trees.

"There," Zipporah said, looking to her left. "Someone is coming."

The three travelers turned to watch two men wearing indigo headdresses walking toward them, spears in their hands. The men looked hardy and healthy, their skin tanned by the sun.

Jethro couched his camel, and Zipporah and Sihon followed suit. Then Jethro reached down and picked up a clump of sand and tossed it into the air, signaling they'd come in peace.

"Stay behind us," Sihon told Zipporah. "If there is any tension, claim that you are my wife."

Zipporah didn't need to be told twice. The Midianites had no recent complaints with the Hur tribe, but there were dealings she probably didn't know about. She pulled her borrowed robe tightly about her shoulders and kept her eyes on the approaching men. Were they friendly? Fierce? Would they be willing to help? What would their price be?

One of the men was taller, and the other more broad, but they both looked as if they could rival Moses and Sihon in a fight.

"We've come in peace," Jethro called out as the men drew near. He made a show of dropping his dagger onto the ground, and Sihon dropped his bow and arrows to the ground as well.

Zipporah inhaled sharply. If the Hurs weren't friendly, or even if they were in a bad mood, her group of three would now be completely at their mercy.

"You are Midianites?" the taller man said, his teeth showing deep stains. "Why have you come this far south?" Their language was more guttural than Midianite, but many of the words were similar.

The shorter man narrowed his eyes.

"We are looking for Asif," Jethro said. "He is a friend of my son-in-law."

The tall man's brows lifted. "Who are you, and who is your son-in-law?"

"I'm Jethro, priest of Midian, and this is my son-in-law Sihon and my daughter Zipporah. But my other son-in-law is an Egyptian man named Moses," Jethro said, looking back and forth between the men. "Do you remember his visit with your tribe some months ago?"

The tall man looked over at his companion, then nodded. The shorter man stepped forward. "We remember the Egyptian. What do you need Asif for?"

"Moses has been captured by the Badrayans," Sihon said, jumping in. "When he arrived in Midian, he fought against some shepherds who overtook the well where my wife and her sisters were watering their flock."

Zipporah was almost sure that one of these two men was Asif. She had to find out, and she had to make them understand. She stepped out from behind Sihon. "I am Moses's wife. We married only yesterday. In the middle of the night, the Badrayans abducted me, taking revenge for Moses defeating them in an earlier skirmish."

The two tribesmen only stared at Zipporah as she spoke, so she continued. "We are here to beg for your help. Moses spoke well of you and of his friend Asif. As you know, Moses is highly skilled, and he is valuable to our family, and—"

"You are fortunate to be alive," the taller man said, focusing on Zipporah. "And now they have taken Moses?"

"Yes," she said, her voice cracking.

"The Egyptian didn't waste much time in finding a wife," the taller tribesman said with a chuckle. He stepped forward and nodded to Jethro, then to Sihon. "I am Asif. Come to my tent, and we will discuss what might be done."

Zipporah felt as if her legs might give way, not only from the horrors of a sleepless night and the trauma of riding the camel, but also from her relief at finding that this man was a friend to Moses. She knew without a doubt that God was watching over her family. She could only pray He would preserve Moses until they could rescue him.

CHAPTER TWENTY-NINE
MOSES

The settlement of Badraya was filled with men, their eyes watchful and calculating. A few of the women looked out of their tents, staying hidden for the most part, their children peeking around their mothers' tunics. The women's eyes were soulful, even haunted, as if they had been through terrible times and could no longer trust in something good.

The children's expressions were too somber for someone so young. Moses didn't see any children laughing or running after each other. It was so different from Midian that Moses could only thank God that he'd arrived at Midian and had been taken in. If he'd arrived at Badraya, his life would have been much different. Here were a people who were downtrodden. Jethro had told him about how the desert fever had ravaged the Badrayans about two years ago and how their community was still struggling to revitalize itself.

Knowing this, Moses understood the haunting watchfulness of the Badrayans. They were a people who had been scourged and beaten. They were trying to survive like everyone else in the desert. But instead of turning to the Lord and diligently seeking a wholesome path, they'd given in to their desperation and had become the predator.

And here Moses was now, completely at their mercy.

The rain had stopped, and Moses looked for the reassuring signs of friendliness typical in Midian—large families, many flocks and herds, neighbors interacting with each other and sharing their goods, fresh water wells scattered about the settlement where the women would meet and talk, and temples where the people could worship and pay tribute to a higher being.

But then Moses realized there were none. Tent clusters spread throughout the valley, and Moses was led past them, his hands tied behind his back. The women averted their eyes as he passed, while the children only watched quietly. No child called after him or chased him as they might in Midian.

The Badrayans were a serious people. A scared people.

Up ahead stood a large building—a temple? The stone structure was more wide than tall. It was well past its days of glory, looking more like a forgotten ruin than the central gathering place of the settlement. One look at it told Moses it wasn't a sacred place of worship.

A young boy sat outside the main entrance, his deformed hand held out for offerings, his sightless eyes turned toward Moses. Moses wished he had something to offer the child and wondered if the child had a home or if he also slept where he begged.

"That child is more fortunate than you, Egyptian," Zur said with a scoff after seeing where Moses was looking. "You'll envy him soon enough."

Moses felt like a beggar, before God at least. His life was in God's hands; that he knew. Miracles had already occurred, too many to deny. Zipporah was safe with her family, and none of the Midianites had been killed in the skirmish. He was confident that Peor and Hobab would fully recover. The Midianites would continue to strengthen themselves, and Moses would take the fall—in order to prevent more attacks and deaths.

Zur led Moses into the building. They stepped into a large open room that might have been a nice gathering place at one time, or even a house of worship. But there were no priests or orderly religious rituals going on here, only filth.

Goats and chickens roamed the stone floors freely, and animal droppings were scattered everywhere. Men lounged on cushions lined against the wall as if they were waiting for something. An audience with the leader?

Two women carried trays with goblets and food upon them, serving the men who were waiting. By the women's scant clothing and bare torsos, Moses guessed they were serving more than food and drink to the men. It was clear that many of the men were drunk, and a few of them even slept amid the chaos.

He shouldn't have been surprised, having lived in Pharaoh's court and knowing the inner system, but seeing such filth out in the open made it seem more brazenly evil. Two guards stood before a massive door at the far end of the room. Zur led Moses toward them.

"I thought you were bringing us a woman," one of the guards said.

Zur laughed. "She wasn't a virgin, so I brought her husband."

The guard shook his head. "Evi will not be pleased." He pushed open the door, and Moses followed Zur into what seemed to be a throne room but which looked more like a treasury.

Not a treasury a pharaoh might have with gold and jewelry carefully cataloged and arranged on shelves, but more like a storeroom. Baskets of grain and animal skins lined the edges of the room. Clay jars were stacked on top of each other. In the middle of the room sat a stocky man on a silk cushion. He was dressed in what might once have been an all-white robe but which was now a dingy gray. He wore a gold necklace and heavy rings on his fingers.

The man rose to his feet, his eyes curious beneath his dark brows. His hair was thick and curly but not long enough to conceal the fact that his right ear was missing.

"Zur," the man said. "What's this?"

Zur gave a half bow. "This is the Egyptian who killed our brother."

Brothers? Zur and this man were brothers. Now that Moses knew this, he saw the similarities in the men's faces.

The man walked forward, his gaze intent on Moses. "What do they call you, Egyptian?"

"Moses," he rasped. The combination of exhaustion and thirst made Moses feel as if he had sand in his mouth and throat.

"Moses . . ." the man said, his tone low yet piercing. "I am Evi, chief of the Badrayans. You are now my property, and for the rest of your life, you will pay for what you've done to my family."

Moses let out the breath he'd been holding, keeping his eyes locked with Evi's.

"I am told that I'm a merciful leader," Evi continued, walking around Moses. "But that is only when I can be sure of payment. What will the Egyptians give me in return for preserving your life?"

"Nothing," Moses said, his voice barely audible.

Evi stopped in front of Moses. "Nothing?" His lips parted into a smile. "You defected from their army?"

"I am a Midianite now."

"Ah," Evi said, taking a step back. He brought his hands together and twisted one of his rings. "You have made fast friends. Tell me, Moses, what will the Midianites give me in return for your life?"

Moses's answer was quick. "Nothing. Do with me as you will."

Evi's smile returned to his face. "You must love your wife very much." He looked over at Zur. "What's the woman's name?"

"Zipporah," Zur said, the sound of her name sounding like a curse.

"Will she mourn your death, Moses?" Evi asked.

Moses didn't move. He wouldn't let this man's words affect him. He would do as these people said, and he could only pray that the skirmishes would stop between the two tribes.

"When I ask you a question, I expect an answer," Evi said, his voice rising.

"Do with me as you will," Moses repeated.

Evi tilted his head back and looked upward as if appealing to the heavens. "I see what needs to be done." His gaze was back on Moses. "Take him to the pit. There he will learn how to answer when questioned."

Moses didn't think his body could feel more pain, but he was wrong. Zur and a couple of other men were all too happy to push him back outside, and with his hands still tied behind him, Moses was led about a hundred paces away from the leader's quarters.

By now, settlers had gathered and stood watching as Moses was led toward the pit. He didn't know what to expect, but as he stood at the edge, looking down, he was relieved that there weren't any wild animals inside of it.

"You are fortunate today," Zur said. "You are still alive. I can't say that about tomorrow yet."

And then Zur shoved Moses in the back, and Moses pitched forward. As he fell, he tried to twist his body so that he'd land on his shoulder and not on his face. The ground came up hard and fast.

Moses landed on his shoulder, and he let out a groan as pain and darkness clouded his mind. After he caught his breath, he tested his movements. Pain ripped through his body, his head, his shoulder. He'd landed on his shoulder all right, and as he tried to move into a sitting position, it felt as if he'd been dragged through a fire.

Someone was shouting above him, but he couldn't see who, and his head continued to throb, drowning out the words The darkness was deep enough in the pit that Moses felt disoriented. Light came from above, but he couldn't make out his surroundings yet. He suspected the depth wasn't much greater than two standing men.

Moses exhaled slowly through the pain, trying not to move for a few moments in order to let the worst of it subside. Once he felt that he wouldn't black out, he tried to sit up again. A jolt of pain seared through him, and he gasped. His shoulder had gotten the worst of the fall, but his neck and chest hurt as well, and his head felt like it had been crushed by a stone.

He closed his eyes and breathed in and out, concentrating only on the air he was breathing in. Damp, spoiled air.

Another shout from above—a jeer—nothing he could fully comprehend. He opened his eyes and waited a few moments as his eyesight adjusted to the darkness. The walls began to take shape, and Moses realized he'd fallen to the side of a pile of rocks. If he'd landed on the rocks, he might not be breathing now.

He carefully rolled onto his side, stopping every so often to let his body adjust to the new positions. When he was half sitting, half propping himself up, he saw that the pit was no larger than the length of a man. If he stood, the edge of the pit would be high over his head, but it would not be impossible to climb out.

Especially if he stacked the rocks.

Moses looked for anything that might have been left behind by another prisoner he could use to cut his lashings. He pushed his feet against the rocks, moving them one by one, looking for a piece of chert or perhaps even a dagger. But as he overturned each rock with his foot, his heart fell a notch. There was nothing.

He bent his legs and leaned forward. His only choice was to hope he could loosen the lashings. He rotated his wrists, nearly blacking out from the pain of the lashings cutting into his skin. But he gritted his teeth and continued to focus on stretching the bindings.

Something fell next to him, and Moses heard laughter from above. He looked up to see a couple of men peering over the edge of the pit. Moses looked over to what had dropped. A desert rat. The thing looked worse than Moses felt. It was nearly skin and bones, and it ran to one of the walls and started to dig.

Moses watched it for a moment, completely unbothered about sharing the pit with a varmint, then he went back to working on the lashings. The men above eventually moved on, although Moses could hear conversations filtering down. Someone must be guarding the pit, but it was hard to know. Whenever Moses looked up, his head started throbbing again and blackness crowded his vision.

The lashings were getting looser, or perhaps it was his imagination. At one point, he had to lie down, but he continued to move his wrists back and forth. He clenched his jaw against the pain vibrating up his arms. He could feel it—they were nearly loose enough to break free.

And then his wrists came loose from the lashings.

Moses gasped in disbelief. He brought his aching arms forward and hung his head while he focused on catching his breath. The desert rat was still clawing at the wall. More voices came from above, but Moses was too exhausted to even look up. He curled up on the wet dirt, telling himself that in moments, his strength would return.

The tribesmen would let him out of the pit, feed him, give him water, and then put him to work. Anything would be better than lying in this dark tomb-like place.

Something landed on his hip—sharp and painful. He lifted his head to see what had happened now.

Several men stood at the edge of the pit above him, carrying rocks in their hands. One of the men smiled as Moses tried to sit up but instead collapsed back to the earth. Another rock landed on Moses, this one hitting his leg. He flinched, which only drew laughter from above. A rock hit his neck, and Moses wrapped his arms about his head as more rocks landed on him.

He'd been thrown into the pit to be stoned.

CHAPTER THIRTY
ZIPPORAH

Zipporah wiped the perspiration and rain from her face. Every part of her body ached, and riding on the camel only increased the pain. But she held on with determination, her body pressed against the camel's back as it strode through the desert.

Her father was behind her, and Sihon and Asif rode ahead of her. There was no slowing down for any of them. Night had long since fallen, and according to Asif, the Badrayans were masters at torture.

"If they had taken you to their settlement, they would have simply sacrificed you," Asif had told her. "It would have been quick and somewhat painless. Ironically, they are kinder to their female captives. But they won't be so merciful to the Egyptian. The Badrayans are a bloodthirsty lot."

Zipporah shuddered to think of it now. They had to find a way to get Moses free before Badrayans killed him. She understood now the desperation that had driven Moses to trade himself for her. She felt the same way. Was it possible to be married for only a few hours yet be willing to trade one's life for one's husband? Yes.

Moses had only defended and protected Midian from the moment of his arrival on their tribal land. But more than that, he was family. He was a part of her. He was her husband. Her eyes stung with tears, even though she'd been sure that she couldn't cry anymore.

The rain had started again, and while it was a gift from heaven to the barren land, it made traveling precarious. The camels were ornery as their footing slipped more than once.

"There," Asif said, slowing his camel and pointing ahead. "That rise is where the Badrayan land begins. There will be no fires tonight to guide us in."

Zipporah and Jethro came to a stop beside Asif.

"That is good for us," Jethro said. "They will be keeping to their tents. Fewer people will witness our arrival."

"Where do we go first?" Zipporah asked, scanning the outline of tents up ahead. The night was deeper and darker than any she'd ever remembered. Clouds covered the moon, and even the stars were hidden.

"You will stay here," Asif said. "Keep the camels together and keep them quiet."

"No," Zipporah said. "If he's injured, you'll need my help." She looked to her father and Sihon for help.

"I'm afraid Asif is right," Jethro said. "The camels are unpredictable in this rain, and if they run off, we'll be captured before we can make it back to Midian."

Zipporah knew that once the men crossed into enemy territory, she'd be left alone. She couched her camel, then watched as the men climbed off of theirs. Asif and Sihon had already slung the goatskins full of strong wine over their shoulders; they planned to give the wine to the guards who watched over Moses. Asif said the specially prepared wine would put the guards to sleep. Her father embraced her, saying in a quiet voice, "Pray for us."

She didn't know if that made her feel better or worse. "I've been praying nonstop for hours," she said, leaning against her father and inhaling his rain-soaked scent. "I won't stop now."

"If I don't return—"

"Father, we've made it this far," she said.

But he grasped her hand. "If I don't return, tell your mother I love her. Tell her I don't regret this mission."

"I'll tell her," she said, her voice tight. She willed her tears back until the men had left her side. Then she crumpled to the ground and covered her mouth with her hand, keeping her tears silent.

The men hurried away with the goatskins of wine over their shoulders and hope in their hearts.

Zipporah burrowed against the camel as the rain started up again. She pulled her robe tightly about her and closed her eyes. She didn't know how long she'd have to wait, and she could only pray that the men would come back with Moses.

* * *

Someone nudged her shoulder, and she realized she'd fallen asleep. Her eyes flew open, and she stared in the darkness at her father's face.

"Moses?" she whispered, looking past him, trying to see if her husband was there too.

"They are meeting us at the edge of the valley," Jethro said. "They're waiting for us."

Zipporah scrambled to her feet, her head spinning from the quick movements. "How is he? Is he alive?"

"He is," Jethro said, his voice strained.

Zipporah grasped her father's arm. "What is it? Is he hurt badly?"

Her father looked away for a moment, then back to her. "He's alive, and I believe he'll recover. Moses is a strong man. We need to get out of here as quickly as possible."

Zipporah held back her many questions. *He's alive*, she consoled herself over and over, letting that propel her into action. She followed her father, riding on one camel and leading the other. Jethro urged his camel into a near run, and Zipporah tried to keep up. She was becoming more adept at riding a camel, but she knew it would take her body days to recover.

What had happened to Moses? she wondered. What had he undergone? And would they be able to get him away safely?

"There," Jethro said, slowing his camel and pointing.

Zipporah didn't see anything except the low sand hills.

He brought his fingers to his lips and gave out a low whistle. Beyond one of the sand hills, a dark form arose. Asif motioned for them to come over. Then Sihon appeared. Was Moses too injured to stand? Zipporah urged her camel up the slope toward the waiting men.

There on the ground lay Moses, unmoving. Zipporah was off her camel without giving it time to kneel, and she rushed to Moses's side. His eyes were closed, and one of the men had covered him with a robe.

She touched his face, whispering, "Moses. Can you hear me? It's Zipporah."

He barely seemed to be breathing. She lifted the robe from his torso, seeing plenty of scrapes and cuts, but nothing that looked serious. "What happened?" she asked Sihon as he knelt beside her.

"They stoned him," Sihon said, his voice bitter. "We have no idea the extent of his injuries. They will manifest themselves soon enough."

"Why?" Zipporah cried out, mostly to herself. "Why did you have to take my place?" She leaned over Moses, resting her cheek against his bare chest. His heart beat strong and steady, and Zipporah took courage. Then she felt a hand on her shoulder.

"Zipporah," Moses said, his voice low and raspy.

She lifted her head to see Moses's eyes open. "You're awake."

His mouth moved slightly upward and he said, "Yes."

"Oh, Moses." She leaned over him and kissed one cheek, then the other.

His smile widened, and he lifted a hand and touched her hair. "You're here."

"I am," she said, feeling like laughing and crying at the same time.

Asif and Jethro crossed over to Moses and knelt down. "How are you feeling?" Jethro asked.

Moses rose on his right elbow, his smile fading as he looked at everyone gathered around him. "Why did you rescue me? This battle will never end if both sides keep retaliating."

"You're family," Jethro said in a voice thick with emotion. "Even before you married my daughter. We won't ever leave you behind."

"They will seek revenge," Moses started to say, but Jethro cut him off.

"It's the way of desert life." He leaned toward Moses and placed his hands on each side of his face. "You can always depend on us."

Moses stared into Jethro's eyes for a moment, then finally nodded.

"There," Jethro said. "You're looking healthier already. Besides, I can't have grandchildren from Zipporah if you are in a Badrayan pit."

Moses pushed himself into a sitting position, his face paling with the effort. "I'm pleased that you brought camels." He looked at Zipporah. "Sihon told me you insisted on going with him to ask for Asif's help."

"She's one stubborn wife," Asif said with a chuckle.

Moses looked over at Asif. "How drunk are the guards?"

"They'll wake with the sun, and when they do, they won't be happy to find you missing," Asif said. He looked toward the horizon that was already beginning to gray.

"I'm ready," Moses said, moving to his feet and exhaling in pain.

Jethro and Zipporah grasped Moses's arms to offer support.

"Are you sure you can travel?" Jethro asked.

Moses's face was still quite pale, and he gripped the staff Jethro handed him. Zipporah took hold of his other arm.

"I'm feeling stronger by the moment," he said in a quiet voice. "I can't exactly account for what happened in that pit. When those stones were coming down upon me, I moved close to the rock pile, and that created a barrier for most of them." He took a shallow breath, leaning heavily on the staff. "I only felt the first few rocks hit, and then . . . nothing."

Everyone was quiet, staring at Moses in wonder.

"Nothing?" Zipporah whispered. "What do you mean?"

"Look," Moses said, pulling his robe open so they could see his torso. "I don't think the bigger rocks hit me. I didn't feel them, and there's no tenderness or bruising."

Zipporah ran her fingers across his chest. "How is that possible?"

His gaze was intense as he focused on her. "It can only be possible through the Lord." He closed his eyes. When he opened them again, he stood taller, straighter. "I was protected in that pit by the Lord. He saved my life. For what purpose, I do not know."

Zipporah wrapped her arms about his waist, and he pulled her close.

The men were quiet, and finally Jethro said, "Let us leave this place and get everyone back home to heal and to rest. We will face tomorrow when we must."

Zipporah watched in wonder as Moses successfully climbed onto the camel. He motioned for her to join him, and she sat in front of him. With his arms wrapped about her waist, warm and firm, she felt safe. Whole.

She leaned against his chest as the camel strode through the desert back toward Midian. "You were truly stoned?" she asked in a quiet voice.

"Yes," Moses said. "I don't think they expected me to survive. And truthfully, I didn't expect to either." His breath stirred her hair. "But I was happy to take your place, and I'd do it again."

Zipporah released a sigh and let her eyes slide shut as she settled into her husband's warm embrace. Whatever the future held, at least they would face it together.

CHAPTER THIRTY-ONE
MOSES

Five years later

"Father!" the young boy said, running toward Moses.

"Gershom, where have you been?" Moses said, holding out his arms. His son ran straight into them, wrapping his arms and legs about Moses in a full embrace.

For a moment, Moses buried his face in the four-year-old's dark, curly hair, smelling sun and sand and damp skin. Even though the sun had just risen and they had finished the morning meal only moments ago, Gershom was already using up more energy than most adults did in an entire day.

"I've been helping Mother cover the morning fire," Gershom said. "Did you know I am four today, again?"

Moses chuckled and set his son down. "You are four *again* today. You're almost old enough to stay overnight with me and the sheep."

Gershom drew back his shoulders and pushed out his chest, keeping his dark brown eyes on his father—eyes so much like Zipporah's. "I'm not scared to sleep in the mountains."

"I didn't say you were scared," Moses said, crouching down to meet Gershom's solemn gaze. "But your mother would miss you too much."

Gershom seemed to consider this information, and a smile grew on his face, accompanied by a pleased look in his eyes. "She *would* miss me too much," he declared.

"*Who* would miss you?" Zipporah's voice came from around the side of the tent. She walked into view, carrying their youngest son, Eliezer, who was nearing five months old.

As soon as Eliezer saw Moses, he reached his arms up and started to fuss.

"He wants his father, it seems," Zipporah said with a smile. "Do you have to leave with the flocks for so many weeks?"

Moses crossed to his wife and bent to kiss her cheek. He lingered for a moment while Eliezer babbled between them. Zipporah handed the baby to him and said, "Your sons miss you when you're gone."

He lifted his brows as he settled Eliezer against his chest. "Do you miss me when I'm gone?" he asked Zipporah in a low voice.

Her face flushed. Moses chuckled, pleased that even after five years of marriage and two sons he could still make his wife blush. If anything, she looked more beautiful than when he'd first met her. After years of marriage, he knew every expression on her face and could interpret them most of the time. Well, some of the time.

"What's wrong?" he asked, not sure how to interpret her wide-eyed expression this morning.

"Nothing is wrong," Zipporah said, ruffling her hand through Gershom's hair. "Why would you say that?"

"Can I hold Eliezer?" Gershom interrupted, bouncing on his toes and reaching for the baby.

"Only for a moment," Moses said, bending down to help Gershom hold his brother without dropping him or making him cry. When Moses looked back up at Zipporah, she'd turned away and was inspecting one of their tent panels.

He took the baby back from Gershom. "Can you make sure the waterskins are filled to the top?" he asked his son.

Gershom grinned and scampered off, disappearing around the tent, where Zipporah had set out the supplies for Moses to take on his journey. He'd only be gone a few weeks, but since the birth of Eliezer, it had been harder to leave Zipporah with two children for even one night. They had set up their homestead not too far from Jethro and Qurayya, so Zipporah had plenty of help if she needed it, although she was usually too stubborn to ask.

Now, with Gershom distracted for a few moments, he crossed to Zipporah and put his arm around her shoulder. "Do you want to tell me what's wrong?"

She brushed a hand against her cheek, and Moses turned her to face him. She blinked rapidly, but she couldn't hide the fact that there were tears in her eyes.

"I just . . ." she started. "Oh, it doesn't make sense. I am just overanxious that you are leaving this time. You've gone into the mountains by yourself more than once, so I know I shouldn't be worried. But you are traveling farther than usual."

Moses didn't have to ask why she worried this time. Since his Badrayan capture, the Midianite shepherds hadn't traveled alone unless absolutely necessary. There had been a few more skirmishes after Moses's escape, but things had been quiet for the past four years since the desert fever had again raged through the settlement of Badraya.

Still, the Midianites rarely traveled alone.

"The Lord will watch over me," Moses said.

Zipporah heaved a sigh. "Yes, I know. But I can't push away this feeling."

Her words were sharp, but Moses knew better than to take offense. She was just concerned about him, and he was grateful for a wife who loved him so much. "I will return safely." He pressed a kiss against her temple.

She leaned against him and wrapped her arms about his waist.

"In a few years, Gershom will be old enough to come with me," he said.

"Maybe I'll become a shepherd as well."

Moses chuckled. "And what would that entail? Packing our tent? Bringing our camels? Your mother and father?"

She laughed, her warmth vibrating against him. "It would certainly be an adventure."

Moses held her tightly against him until Eliezer started to squirm between them. "Someone needs to feed the flocks, unless you want me to become a traveling merchant."

Zipporah tilted her face upward. "I could travel. You could show me your homeland."

Moses shook his head and smiled. "It would take an act of God to get me to return there." He brushed his fingers along her cheek. "I will be fine in the mountains. God will watch over me, and you, here at home. We need to have faith in that. If we didn't have faith, neither of us would ever leave our tent." He bent to kiss her softly.

"Would that be such a terrible idea?" she asked, then kissed him back.

"We would starve and waste away," Moses said, his voice growing quieter.

Zipporah smiled. "But at least we'd be together."

"What about Gershom and Eliezer?"

"Hmmm." Zipporah cradled Eliezer more tightly against her chest. "I guess we should feed our children."

Moses bent down and kissed the baby's head. "I suppose we should." He grasped Zipporah's hand. "I will return before you know it."

"I know you will," she whispered, looking down at their clasped hands.

"It's finished, Father!" Gershom shouted, running around the corner of the tent. "And I didn't get any sand in the water this time."

Moses released his wife and laughed. "Thank you, son." Moses knew very well that there would be plenty of sand mixed in with the water. It wouldn't matter though—it would just make him think of his oldest son while he was spending the days alone in the desert.

"Can I walk with you to the well?" Gershom asked. "I promise to run straight back home to Mother."

"Not this time," Moses said, looking over at Zipporah. The relief on her face made it evident that he'd said the right thing. He'd be traveling to the valley of Horeb, farther than he'd gone before. But the lush valley reported to be there would be ideal for grazing the flock for a few weeks. "Mother needs your help. Aren't you going to visit your cousin Oreb?"

Gershom's face brightened. "Yes! We're going today to visit him."

Moses chuckled and tousled his son's hair. Then he kissed the baby and pulled Zipporah in for one more embrace.

"Take care of your mother," he said to Gershom, who gave a stiff nod.

Moses slung his bow and quiver of arrows over his shoulder, then grabbed his satchel of food and took his staff in hand. The sheep were waiting, and the sun was only rising higher, growing hotter.

He left the family homestead and headed first toward the sea, then beyond it, toward the mountains. Over the past five years, he'd become a part of Midian, and he loved the people and the desert life. Jethro had entrusted him to watch over his large flock of sheep, and it was with honor that Moses had cared for them. Now, with sand beneath his feet and clothed in a simple tunic, walking with the sheep was akin to a religious ritual for Moses. He'd miss his wife and two sons, but spending time alone in the desert was rejuvenating.

He'd grown to love the absolutely quiet nights when his thoughts expanded well beyond himself and all the way up to the heavens. He was able to contemplate the nature of God and how all things came together for the benefit of righteous men. Moses had no doubt that the Lord had protected him during the multiple skirmishes with the Badrayans. God had also preserved his wife and was now blessing him with sons.

Sons who were a mixture of Hebrew and Midianite. And it was during his trips with the flocks that he allowed himself to think about his Egyptian mother, Bithiah. Had she ever married? Would she ever have children of her own? He also thought about the family he'd never met—his Hebrew mother and father. He wondered whether he had any siblings. Perhaps he had sisters who had been spared during Pharaoh's edict to kill all male infants.

Moses spent the next several days driving the flocks toward the sea, then continued on. On the fifth day, as Moses approached the mountain range far from his home, familiar misgivings started in his chest. He'd spent a lot of time in other mountains fighting for his life, mountains that rose from the desert floor as these did, imposing in their sharp austerity.

Moses thought about the last time he'd seen Asif—a few months before. The two men reunited a couple of times each year. They had a bond that could never be broken, and Moses was grateful that somehow he'd happened upon men of integrity. He could very well be a slave in a settlement somewhere or, more likely, dead.

As the sun climbed in the sky, Moses started up one of the slopes that would soon lead to a fertile valley where the sheep could graze. The rainy season had recently ended, and there was plenty of desert grass to be found. Traditionally, the tribes throughout the area were more inclined to be peaceful during the months of plenty. It was when food and water were scarce that desperation set in.

A sheep knocked against Moses's leg, hurrying ahead as it bleated. The other sheep picked up their pace as well, smelling the abundant grass ahead. Moses smiled as he watched them shift against each other through a narrow passage that led to the valley of Horeb.

After traveling farther than he ever had, he followed the sheep into a lush valley. The beautiful greens and browns spread before him like a finely woven rug. The deep, rich colors reminded him of the tapestries hung along the palace corridors in Egypt.

Moses moved up the opposite slope to where there was a collection of bushes and trees with plenty of shade. The trip to this distant place had been worth it. He sat in the shade of the trees where he could watch the sheep as they meandered the valley, eating their fill. He opened the goatskin and took a deep drink of water. There wasn't any taste of sand yet. That would come as he neared the end of the water, as he had learned the last time.

As Moses sat and watched the flocks, the sun slid across the sky, and the shade shifted. It was remarkable, he thought, how time moved and how the earth provided sustenance for all living things.

Moses closed his eyes for a moment, contemplating all that he was grateful for. He had a new family—a large, extended family—and he couldn't be more content. Jethro's flocks were doing well under Moses's care and increased each year. Zipporah was a wonderful mother, and his boys would soon grow into strong and intelligent men. There was nothing Moses lacked or needed.

His questions about his birth family might never be answered, but not every man was as fortunate as he. And that would be enough for him.

"Moses." The whisper came deep and soft, almost inaudible, yet tangible.

He opened his eyes, certain he had started dreaming and nearly fallen asleep sitting up. The heat had suddenly become too strong, although he was still beneath the shade. Moses moved to his feet, feeling more tired than he'd expected.

"Moses." It was the same voice. Clear, deep, vibrating, sounding like it came from somewhere deep within Moses, but that was impossible. Moses hadn't spoken, and he was completely alone on Horeb's mountainside.

Moses brushed his hand against his forehead and found himself perspiring. It was as if the sun had moved closer to the earth and was baking against his back. He turned to pick up his goatskin of water, then stopped. The bush he'd been sitting near was on fire. Flames reached upward and crackled with fervor.

He knew that on the hottest days sometimes a dry plant or bush might burst into flames, but today was particularly mild. Moses took a couple of steps back, knowing that the water in the goatskins he'd brought with him was too precious to waste on a desert fire.

The sheep were far enough away that they wouldn't fret and stampede. But would the fire spread? And if so, how quickly? Moses scanned the mountainside and saw that the surrounding bushes, grass, and the nearby trees were quite green. They wouldn't burn too fiercely, and perhaps that meant the fire wouldn't spread along the mountainside.

Still, Moses stepped back even farther, and then he noticed that although the bush was on fire, the branches and leaves weren't actually burning. He furrowed his brow and looked more closely. Perhaps he was asleep and was dreaming. What he saw before him was impossible.

Now he took a few steps closer, holding his hands out in front of him. Sure enough, the heat of the flames increased as he moved closer. The flames snapped and crackled, and a few sparks flew out into the air, extinguishing themselves before they landed on the ground.

And then Moses knew he must be dreaming because of what he saw next. A man appeared, standing above the bush, the flames rising to surround him. He was clothed in brilliant white—more brilliant than the sun, and Moses squinted to see the image before him. What a strange dream.

Moses rubbed his eyes, then blinked rapidly, clearing his vision. Was he awake, or was he dreaming? If so, it was a strange and wonderful dream—seeing persons and bushes that were afire but not blackened with burning.

He crouched to see if there was anything under the bush that might make it burn so strangely.

"Moses . . ." That voice again. "Moses."

Moses rose and looked up at the image, or man, hovering above the bush. He opened his mouth to question the person, or the heavenly being—bumps rose along his arms at the thought.

"Here am I," the voice said. It was no longer a voice in his head but the messenger speaking to Moses.

He didn't know what to do; he still didn't know if he was dreaming or if he was awake. Drawn toward the bush, he took a few steps forward, feeling the heat increase again.

"Draw not nigh hither," the messenger said. "Take off thy shoes from thy feet, for the place whereon you stand is holy ground."

Moses's mind spun in a hundred different directions. This man, this image, was real and not just in his imagination. A holy being from heaven. How else was any of this possible? Moses slid his sandals from his feet. He didn't know where to look, what questions to ask. He could only stare at the floating image before him.

"I am the God of thy father, the God of Abraham, the God of Isaac, and the God of Jacob," the being said, His words rocking Moses.

God? The God of my father, of Abraham? Isaac? Jacob? The words wrapped around Moses's soul. *I am Hebrew, and this is the Hebrew God. That means He is my God.*

Moses could no longer believe that what he was seeing was a dream. For this was God. The God of the world and of the heavens. Moses covered his face, his breath coming short, afraid that God would see every thought and know every word and it would be enough for Moses to cease living.

But the voice continued. The voice of *God*, Moses reminded himself.

"I have seen the affliction of my people which are in Egypt," the voice said.

Egypt. The word reverberated through Moses's mind. *My people. God is speaking about the Hebrews as His people.*

"I have heard their cry by reason of their taskmasters, for I know their sorrows," God continued.

Moses sank to his knees. God knew everything, and that meant He knew about Moses killing the Egyptian taskmaster. *I have seen the Hebrews' sorrows as well*, he thought. The air around him pulsated with energy. The fire that sprang from the bush and encompassed God's image continued to burn without consuming anything.

"And I am come down to deliver them out of the hand of the Egyptians," God said. "I will bring them up out of that land, to a land that flows with milk and honey—to the place of the Canaanites, the Hittites, the Amorites, the Perizzites, the Hivites, and the Jebusites."

As God spoke of the peoples that populated the lands northward, Moses tried to imagine how God would bring these events to pass. Would it be a large-scale battle? Many of those tribes had fierce natures, and Moses had learned of their battles and conflicts through his studies in the palace.

God continued to speak, His words vibrating through Moses's very soul. "Behold, the cry of the children of Israel is come unto me, and I have seen their oppressions by the Egyptians."

Moses inhaled. He had seen the oppression of the Hebrews as well—he had lived among it his entire life.

God's voice changed then, growing softer yet firmer at the same time. "Come now, and I will send thee unto Pharaoh, that thou mayest bring my people the children of Israel out of Egypt."

Moses felt the breath leave him. God was asking *him* to bring the Hebrews out of Egypt? "Who am I?" Moses said, his voice barely above a whisper. He didn't know if he could even speak in God's presence, but when he tried, the words came out. "Who am I that I should go to Pharaoh and bring the children of Israel out of Egypt?"

Moses had run away from his home and people and way of life. He'd been gone for years, and even if there had been a calamity and his loved ones had been killed, there was still an edict for his death. And an edict by a pharaoh could never be changed until a new edict replaced it.

Moses was a Midianite now, far from the Egyptian royal he used to be.

But God was before him, and God ruled the heavens and the earth. Moses felt a shudder pass through his body, like an intense warmth that made him feel as if he could rise off the ground with only a thought. And that was when God's next words came.

"I will be with thee, and when thou hast brought the people out of Egypt, you shall serve God upon this mountain."

Moses tried to comprehend what God was telling him. He was to rescue the Hebrews and bring them here. The Hebrew slaves numbered in the thousands . . . perhaps hundreds of thousands . . . and Moses was a shepherd from Midian. A simple man who had a wife and two young boys. A man of the desert who spent his days herding his father-in-law's flocks.

He raised his eyes to see God. The image remained, and deep inside God's gaze, Moses saw himself for a moment as God must see him.

And Moses saw that all possibilities were truth in God's eyes. And they were without number.

CHAPTER THIRTY-TWO
ZIPPORAH

Zipporah stood facing the wind. The desert was angry today, pushing the sand up from the earth and blasting it against the trees and tender green grass. By her calculation, Moses should have returned last evening, but now it was the following afternoon.

Not being able to stand it any longer, Zipporah had taken her children to her mother and walked out into the desert to a location where she could still see her family tent yet be on the lookout for Moses.

"Where are you, Moses?" she said, throwing her words against the wind. It wasn't yet time to worry, but she did. Any number of events could have delayed Moses. A sick sheep, a visit with another shepherd, or an encounter with a Badrayan tribesman. Zipporah tried not think about that. Things had been quiet between the tribes for a few years.

Zipporah cataloged what Moses had taken with him—plenty of water, enough food, his bow and arrows, his dagger, his staff . . .

She brought her hand up to shield her eyes from the blowing sand. *Any moment*, she thought. *Any moment*, she pled, turning her thoughts into a prayer.

And then she saw him . . . at least she hoped it was Moses. She waited, holding her breath as the figure came down a ridge and headed toward Midian. Relief flooded through her as she picked out the sheep trailing behind him. They must be gorged if they were moving so slowly.

As Zipporah watched, shielding her eyes from the increasing blowing sand, she realized Moses was walking differently. Much slower than she expected. Had he been injured? Had he encountered hostile tribesmen after all?

He seemed to stand straighter though, and there was no evident limp as he walked. So then why did looking at her husband feel different?

"Zipporah!" her father's voice called out, and she turned to see him approaching. He had his headdress wrapped around his nose and mouth, leaving only his eyes to peer out.

"He's coming," she told her father.

His eyes crinkled, telling her that he was smiling. Zipporah believed that her father was as relieved as she was, even though he'd told her over and over not to worry.

Her father joined her, and together they watched as Moses approached. By her father's silence, she knew that he was noticing the changes in Moses as well. He was closer now, and Zipporah could see that the differences were indeed real. Moses wasn't wearing a headdress, and the dark hair that had grown from its shaved Egyptian style to the long locks of a shepherd had changed in color. Instead of the deep brown, it was now streaked with white. The skin that had been deeply tanned by the sun now appeared golden, almost alabaster.

"What's happened to him?" she said in a quiet voice.

"I don't know," Jethro said. "If I hadn't known Moses as my son-in-law for the past five years, I would have said he is a different man."

"It *is* Moses, isn't it?" Zipporah said.

"Yes," her father said.

It was Moses's face, his height, and his broad shoulders, but his skin and hair were different. Zipporah stared, unable to look away.

It was as if he could see right into her soul and know her thoughts in the blink of an eye. Why she had this impression she didn't know. Her father clasped her hand in his, and she gripped his hand back.

Something had happened to Moses, and they were witnesses to his changed countenance.

He was within hearing distance now. The sheep started to pick up speed, recognizing their home area. They passed Moses, but he didn't seem to notice. He continued forward, shouldering his satchel, goatskins, bow and arrows, his hand gripping his staff.

His stride was long and sure and measured. It was as if he walked with no effort and could continue walking for another day and night.

She gripped her father's hand tighter. As Moses neared, Zipporah felt out of breath for some reason. She didn't know what to say. She didn't know if she could embrace him or even touch him. Had he been ill? Had he been scorched by the sun—or the opposite—illuminated somehow? It was like the moon was walking toward her.

"Moses," Jethro said, finding his voice. "What's happened, son?"

Moses didn't reply but stopped in front of them both. He was silent for a moment, yet Zipporah could feel the energy thrumming from him as if he were a bird waiting to burst into flight.

"Moses?" she whispered, stepping forward, reaching out her hand.

He enclosed her hand in his, then brought it to his heart. There she felt it beating a steady rhythm.

He was home. Whatever he'd been through didn't matter, so long as he was here, with her, and safe.

Finally Moses spoke, and his voice was deeper, yet softer than Zipporah had ever heard it. "I saw the face of God."

The wind that blew around them carried his words in circles, spinning about Zipporah and her father. She wasn't sure if she could remain standing. But Moses was holding her hand, and it was as if his strength and surety were flowing directly into her.

"He appeared to me in the midst of a burning bush on Mount Horeb," Moses said.

All other sounds faded as Moses told her about God's request that he return to Egypt to deliver His people, the children of Israel. The Hebrew slaves. Moses's people. Moses's family.

"How is this to be done?" Jethro asked, his voice barely above a whisper. "How are you to deliver the children of Israel from the pharaoh of Egypt?"

"I asked God the same thing," Moses said. His gaze fell for the first time since Zipporah spotted him walking toward her. "God told me to tell the Hebrews that the God of their fathers has sent me. And when they ask for proof, and they ask me for God's name, I am to tell them that I was sent by *I Am*."

Zipporah stayed silent; she couldn't speak a word as Moses continued. "God said I should tell the children of Israel that the Lord God of their fathers, the God of Abraham, the God of Isaac, and the God of Jacob, has sent me."

Jethro reached toward Moses and touched his shoulder. Moses placed his hand over Jethro's. "God wants me to gather the elders of Israel together and tell them that the Lord has visited them and has seen what is being done to them in Egypt. God will bring them out of their affliction and lead them to the land of the Canaanites, a land that flows with milk and honey."

"The elders of Israel who live in Egypt?" Zipporah asked, her mind trying to catch up with all that Moses was saying. She didn't doubt that he'd seen the face of God, for Moses was so changed.

"Yes," Moses said, his gaze moving to her. "The pharaoh who sought to take my life is now dead, and his son Ramses rules over Egypt. I am to accompany the elders of Israel and visit the pharaoh of Egypt and beseech him to allow the Hebrews to journey into the wilderness that they may sacrifice unto the Lord."

"How can the new pharaoh just let all of those slaves go?" Jethro asked.

"He won't, at first," Moses said. He stepped toward Zipporah and linked his fingers with hers. "Pharaoh will not let the children of Israel go, but God will smite Egypt with all of His wonders. And after the wonders, Pharaoh will let the Hebrews go."

"What sorts of wonders?" Zipporah asked.

His grip tightened on his staff, and his words seemed to falter. Jethro motioned toward him. "Come into my tent, out of this wind, and tell us what else God told you."

"My tent is empty," Zipporah said. "The boys are with Mother. Let's go there."

As she led the way, Zipporah felt her legs tremble. If she hadn't seen Moses's changed countenance, would she have believed his words? She knew she would. But *Egypt*? She wondered how much things had changed since Moses had lived there. Would his friends remember him? Her skin prickled at the thought.

Zipporah breathed easier. If Ramses had been Moses's friend in the past, perhaps he'd remember him with fondness. As it was, Zipporah could hardly imagine any pharaoh of Egypt releasing all of the Hebrew slaves without some sort of compensation.

They reached her tent, and as they stepped inside, she was grateful the boys were with their grandmother. Inside it was quiet, protected from the wind, and it gave Zipporah a chance to take a much-needed drink of water. She offered water to Moses, and he drank it down as if he hadn't had a drink in days.

"Are you all right?" Zipporah asked him. "Do you need something to eat?"

"No, the water is fine," Moses said. "I have been so occupied with thinking over what God told me I haven't paid much attention to my body."

"You are changed, Moses," Zipporah said in a soft voice. "Your hair is different, and your skin shines like polished brass."

He was quiet for a moment, looking from Zipporah to Jethro, then he said, "I have changed on the inside as well. The Lord told me that the Hebrews will not leave Egypt empty-handed." He looked down at his hands. "Still, I doubted the Lord's mission for me. I told Him that the Hebrews would not believe that I'd seen and spoken to God."

"And what was His response?" Jethro asked.

"The Lord told me to cast my staff upon the ground," Moses continued. "When I did, it turned into a serpent."

Zipporah stared at Moses.

Moses offered a half smile. "It was as real as any snake I've ever seen. I jumped out of its way, but the Lord told me to pick it up by the tail."

She gasped. A snakebite was the most fatal of all the desert calamities.

"When I picked up the tail of the serpent, it became a rod again." He reached for the staff he'd brought into the tent with him. "This was a serpent four days ago."

"And this will prove to the Hebrews that you have seen God," Jethro stated. "So you will perform this miracle for those people."

Moses nodded. "But that's not all. The Lord told me to put my hand into my robe, and when I removed it, it was as leprous as snow." He lifted his hand to show Zipporah and Jethro that it had changed back. "After I again thrust it into my robe, my hand turned back to healthy flesh."

She reached for Moses's hand and examined it. There was no sign of leprous sores.

"They will believe you," Jethro said. "I believe you."

Moses fell quiet, and the silence thickened in the tent until Zipporah said, "That's not all the Lord told you, is it?"

"The Lord told me that if the Egyptians don't believe the first two signs," he said, "then I am to give another sign. I will gather water from the River Nile and pour it onto the ground. There it will turn to blood upon the dry land and then spread into the River Nile and canals."

Zipporah looked over at her father, whose face had paled.

"I told the Lord I am not eloquent in the Hebrew language. How am I supposed to convince the elders of Israel of my mission?" Moses said. "Your family accepted me right away and were patient in teaching me your language. But the Hebrews will look upon me as an Egyptian—a royal Egyptian. I know only a few Hebrew words, and I'm not familiar with their beliefs and traditions. Why would they trust me?"

Jethro nodded and started to say, "The Lord will provide a way—"

"Yes," Moses said, his face reddening. "I was sorely rebuked by God. He told me that He created man's mouth, that He made people deaf, dumb, seeing, or blind. God said that I will be His mouthpiece and that He will tell me what to say."

Zipporah's skin prickled despite the warmth inside the tent.

"I am a stubborn man, though," Moses said. "And God grew angry with me when I was still not convinced that I should be His spokesman. He told me about Aaron the Levite and called him my brother." Moses met Zipporah's gaze. "Do you think God meant that this Aaron is my true brother, or a brother in heritage?"

"I don't know," Zipporah said. "You never found out who your true parents were. But if God called him your brother, then perhaps Aaron the Levite is your brother."

Moses ran his hand slowly over his hair. "God told me that Aaron the Levite speaks well and that he will come to meet me on my journey to Egypt. And when Aaron sees me, he will rejoice in our meeting."

"He must be your brother, then," Zipporah whispered, feeling the tears burn in her eyes. Moses had a brother, a brother he'd never met. "God doesn't only want you to bring the Hebrew slaves out of bondage; He wants you to rescue your family."

Moses exhaled slowly. "I am to tell Aaron what the Lord wants him to say, and Aaron will act as my mouthpiece." He gripped the staff he was still holding. "I will perform the signs from the Lord with this rod."

Zipporah nodded, her head and heart pounding. Was Moses really going to travel to Egypt and plead for the Hebrews' release?

"The Lord also had another request of me," Moses said in a quiet voice. He rubbed his hand across his face. "He told me to circumcise our son."

"Like the Hebrews do to their sons?" Jethro asked.

Moses's face paled. "Yes."

Zipporah looked between the men. She'd heard of this circumcision done by other peoples to their male infants. It would be a harsh thing to perform with an older child. But if the Lord had commanded it, how could they not obey?

Moses exhaled, saying nothing more about it. He looked at Jethro. "You have been a good father to me, but I need to return to Egypt and fulfill the Lord's wishes. I will be taking my wife and sons with me, for I know not when I will ever see Midian again." His voice trembled. "Pray, let me go."

Zipporah choked back a sob, wondering if she were fully comprehending all that her husband had confessed to her. She'd be going with Moses, but she'd be leaving her family behind. Would she ever see them again?

Jethro wiped the tears spilling from his eyes and said, "Go in peace, my son. And may the Lord bless and protect you." He reached for both Moses's and Zipporah's hands. "May the Lord bless you both."

CHAPTER THIRTY-THREE
ZIPPORAH

Zipporah woke well before the sun rose and slipped out of the tent. The air was cool yet, but the promise of a hot day was apparent in the cloudless sky and the telltale dry wind. She adjusted her shawl about her shoulders and walked past her tent and past her parents' tent until she reached the goat enclosure. The goats raised their sleepy heads and bleated out greetings.

She still milked the goats each morning while Moses tended to her father's flocks and other duties. She would miss this early-morning routine.

Life had been chaotic for Zipporah and her family the past few days, and now, finally, the morning of their departure had arrived. They would be traveling with a Midian trader who was transporting myrrh to Gilead. They'd journey with him and a large caravan as far as an inn near Egypt's border before the caravan split off. Since they'd be crossing through many different tribal lands in the northern Sinai area, they needed the extra protection a larger caravan would bring.

Zipporah scratched the head of the first goat to reach her, then she settled into her routine. As she milked each goat in turn, she thought of the years since Moses had arrived at Midian. He had arrived without a sure conviction of the true God. But he'd opened his heart and mind and started praying. In their early marriage, he'd insisted that they begin and end their days in prayer together.

Since then, she'd seen him slowly and consistently begin to rely on God and to recognize His hand in all things. But this request was beyond anything that Zipporah could have ever imagined or dreamed. She exhaled, letting the memories of what he'd told her about events on Mount Horeb wash over her.

She'd been drawn to Moses from the start—his willingness to help and defend others, his willingness to serve at his own peril, and his humility. She realized that Moses was perhaps the best man God could select for such a momentous task. And Zipporah had no doubt that it would be momentous indeed. Moses had formal training in the royal court's military skills, negotiation, and languages; and he possessed knowledge of the inner circles of palace politics.

And . . . he would have a chance to meet his family. His brother, Aaron. Zipporah felt overwhelmed every time she thought about it. She knew how important her own family was to her and realized that Moses had known only his Egyptian mother.

Zipporah wiped at the tears straying from her eyes. It would be hard to leave her homeland and travel to the unknown. She looked forward to seeing a new land, but she was afraid and anxious as well.

She knew she had to put her supreme faith in God. That was the only way she could push back her fears and doubts about the journey. Her boys were coming with her, and that would be a great comfort, although she'd deeply miss her sisters and brother and their children, as well as her parents.

"Zipporah." Moses's voice cut through the quiet morning.

She turned and smiled to see him walking toward her, much like he had in the days before their marriage. This early-morning reunion was always sweet when they could be alone for a short time before the rest of Midian awakened.

She rose as he neared her, and within moments she was in his arms.

"Are you ready to journey to Egypt?" he whispered into her hair.

Through her clothing, she felt the quick drumming of his heart. He was nervous, she realized, and she knew it must have been difficult for him to accept what God wanted him to do. To leave Midian and travel back to a place he thought he'd never revisit. To meet a family he didn't remember and to learn about his heritage.

"I'm ready to go wherever you go, Moses," she said, tightening her arms about him.

He held her for several moments, saying nothing. Then he kissed the top of her head and said, "Thank you."

She drew away from him. He was a changed man since his experience on Mount Horeb, but he was still her Moses, her husband. "Now help me with these goats, then we'll go wake the boys."

Moses smiled and released her, then collected a couple of jugs by the clean-water well. They made quick work of the rest of the milking and were back at their tent before either of their boys stirred.

Zipporah had already packed what they were going to take, so the inside of her home looked bare and lonely. It was no longer the same. It was as if they'd already departed Midian.

Gershom lifted his head up from where he was curled on his mat and said in a sleepy voice, "Is today here yet?"

"It is," Zipporah said, crossing to her young son. "The sun is coming up, and we are leaving for Egypt."

A smile lit his face, then he rubbed his eyes and yawned.

"Come on, son," Moses said. "We need to load the donkeys and the camel. The family will be here soon to see us off."

As Gershom skipped after his father, little Eliezer stirred and blinked his eyes open. Zipporah was grateful for the quiet moment to nurse him. They had many days of traveling ahead of them, and Zipporah didn't know how her baby would fare on the journey. She was glad she was breastfeeding him so that he could at least take comfort in that familiar routine.

When she finished with Eliezer, she carried him outside to see what else needed to be done. Moses, with Gershom trying to help, had the two donkeys nearly loaded, and a camel was loaded with the small tent they'd be taking. Her father was securing the bundle on the camel, and Zipporah smiled at the sight. And then the tears started.

She chastised herself for crying so early; more people were yet to come. One by one, family by family, everyone arrived. Her brother and sisters, their spouses and their children. And finally her mother, who hurried toward them carrying a wrapped bundle.

Qurayya pressed the bundle into Zipporah's hands. "Do not open this until you are well away from Midian." Her voice trembled.

"Oh, Mother," Zipporah said. "What did you give me?"

Her mother offered a tremulous smile. "You will have to wait to find out." Qurayya pulled Zipporah into an embrace, and the two women stood there for several moments.

"Let's have a family blessing," Jethro said over the commotion of such a large gathering. Everyone quieted and bowed their heads. Once the final few children were ready, he called upon the Lord, beseeching Him for the safe travel and protection of Moses and Zipporah and their children.

Warmth washed over Zipporah at the sound of her father's sacred prayer. She knew it would be the last she'd hear for a while, so she cherished every word. When the prayer was finished, Zipporah took the time to embrace each of her family members.

It was impossible to hold back her tears, so she didn't even try. After bidding a tearful farewell to her brother and his wife, as well as her two older sisters and their husbands, she spent extra time hugging her nieces and nephews, not sure how much older they'd be when she saw them next. When she reached six-year-old Oreb, she kissed him on the forehead, and he scrunched up his face.

"Don't worry, Oreb," she teased. "You'll get a break from your aunt's kisses for a while." Her voice broke, and she had to turn away.

She hugged her three youngest sisters tightly, then finally it was Cozbi's turn, and the two sisters shared a long embrace. "We'll be praying for you every day," Cozbi said.

"And I'll be praying for you as well," Zipporah said, wishing she didn't have to let her sister go.

"Come home to Midian soon and safe," Cozbi said.

"We will," Zipporah promised, wiping the moisture from her cheeks. And then it was time to hug her father farewell. He held her for a long moment, patting her back. Finally he released her, and Zipporah wiped her eyes one last time.

She crossed to where Moses was loading Gershom onto a donkey. Moses would be riding the camel, and Zipporah would sit on the other donkey with Eliezer.

Moses grasped her hand and squeezed it, then said, "Hand me the baby so you can get settled."

With the rest of the family watching, Zipporah climbed onto the donkey, then held out her hands for Eliezer. He nestled against her chest, and she pulled him close, reveling in his soft body since it was something she could still hold on to.

Moses was the last to mount his camel, his staff in hand—the rod that would perform the miracles of God for the pharaoh of Egypt. Was this all really happening? Zipporah wondered. The animals started moving, and Zipporah turned and waved to her family several times before they were too far away to hear any more farewells.

She faced forward at last, resecuring her scarf about her head to keep out most of the wind. She felt Moses watching her, and she turned her head toward him.

"How are you feeling?" Moses asked, his eyes intent on hers.

"Excited but nervous," Zipporah said. "Maybe even a little bit scared."

He nodded and maneuvered the camel closer to her donkey. "I feel the same way; I don't know what to expect."

"We can only have faith," Zipporah said.

He smiled. "Now you are starting to sound like me."

They reached the crossroads where Ishmael the trader was already waiting with a caravan of about twenty camels loaded with goods. Three other men traveled with him, and Zipporah felt relieved that there would be several men in the group.

"It's a good morning," Ishmael said, his tone jovial.

Moses greeted him, and Ishmael nodded, then smiled over at Gershom. "Riding your own donkey," he said. "You must almost be a man."

Gershom beamed. Then, as the caravan got underway and they settled into a comfortable pace, Gershom proceeded to ask the trader questions about what kind of adventures he had on his journeys.

Zipporah half listened with a smile on her face, but mostly she was thinking about her family and her home. Moses talked to the other men in turn; it seemed he knew everyone in Midian now, especially since he'd offered most of the men battle training. Eventually, Gershom's questions and Ishmael's tales fell silent. For Zipporah, it felt surreal to be riding a donkey across the desert. Instead of stopping at one of the mountains, they would be continuing on. Zipporah realized that they'd spent days preparing and thinking of nothing else but getting ready to leave. And now that they were actually on the journey, it was as if they could finally allow themselves to comprehend what they were really doing.

It didn't seem possible that Zipporah had truly said good-bye to her family, but the endless stretches of desert now behind them confirmed that they had indeed left her homeland of Midian behind.

Midafternoon, they stopped at a small oasis dotted with palms and a rather forlorn-looking well. Zipporah was grateful to climb off the donkey and stretch her legs. Her back and neck ached from holding Eliezer for so long. The men of the caravan quickly spread out, finding shade for their naps.

Eliezer was plenty hungry, and Zipporah found her own shade and sat with her back against the trunk of a palm, where she nursed him until he fell asleep.

Moses and Gershom explored the oasis, then eventually lay down on a rug Moses had unpacked and took a nap. Zipporah took the solitary moment to open the bundle her mother had given her. She slowly untied the rope, then lifted the coarse linen wrapping. Within the folds was an intricately woven shawl of the most lustrous shade of blue. Tears pricked Zipporah's eyes because she knew the silk thread would have cost her mother a fortune. She must have traded for it with one of the caravans traveling through Midian. Zipporah could only guess at the price—a sheep, even two—her mother had paid for the dyed silk from the East.

She brought the shawl to her face and breathed in the scent of home. She imagined her mother's aged hands weaving each weft and warp in careful rhythm. The cloth was too delicate for the desert wind, so after a few moments, Zipporah wrapped it up again in the coarse linen bundle. Perhaps she could wear it on Sabbath in Egypt. Her heart full, she lay down next to her napping husband and children, and soon she also fell asleep to the sound of the desert wind and buzzing insects.

She woke a short time later and sat up, her back soaked with perspiration. Although she was in the shade, she wasn't used to being at the mercy of the desert at the hottest time of day. The men in the caravan were still sleeping—oblivious to the heat and insects.

She looked over at Moses and found that he was sitting too, his legs pulled up, a somber expression on his face.

"What are you thinking about?" Zipporah asked, wondering if they'd left something important back in Midian.

"There are other things the Lord told me," Moses said, meeting her gaze. "He said that even when he sees the wonders and miracles the Lord will perform through me, Pharaoh will still harden his heart and won't let the children of Israel go."

Zipporah rose to her feet and crossed to him. Sitting by Moses, she grasped his hand. "Then all this . . . are we doing it for naught?"

"No." His voice was a whisper. "There is another sign I am to perform. If Pharaoh won't let me and the children of Israel leave Egypt, the Lord will slay not only the firstborn of the pharaoh but also the firstborn of all Egyptian families."

Zipporah brought her hand to her mouth.

Moses exhaled and closed his eyes.

"And then Pharaoh will be devastated and beyond grief," she said, mostly to herself. "He will then let the Hebrew slaves go free." She leaned her head against his shoulder, and Moses wrapped her in his arms.

"I don't know if I can do this," Moses said. "My arrival in Egypt will set in motion some terrible events."

"But your people are in bondage," Zipporah said. "And they are your people, Moses. They are your family."

Moses said nothing, only tightened his embrace.

* * *

The days of travel blended together in heat and wind and brilliant blue skies as they crossed the Sinai Peninsula. Gershom became fast friends with Ishmael and the other men. Eliezer clung to Zipporah for the most part but occasionally let his father hold him.

As the sun set on their eighth day and they neared an inn at the crossroads leading to Egypt's border, Zipporah realized she'd become accustomed to many of the desert-living nuances: sleeping in a different place each night, having sand constantly in her hair and beneath her nails, and being the only woman in the caravan. They'd been traveling for over a week now, and her body had adjusted to the physical changes of sparse meals and constant travel.

"We're nearly there," Ishmael called out, pointing up ahead.

From her position in the caravan, Zipporah heard him and eagerly looked for signs of civilization. The inn was a series of stalls covered with goatskin panels for a roof. It served more as shade than anything else.

A large tent seemed to be the inn's center, and other traders and caravan masters were milling about, speaking to each other. Some looked as if they had entered into trade negotiations for gum, balm, and myrrh. Some were even negotiating the trading of slaves. Nearly two hundred camels were resting outside the tent, creating some excitement for Gershom.

Moses couched his camel and walked over to Zipporah to take the baby so she could climb off her donkey. "I'll rent us a stall so there will be some privacy for us tonight." He looked over to the main tent. "We should be able to purchase some fruit and other foods as well as fodder for the animals."

Zipporah could already feel her mouth salivating at the thought of something other than the dried fruits and hardened bread they'd brought.

While Moses went over to the tent, Zipporah crossed to Gershom, who had fallen into an animated conversation with one of the caravan men, asking him about jaguars in Egypt. "Can you fill our goatskins while I feed Eliezer?" Zipporah asked Gershom. She pointed to the line that had formed by the well, and Gershom hurried off with the goatskins.

Moses returned and led her to the stall he had rented. It consisted of walls made of palm timber with goatskin panels for the roof. It was completely open on the side that faced the large tent, but there was a flap they could lower. Zipporah handed Eliezer to Moses and picked up the two rugs that were on the ground of the stall. She shook them, then spread them out again. She took Eliezer from Moses and settled into the back corner, where there was the most privacy, and started to nurse him.

Moses set about arranging their bedrolls. "There's a stand selling oranges and another selling fresh bread," he said.

Just the thought of the food made Zipporah feel like she was suddenly starving.

Gershom went with Moses to purchase food and to water their animals. It was nearly dark by the time they returned with the oranges and bread, along with cucumbers and a chunk of meat. Moses built a fire, and while Eliezer slept, Zipporah prepared tea and cut the vegetables and meat Moses had purchased. She made a simple stew, but it was delicious.

Gershom fell asleep quickly after the evening meal, and Zipporah lay down next to her son, exhaustion taking over.

She'd barely closed her eyes when Moses cried out. Zipporah sat up with a start. Moses looked as if he were being restrained by someone or something, but she couldn't see who it was.

She grabbed the dagger she'd removed earlier from her waistband and placed next to her bedroll. "Moses! What's happening?"

"The Lord," Moses gasped out. "He is chastising me for not circumcising Gershom." He took great gulps of air, and as Zipporah watched, the color drained from his face. His breathing grew shallow, and he collapsed back onto his bedroll.

"Moses!" Zipporah leaned over him. His face was turning purple as if an unseen hand were choking him.

"We have to—" Moses gasped.

Zipporah gripped the dagger in her hand and turned to the sleeping Gershom. She squeezed her eyes shut for a moment, then flew into action. Removing the rug covering his small body, she lifted his clothing. He started to wake as Zipporah used the dagger to cut off his foreskin. Gershom started crying, and she turned and showed Moses the foreskin.

"Tell the Lord that I've circumcised our son," she said in a trembling voice.

Moses jerked on his bedroll, gasping for air. Then his eyes flew open, and when he raised them to meet Zipporah's, they were wet with tears. "Thank you," he told her in a hoarse voice. "Thank you."

Zipporah pulled Gershom into her arms, rocking him back and forth as he cried.

CHAPTER THIRTY-FOUR
MOSES

Moses studied the terrain leading the rest of the way to the Egyptian border and the Nile Delta. They'd traversed several hills and had one more mountain to ascend.

"This is where we must turn north," Ishmael told Moses.

Moses was grateful they'd been a part of the caravan this long. It was only another day's travel into Egypt, and with the increased number of caravans and travelers, they should be relatively safe.

"Thank you for offering your protection," Moses told Ishmael and his men.

Ishmael crossed to Gershom and gave him a colored stone as transparent as a gem. The young boy smiled, and Moses was glad to see it. Gershon had been quiet the past couple of days, and Moses knew it was because of the circumcision. Moses had explained the necessity of circumcision to Gershom, but that hadn't lessened the trauma Gershon's small body had experienced. Moses regretted procrastinating the Lord's command, and it humbled and pained him to know he had been so negligent.

Gershom's pain was his pain, so Moses was pleased to see the boy smiling over the trader's gift.

As Ishmael and his caravan moved north, Moses led his little family through a ravine, then up the slope of the next mountain. He kept watch on all sides and saw that Gershom was doing the same thing.

It was nearing the hottest part of the day when they found an area shaded with several trees where they could stop and rest. Moses took Eliezer while Zipporah climbed off her donkey. Gershom wanted to explore, but Moses refused him permission since they were no longer with the caravan.

"We must stay close together on this mountain," he told Gershom. "We'll be in Egypt soon, and there will be many new things to see and explore." He wondered about the Hebrews' reception of them. He'd come all this way now, and the time had nearly arrived when he was to carry out the Lord's command.

Moses looked over the valley below and saw movement a ways off. He was surprised to see a person traveling along, riding a donkey. "Zipporah, look," he called softly to his wife.

She came to stand next to him. "He's coming this way."

Sure enough, the traveler started up the slope that led directly to their resting place. It was almost as if the man had spotted them and meant to come and speak to them.

"Why is he traveling alone?" Zipporah asked, echoing Moses's thoughts.

Moses's heart drummed as the man drew closer. He appeared to be a tall man, and his beard as well as the thick hair showing beneath his headscarf made it clear that he wasn't Egyptian. Was he Hebrew? Moses's pulse raced faster as he wondered if it could possibly be the man named Aaron the Lord had told him about.

For some reason, Moses didn't feel that this man was a threat to his family, especially since he was traveling alone, and there was something in his appearance and the way he sat upon the donkey that felt familiar.

Zipporah's hand grasped his arm. "He has similar features to you," she said in a quiet voice.

Moses's mouth went dry. He was about to meet his brother—a man he had no memory of.

By the time the donkey reached them, Gershom was standing between Moses and Zipporah, gripping both of their hands.

DELIVERANCE

The man pulled his donkey to a stop, then climbed down. He looked from Moses to Zipporah to Gershom, then back at Moses.

Then he smiled broadly, seeming to contradict his serious brown eyes. Moses felt tears start in his own eyes. He realized he'd seen this man before . . . during the Libyan battle when they'd enlisted hundreds of Hebrews to fight. He had been among that group.

"Moses," the man said in Egyptian. "I am Aaron, your brother."

"Yes," Moses said, as tears no longer held back dripped down his face. "The Lord said you would come to meet me. I now remember you from the Libyan battle."

"That's right," Aaron said. "Oh, how I wished I could have confessed who I was." He stepped forward, his eyes searching Moses's face, then he embraced him and kissed him on each cheek. He drew away and looked at Zipporah. "This is your family?" Aaron asked.

Moses wiped at his tears with a trembling hand. "Zipporah is my wife, and our sons are Gershom and Eliezer."

"It's an honor to meet you," Aaron said in a mix of Hebrew and Egyptian, then he kissed Zipporah and Gershom and the baby.

Moses blinked back more tears at the sight of his brother greeting his wife and children. He marveled that here was a man with whom he shared blood. He'd been envious of the close relationship Zipporah had with her siblings and had truly cherished his own budding relationship with her family.

Moses studied his brother's face, taking in the long straight nose, the eyes that were darker brown than Moses's, and the thicker beard and tamed hair. Gray strands ran through Aaron's hair and beard, and there were more lines around his eyes and mouth, lines deepened by years of servitude. But Zipporah had been right. Moses and Aaron looked like brothers.

Aaron moved back to Moses's side and clapped his hand on his brother's shoulder. "I have not seen you for many years," Aaron said in Egyptian. "And when I did see you, it was from afar, and you certainly didn't look like this."

Moses chuckled, then he translated for Zipporah. To Aaron, he said, "I think of all those years I spent in the palace not knowing my true identity. I feel as if I wasted much of my life."

Aaron stayed quiet for a moment, then his voice was somber when he spoke. "You learned more about Egyptian law and culture than you could have as a Hebrew slave." He met Moses's gaze. "It was the only way you could have survived, you know."

"I know," Moses said in a thoughtful voice. "Come, sit and rest with us. Tell me of your life, my brother."

Aaron followed the small family to where they'd set up their bedrolls in the shade so that they might rest during the hottest hours of the day. Zipporah brought out dried figs and bread still soft from their time spent at the inn.

With Gershom and Eliezer settled to take a nap, Aaron began to speak. "You have a sister named Miriam, and both of our parents are alive and well. Father's name is Amram, and he's of the tribe of Levi. Mother's name is Jochebed."

Moses repeated, "Miriam, Amram, and Jochebed." The names warmed him through. He translated Aaron's words for Zipporah.

"Miriam used to watch you," Aaron said. "Spy on you, actually, during the times you were at the river with Ramses and Pentu."

Moses looked at his brother sharply. "*Spy* on me?"

"She's a bit stubborn and set in her ways," Aaron said, looking over at Zipporah with a smile. "I'm sure you have more peaceful women in Midian."

Once Moses translated, Zipporah laughed. "Some of them are. None of my sisters, though."

"Wait," Moses said, his breath feeling like it had left his chest. "Miriam—the Hebrew woman. I . . . Was she once betrothed to a man named Caleb?"

"Yes, they are married now."

"But . . ." Moses paused. "I remember her. She disappeared one night on the battlefield. Ramses organized a search for her. We thought—I thought she'd died."

"No." Aaron's voice was soft. "She spent weeks in the wilderness and was rescued by a desert dweller named Katu. He brought her back to our village. She married Caleb, and they have a daughter now."

Moses leaned back, blowing out a breath. "She's alive? And she's my sister?" He thought of all that had transpired when Caleb had been wrongly accused of theft and the pharaoh had sentenced him to death unless Caleb could find the true thief. He thought of Caleb's strength and courage and his devotion on the battlefield. Miriam had helped his mother, Bithiah . . . Miriam had been at his mother's side for days, attending to the wounded. And all that time, she'd said nothing. Aaron had said nothing, although they'd both known the truth about Moses's birth.

"And our parents?" he asked. "How are they?"

"They are aged and have slowed considerably but continue to work as much as they are able," Aaron said. "But as you know, the elderly taking on less work just increases the burdens of the surrounding village. We still have to do the same amount of work regardless of whether someone is elderly or ill."

Moses nodded.

"And what about you, Aaron?" Zipporah asked. "Do you have a wife and family?"

"My wife's name is Salome, and we have a son and a daughter." He folded his hands together. "Everyone will be overjoyed to see you, Moses, and to meet your family."

"Do they know you came to meet me in the desert?"

Aaron shook his head. "I told Father and my wife, but no one else. When the voice of the Lord came to me, I was afraid and unsure whether I would truly see you. I didn't want our mother and sister to be upset if it turned out to be my imagination." He looked down at his hands. "Of course, there is now proof that it was the Lord Himself who spoke to me. Here I am, and here you are."

"I understand your doubts," Moses said in a quiet voice. "For I have seen the face of God, and yet, I have still been found weak in faith and obedience."

Aaron stared at him. "Tell me what happened, Moses. Tell me why the Lord has brought us together after all this time. Do you intend to relocate to a Hebrew village and work as a slave? Do you think you can kidnap the entire family and bring us to Midian to start a new life?"

It was Moses's turn to clasp his hands together and stare at them for a long moment. "God appeared to me on Mount Horeb, south of here, while I was tending my father-in-law's flocks. He told me He's seen the affliction of His covenant people and that He knows your sorrows." He looked up. Aaron was leaning forward, listening intently. "The Lord has seen your oppression by the Egyptians, and He has sent me to deliver the children of Israel out of Egypt."

Aaron stared at him for several moments, then blinked his eyes a few times. "Tell me, my brother, how will you deliver thousands of Hebrew slaves away from the pharaoh of Egypt?"

Moses reached for his staff and stood up, moving a few paces from where Aaron and Zipporah sat.

He threw the staff upon the ground, and immediately it transformed into a snake.

Zipporah gasped, and Aaron leapt to his feet with a cry.

Moses simply reached down and picked up the snake by its tail. As his hand made contact, the curving snake straightened and formed into a rod again. Aaron was absolutely quiet, standing before Moses, as he stared at Moses's staff.

"Despite your awe over the Lord changing my staff into a snake," Moses said to Aaron, "it will not be enough to convince Pharaoh." He looked over at Zipporah, who nodded. "Sit down with me, my brother, for I have many things to tell you."

* * *

Moses slowed his camel as they neared the Nile Delta. They'd be crossing through a gap in the hills, a place with which Moses was vaguely familiar. It had been many years, but the terrain remained unchanged. The flooding season was still months away, and the desert was heading into its driest season. The valley spread before them, and new buildings and edifices had been erected—by Hebrew slaves, no doubt. Temples and tombs and sanctuaries dotted the distant landscape amidst rolling fields of grain and groves of date palms.

The setting sun cast its golden glow across the land, and Moses felt a pang of longing . . . he'd once enjoyed all the riches of Egypt, had lived right in the midst of it. He'd benefitted from the work of the Hebrew slaves, most likely at the cost of their health and even their lives. Standing there, gazing over the magnificence of Egypt,

Moses wondered if his former best friend, Ramses, who was now Pharaoh, would ever give up the Hebrews.

Moses knew without a doubt that it could only happen by the hand of the Lord, through great and terrible events. No pharaoh in his right mind would break apart his economy at the request of a childhood friend—now a simple shepherd from Midian. Moses swallowed against his dry throat, anticipating the massive task ahead of him. Not only with convincing the children of Israel to allow him to lead them to deliverance but also convincing Pharaoh to allow them to go free.

The two days and night they spent with Aaron passed quickly, and now it was almost time to meet Moses's family. Moses also wondered how his Egyptian mother, Bithiah, would react upon seeing him again when he went to plead with Pharaoh. Over the past two days, Moses had a lot to tell his brother, not only of what God had revealed to him but of his early life in the pharaoh's palace and his present life in Midian.

Aaron had marveled at the many ways Moses's life had been spared, from his beginning as a child, to escaping Egypt with his life after killing the Egyptian taskmaster, to the various battles with the Badrayan tribe.

Aaron also told Moses about what it was like to grow up in a Hebrew slave village and about the oppressions he'd faced, the oppressions the children of Israel had endured for four hundred years. And now Aaron was willing to be spokesman for Moses as he presented the Lord's plan to them.

Aaron pulled his donkey next to Moses's camel and pointed across the narrow channel of the River Nile toward a collection of huts and paths that wound through them. "That's our village. It's the middle of the day, so Father and Caleb will be working at the stone pit, shaping stones for the newest temple. But Mother will be helping Miriam with her weaving. Our sister is known as one of the finest weavers in Egypt."

What would it be like to finally meet his mother? And to see his sister again—this time knowing that she was his sister? *Miriam.* He already knew she was a courageous and headstrong woman. He wondered what Ramses would do if he knew she was still alive and had evaded him all these years.

"Are you ready, Moses?" Zipporah asked in a soft voice as she came to a stop next to him. He looked over at his wife and sleeping baby. Soon he'd be able to introduce his wife and children to their grandparents and other relatives.

"I am," he said and reached down from the camel as she reached up from her donkey. They clasped hands for a moment, then Moses released her hand. They followed Aaron as they splashed through the slow-moving water of the river channel and approached the village. An elderly woman came out of her hut to watch them pass by. Moses supposed most of the Hebrews were out working for the Egyptians.

When they arrived at a modest hut, Aaron stopped his donkey and climbed off. He lashed his animal to a tree. Moses followed suit with his camel and the two other donkeys. With Gershom's hand in his, Moses, along with Zipporah and Eliezer, followed Aaron through the worn gate and across the square courtyard to the hut.

"Is this where my grandmother lives?" Gershom asked, tugging on Moses's hand.

Aaron confirmed, "Yes, and your grandfather. Your aunt Miriam should be here working with her loom. Miriam has a daughter about your age."

"Is it Sarah?" Gershom asked.

"Yes, just like I told you earlier," Aaron said.

Before Gershom could ask any more questions, the door opened and a woman stepped out. She looked to be about sixty years old, although her thick, abundant hair was that of a younger woman. She stared at Moses with her large, dark eyes that were set on a round, pleasant face. She was thin but seemed sturdy, far from frail.

Moses didn't know what he expected to feel when he met his birth mother, Jochebed, but it was hard to form into thoughts. He knew her eyes didn't miss anything, not his shepherd's clothing, his long hair streaked with white and tied back with a leather strap, his headdress, or his short beard.

Jochebed's mouth opened, then shut again, her lips trembling as she pressed them together. Her dark eyes filled with tears. "Moses," she whispered. Then louder, she said, "Moses! My son!" She grasped his face and kissed both of his cheeks, then kissed them again.

"You've come home at last," she cried in Hebrew.

"Mother," Moses said, but he was unable to say anything more as his voice failed him.

His mother's thin arms wrapped around his neck and embraced him. Moses held her against him, feeling as if his soul had connected with hers, and he realized that it had always been connected. If there was one thing in his life Moses realized about this woman, it was that she loved him fiercely. He could feel it in her embrace and see it in her eyes.

He knew his Egyptian mother loved him as well, but his Hebrew mother had done a remarkably hard thing—she'd given him up in order to save his life.

Jochebed drew away and patted his cheeks, speaking in Hebrew so rapidly that Moses couldn't follow what she was saying.

Then she moved to Zipporah and embraced her, following which Gershom was showered with many kisses. Then it was Eliezer's turn, and he was wide awake for all the greetings.

Another woman came through the door, a young girl at her side.

Moses recognized Miriam, even though it had been years since he'd seen her. With her round face and thick hair, she closely resembled their mother. A smile broke out on her face.

"What's this?" she asked, looking from Moses to Aaron, then back at Moses with disbelief. Then the tears started and she shouted, "You're alive!"

Even he could understand that much Hebrew.

Miriam stepped forward to kiss and embrace him. Pulling back, she scanned his face. "Where did you go? How have you been?"

He wasn't sure he understood all of what she was saying, but he could very well guess. "I fled to Midian," he said slowly in Midianite, "and this is my wife and our two sons. I have taught her what little Hebrew I know, so you may be able to understand each other a little."

Miriam looked upon his family, grasped Zipporah's hand for a moment, and patted Gershom's head. "Welcome to Egypt." She tugged the young girl at her side forward until she was standing in front of Miriam. "This is my daughter, Sarah," she said in Hebrew. "She's just turned four years old." She used her fingers to show the number four.

Gershom's eyes lit up, and he lifted his chin. "I'm four years old too."

Miriam smiled at him, tears shining in her eyes. "You two will be great friends, then."

Sarah seemed extraordinarily shy. She tried to move to her mother's side again, but Miriam held her in a firm grasp.

Jochebed motioned them inside the hut, where she and Miriam told them to sit on the cushions in the tiny gathering room while they made tea. When the tea was ready, Miriam convinced Sarah to take Gershom outside and show him around. Then she leaned forward.

"It's a wonder to see you back in Egypt," she said, her eyes gleaming with happiness. Aaron translated his sister's words into Egyptian for Moses. "You do not know how many prayers we've offered in your behalf."

Moses nodded. "I've been blessed greatly. Thank you for your prayers."

Miriam tilted her head in Zipporah's direction. "You are from Midian?"

"Yes," Zipporah said, grasping her question. "I was born there, as well as my father, and his father."

"Ah," Miriam said. Then, without asking any other questions of Zipporah, she turned back to Moses. "As wonderful as it is to see you, I don't understand why you would leave your new home and bring your family to Egypt. Surely you don't think Pharaoh won't recognize you?"

"He plans on that," Aaron said.

Both Miriam and Jochebed looked at Aaron in surprise.

"You want Pharaoh to know you are here and to discover your true heritage?" Miriam asked, shaking her head. "Are things so desperate in Midian?"

"I care for my father-in-law's flocks in Midian," Moses said. "Our life in the desert is hard but fulfilling. And I have two healthy sons and a wife whom I love dearly. So you may question why I would ever want to return to Egypt, except for the opportunity to meet my true family."

Jochebed reached out and grasped Moses's hand. "Whatever your reason, you are welcome to all that we have."

Miriam's gaze narrowed. "You'll be put to work, you know. The taskmasters will hear of your arrival within a day, and then they will seek you out. A strong healthy man is in much demand for the building of Ramses's new temple."

Letting out a breath, Moses said, "You are right, but I have come for something other than a reunion with my family or introducing my children into an oppressive life with the children of Israel." He looked over at Aaron, who nodded. "I have come on the errand of the Lord to deliver the children of Israel from their bonds."

CHAPTER THIRTY-FIVE
ZIPPORAH

Zipporah rose from her bedroll they'd laid out in the gathering room of Jochebed's home. Although it was well after midnight, she couldn't sleep. Next to her, Moses's breathing was soft and even. It was a relief to Zipporah that he was finally resting. She didn't think he'd slept more than a few hours each night since leaving Midian.

Thoughts of the reunion with Moses's family still brought tears to her eyes. When she'd witnessed father and son embracing, everyone in the room had been crying. Zipporah knew that her husband had longed for his true family ever since learning that he'd been adopted by Bithiah.

Zipporah slipped out the front door of the hut and breathed in the fresh night air. The village was quiet, and the stars seemed so close it was as if she could touch them if she reached up high enough. Gershom had been delighted to play with little Sarah and to meet Aaron's children as well.

It was plain that the family lived in very confined and humble circumstances, yet they were close and loving. They cared deeply for each other and appreciated the small, simple things. These were people who had lived out their lives as slaves controlled by their taskmasters' whims and facing their challenges while overcoming their continued fears of oppression.

Tomorrow was the Sabbath, and Aaron and Amram would take Moses before the elders of the children of Israel, where Moses would tell them of his mission. Zipporah pulled her robe more tightly about her as a breeze pushed against her skin. Her dark skin. Her coloring had never bothered her, so she was surprised to see Miriam's critical eye on her more than once.

Miriam had also asked her several questions about how her family felt about her marrying a foreigner, simplifying her Hebrew language so that Zipporah could grasp most of her words. Miriam then proceeded to tell Zipporah that the Hebrews didn't intermarry those from other cultures or religions. "That is why," Miriam had told Zipporah in a soft voice, "if a Hebrew woman is forced into Pharaoh's harem, there is no life for her to return to."

Zipporah understood the logic, but she was also bothered by Miriam's continued scrutiny. She and Moses loved each other, and he'd been a foreigner in Midian, yes, but did his sister expect Moses to return to a life of slavery so he could marry a Hebrew woman? She didn't dare talk about it with Moses yet—he had enough to be concerned about without being bothered with her assumptions of Miriam's opinion of her. And Zipporah hoped they were only assumptions.

She walked across the courtyard and stopped by the gate. She missed her home and her family. She missed Midian. Her sisters, her parents, her goats. She could only hope and pray that the elders of Israel would receive Moses and support his work. And then she could only beg for the Lord's guidance and protection as Moses went before the pharaoh of Egypt. Would Ramses listen to his former friend? Or would he be angry and feel betrayed by the man he'd grown up with and who now lived as a humble shepherd in Midian?

"Zipporah?" Moses called out to her in the darkness.

She turned to see him coming out of the hut. He crossed the small courtyard and slipped his arms about her.

"What are you doing out here?" he asked, his whisper tickling her ear.

"I couldn't sleep," Zipporah said. "I didn't want to wake you, so I came outside for a while."

"I didn't think I'd be sleeping much tonight anyway," Moses said. "Tomorrow will be an important day."

Zipporah turned toward him and wrapped her arms around his waist. "Are you anxious?" she asked.

"I am intimidated more than anything," he said. "Here are men, the elders of the village, who have lived their entire lives in bondage. Who am I to tell them I've come to set them free? If the roles were reversed, would I believe the stranger?"

"You are no stranger," she said. "Miriam said that both Egyptians and Hebrews know of you, and when they see your conviction and sincerity, they will believe you."

"I hope you're right," Moses said. "I'm grateful that Aaron will act as my spokesman. If I can't even speak their language properly, how am I supposed to be their leader?"

Zipporah chuckled softly. "I watched you commit yourself to learning Midianite. You'll learn Hebrew in no time. Besides, there are a lot of similarities to Midianite."

Moses stroked her hair, pulling her closer. "I hope you're right. We can only put our trust in the Lord, for it is He who sent us here."

Zipporah closed her eyes as she leaned against her husband. It was so quiet now, so peaceful. Yet their future would be far from peaceful. First, Moses had to convince the elders of Israel that he was the Lord's representative, come to deliver them from bondage. Then he'd have to persuade Pharaoh to release the slaves—a major commodity.

And the signs and plagues the Lord would send through Moses's lips would be astonishing and devastating. She held on to Moses a bit tighter. Tonight, this hour, this moment, might be the last calm moments they had together before the terrible storm brewing before them broke.

CHAPTER THIRTY-SIX
MOSES

Moses pulled on the robe he'd brought with him from Midian—the one that he'd kept with him since that fateful night he'd first fled from Egypt and which he'd worn on his wedding day. The lustrous colors of red and blue and yellow shimmered in the early afternoon light. He thought of the woman who'd made the robe—his Egyptian mother, Bithiah—and wondered when he would see her again. Perhaps she'd be in Pharaoh's court when he went to plead for the release of the children of Israel. What would she think of his return?

But first Moses must face his most critical audience—the elders of Israel. If they believed Moses, then they would take his message of deliverance back to their homes and villages and congregations.

It seemed Moses was praying with every breath he took since leaving Midian with his family. He knew that his wife, mother, and sister would be waiting anxiously for news of how the meeting went with the elders, and he hoped that news would be good.

Moses exhaled and grabbed his staff from where it leaned against the wall. Then he shouldered a goatskin and left the cramped bedchamber, where he'd readied himself. The women greeted him as he came into the cooking room, and his mother brought a hand to her mouth. "Oh, Moses, that's beautiful."

"Princess Bithiah made it for me," Moses said.

His mother crossed to him and grasped his hands. "I'm so grateful that a good and kind woman raised you as her own. You must visit her soon."

Moses nodded. "I would like to, but I'm not sure how I'll be received in Pharaoh's court or if I'll even be allowed to speak with Bithiah." It was strange to refer to her as Bithiah since he'd known her only as Mother his entire childhood.

"Has she married?" he asked his mother.

"No," Jochebed said. "I have only caught a glimpse of her a few times, but she did not ever marry."

Jochebed and Miriam exchanged glances.

"What is it?" he asked. "Has something happened?"

"There have been rumors," Miriam said, her eyes narrowing. "In the village, for years. Mered, the Hebrew scribe at the palace, has struck up a friendship with her."

Moses remembered Mered and wasn't surprised that Bithiah would be kind to him, but what Miriam and his mother were implying was something much more. It would be dangerous for Bithiah to enter into any sort of alliance with a Hebrew, even if he were an educated palace scribe. Pharaoh held his family connections very close, and marriages were always arranged.

"Don't worry," Jochebed cut in. "Mered would never force her to make a choice. They would both be content at passing each other once in a while in the corridor. You won't find two more loyal people."

"Bithiah protected me for a long time," Moses said. "It wasn't until I confessed about the Egyptian taskmaster that she told me the truth about my heritage."

"She can be trusted," Miriam said in a quiet tone. She crossed to Moses and kissed him on his cheek. "Now go speak to those elders. They will believe you, just wait and see. Before you know it, we'll all be on our donkeys and journeying into the wilderness."

Moses returned the kiss on Miriam's cheek, then kissed his mother's cheek as well. "Thank you both." He left the cooking room and stepped outside. Zipporah was waiting for him in the courtyard with Gershom and Eliezer. Aaron and Amram stood at the gate. Zipporah smiled at him as he crossed to her, but he could see the nervousness in her gaze.

"May the Lord be with you," she said, embracing him.

He held her close, Eliezer nestled between them, then he released her. Zipporah wiped tears from her eyes as Gershom wrapped his arms around Moses's legs. "I'll be back soon," Moses told him.

Finally he was ready. He turned toward his father.

"Ready, son?" Amram said as Moses joined him at the gate.

"Yes," Moses said and walked with his father and Aaron out of the courtyard. Moses turned a final time to wave to Zipporah and his boys. It felt like he was dreaming as he gazed at the sight of his wife and sons standing in front of a village hut in Egypt. He took a deep breath and continued on with Aaron and Amram.

Amram clapped his hand on Moses's shoulder. "You are about to change thousands of lives," he said in a voice thick with emotion.

Moses could only nod, could only pray, could only believe.

The gathering place sat in the center of the village and looked like an oversized hut. Moses was pleased to see that they had such a place to meet together. His heart was thundering in his ears by the time they stepped through the door. Row after row of men were seated on the ground, some on cushions, others on rugs.

Dozens of dark eyes turned toward Moses. Eyebrows raised, and lips moved in speculative whispers. Moses didn't think there was a man younger than fifty or sixty in the gathering. Moses walked all the way to the back of the building, keeping his gaze forward. When they came to a stop and turned around, Moses found himself awed by the aged faces that peered back at him.

These were men who'd spent their whole lives in captivity but had managed to hold together a thriving village, who clung tightly to their faith.

Moses felt like a multicolored bird standing before them, wearing such a fine robe. Nothing these men wore even came close to the luxury Moses had been able to preserve.

Amram held up his hands for absolute silence, then, addressing the gathering, said, "Thank you for coming today to this meeting. I would like to introduce my youngest son to you—Moses."

Conversation buzzed among the men, and Amram waited again for silence. Moses concentrated fully on his father's words, hoping to understand the language.

"When Moses was born, Pharaoh Seti sent an edict throughout the land that every male child born should be put to death." He looked over at Moses and then continued, his voice shaky. "The Lord saw fit to preserve his life when my wife hid him in a basket and sent him down the River Nile. He was found by the Princess Bithiah and raised as her adopted son."

Amram paused, letting the murmuring subside. "He departed Egypt many years ago after a tragic event and found himself a new home with the tribe of Midian. He now has a wife and two sons."

More conversation.

"My son has returned to Egypt with his family under the direction of the Lord," Amram said.

Brows pulled together and a few men scoffed. "He's an Egyptian!" one man protested. "He's not a Hebrew! Look at that robe."

Moses had expected the questions, the suspicions, but now that he was in the center of it, his doubts began to grow.

"You mean he's a Midianite now," another man cried out. "He has not lived our covenants."

"Is he here to set new rules upon us?" a third man asked.

Aaron stepped forward now, raised his hands, and said, "Enough! You will hear my brother's message. He has traveled very far at his own peril to come to our people's aid."

"What do you mean?" one of the elders said.

Aaron kept his hands raised until everyone fell silent at last.

Now Moses could wait no longer. He set his staff against the wall and stepped forward, speaking slowly, methodically, letting Aaron interpret for him.

"My father has spoken the truth," he said in broken Hebrew. "Yesterday was the first time I ever remember laying eyes upon my mother and father. They have lived among you and worked alongside you. They are good people. When I arrived in the village last night, they had no idea that I was coming."

All eyes were fastened on Moses.

"This robe I'm wearing was made by my Egyptian mother, a woman I love very much." He tugged at one of the sleeves and drew his arm out, then his other arm. "But I am no longer an Egyptian royal. I do not worship their gods."

Moses paused, letting Aaron interpret his words, making them stronger and more powerful.

Moses held out the multicolored robe. "I will always treasure this part of my past, for it saved my life in order to accomplish the Lord's errand."

Several whispers started again, but most of the men were listening intently.

"I have seen the face of God," Moses said. The men went silent.

"God appeared to me on Mount Horeb and told me He has heard your cries," Moses said in a clear voice. "He's seen your afflictions, and He will deliver you from Egypt."

The men stared at Moses as Aaron repeated his words. It was as if they understood Moses just as well.

"The Lord has commanded me to free the children of Israel from slavery and lead you out of Egypt." He reached for his staff and threw it on the ground. It immediately transformed into a snake. The elders gasped and drew back. Several scrambled to their feet. "The power of God is made manifest in me," Moses said, reaching for the snake and turning it back into a long wooden rod.

"See my hand," Moses said, stretching out his hand. "The flesh is healthy and whole." He moved his hand inside the opening of his robe, then drew it out. The skin had turned white and red, mottled with leprous sores.

The elders stared at his hand, their eyes wide in astonishment.

"And now the Lord will remove the leprosy." He put his hand inside his robe again, and this time when he drew it out, the leprosy had disappeared. The skin of his hand was healthy and clear.

In the absolute silence, Moses picked up the goatskin he'd left on the ground and started to pour the water out. It fell in a long, clear stream toward the ground, but once it hit the earth, it turned into dark red blood. The men leaned forward, their eyes wide, their mouths open.

"The Lord will send plagues upon Egypt and its inhabitants as a warning to Pharaoh to let His people go," Moses said, and Aaron repeated his words.

Moses continued telling the elders about the Lord's instructions on Mount Horeb. The men stared at him in awe, many with tears running down their faces. The Spirit permeated the room, touching hearts and opening minds. The elders nodded, clasping their hands together in gratitude as Moses spoke. Finally, he told them of the plagues that would come and of the last and most terrible curse. Every firstborn of the Egyptians would be put to death by the hand of the Lord.

"And only then," Moses said in a quiet voice that could be heard all across the hut, "will Pharaoh release all the Hebrew slaves from bondage."

His voice caught as he said the next words. "I have come to Egypt as your humble servant. I am here at the Lord's request, and I will do everything He asks of me. The Lord sent me to deliver the children of Israel, and I am here to do His will."

Aaron did not interpret these last words. The more words Moses spoke, the more his language was transformed. Heads bowed, knees bent, and the elders praised Moses as their prophet, their deliverer.

Tears fell down Moses's face as he looked over the congregation of elders, men he didn't know but men whom he could clearly feel the Lord's love for. The Lord was willing to send destruction and death to the entire land of Egypt to rescue His beloved people. They had suffered in their afflictions for over four hundred years, and now the time had come for the children of Israel to be delivered.

And it all started now.

The deliverer had arrived.

End of Book 2

ACKNOWLEDGMENTS

As with any second volume in a series, a precedent has been set. I'm most grateful to the readers and reviewers who read and enjoyed *Bondage*. Your words of encouragement always mean a lot.

Many thanks to my parents, Kent and Gayle Brown, who read the initial draft and offered excellent guidance. With my father's expert knowledge of Biblical topics and of the various locations in the Middle East, I always try to see if my research matches up to his insights. It's great when I can prove myself a little, but I also appreciate any corrections.

I'm grateful for my publisher's support with this series and all of the many hands this manuscript has passed through. From the initial editing to cover design to marketing and distribution, it truly takes a tribe of excellent people to bring a manuscript to the bookstore. Thanks to managing editor Kathy Gordon and project editor Samantha Millburn for always believing in my work. Thanks to copyeditor Shauna Humphreys, who freelanced for this book and dug deep to bring out the best of the story. Shauna is the former managing editor who accepted my first book with Covenant. Thanks to Stephanie Lacy and Robby Nichols for their hard work in marketing and sales. And many thanks to art director Margaret Weber-Longoria and her design team.

My critique group continues to be an integral part of my writing life, namely Michele Holmes, Annette Lyon, Sarah Eden, Rob Wells, and J. Scott Savage. In 2015, critique group member Lu Ann Staheli passed away. I dedicated *Bondage* to her before knowing of her dire health condition. These past months as I've continued on my writing journey, I've realized how truly integral she was to my growth, both as a mentor and as a friend. Lu Ann was a rare gift indeed, and I've been blessed to know her for the twelve years we spent together. She was one of the first to encourage me to submit *Of Goodly Parents* to Covenant in 2003. She said it was "good enough to be published." This book, *Deliverance*, will be the first work Lu Ann hasn't read.

I appreciate the enthusiasm of my many family members, including my father-in-law, Les Moore, who continues to be a great encourager of my work. Thanks to Susan Aylworth for her willingness to swap manuscripts. Her edits are always insightful. And my husband and children have my endless thanks for all of their support.

ABOUT THE AUTHOR

Heather B. Moore is a *USA Today* best-selling author of more than a dozen historical novels and thrillers written under the pen name H.B. Moore. She writes women's fiction, romance, and inspirational nonfiction under Heather B. Moore. This can all be confusing, so her kids just call her Mom. Heather attended Cairo American College in Egypt and the Anglican School of Jerusalem in Israel and earned a bachelor of science degree from Brigham Young University in Utah. Visit Heather's website here: www.hbmoore.com.